LOVE FOR SAIL - A CONNIE BARRERA THRILLER

THE 1ST BOOK IN THE CARIBBEAN MYSTERY AND ADVENTURE SERIES

C.L.R. DOUGHERTY

Copyright © 2014 by Charles Dougherty

All rights reserved.

No part of this book may be reproduced in any form or by any electronic or mechanical means, including information storage and retrieval systems, without written permission from the author, except for the use of brief quotations in a book review.

rev. June 2017

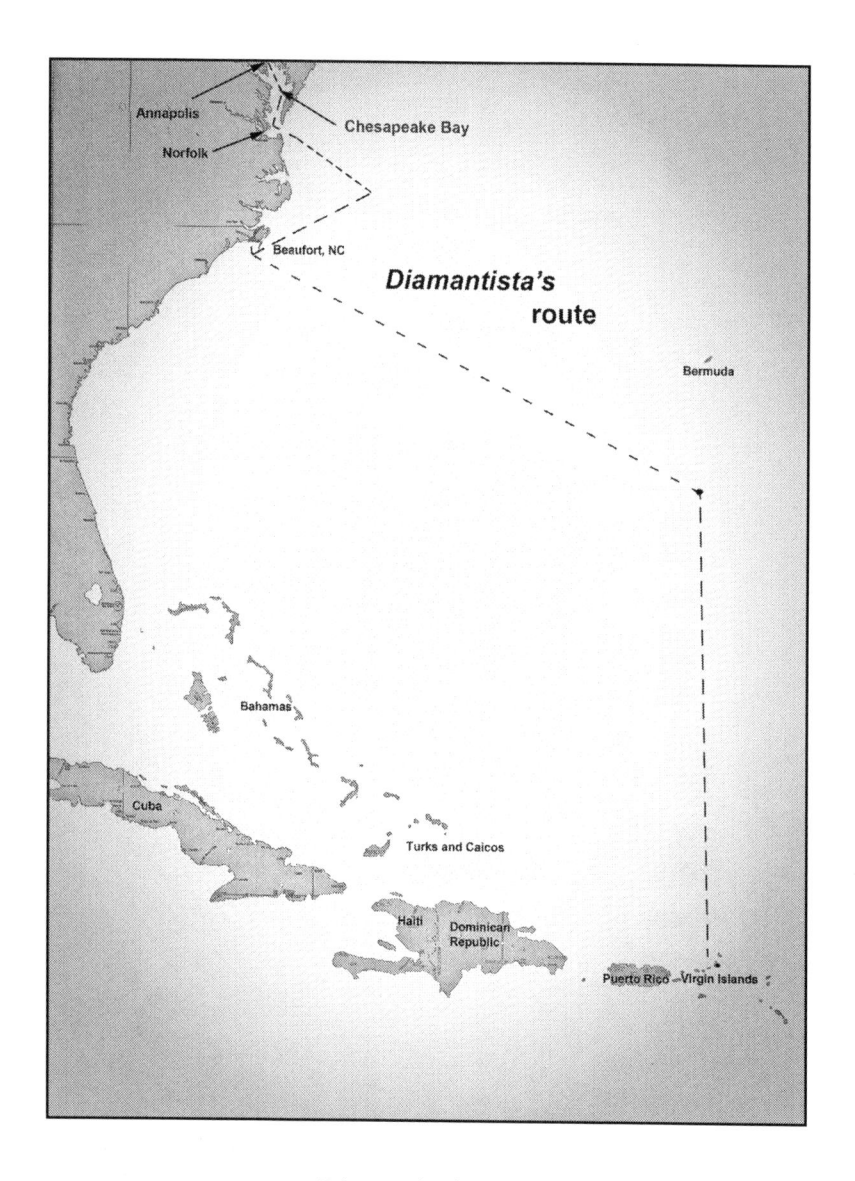

Diamantista's Route

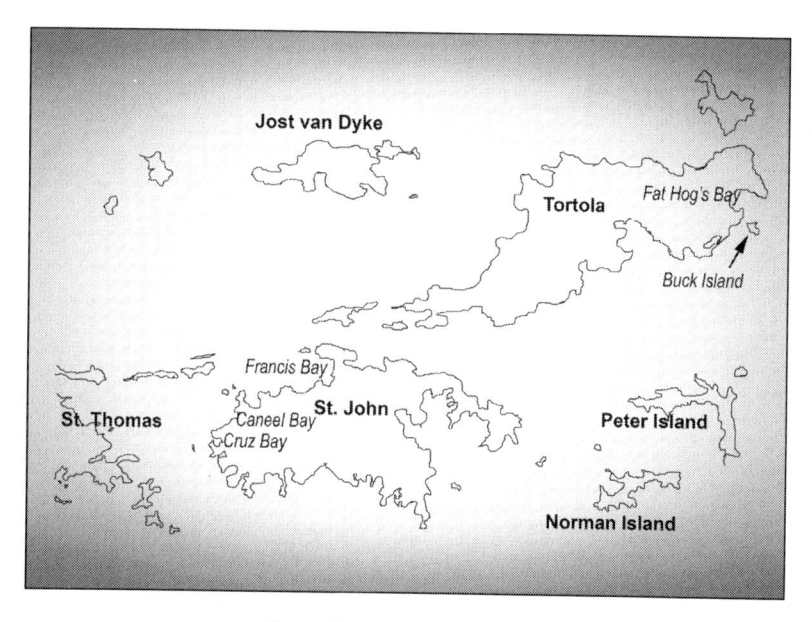

Sketch Chart of the Virgin Islands

1

Connie clenched her jaw so hard she thought her teeth would crack. She was intent on the heavy straps, imagining what would happen as they were pulled tight. From the corner of her eye, she could see the man with his hand on the control lever. The other man, the one standing in front of her, nodded his head. The machine groaned and creaked as it pulled the slack from the straps. She flinched and bit back a scream of anguish as the man in front of her waved his arms frantically.

"Stop!" he yelled, over the noise of the machine.

The other man pushed the lever back, easing the pressure, and Connie started breathing again. "What's wrong?" he asked as the noise abated.

"We're gonna break her back if you don't watch it. Forward sling's gonna slide right off her bottom. We gotta tie 'em together, or she'll slip right out 'n' bust like a watermelon."

Connie watched like a mother lion as the workers repositioned the straps under *Diamantista* and prepared to lift the 49,000-pound boat and move her to the launching area. She knew that the crew launched as many as ten boats per day during the busy season and that they never dropped one or even scratched the paint, but none of those other boats was hers.

She was surprised at how attached she had become to *Diamantista* in the short time she had owned her. She'd never been one to care about possessions; she was more into collecting experiences than things. She knew that was ironic, given her impoverished childhood. Most people who struck it rich after growing up in desperate poverty were acquisitive, but she was a 'take nothing but memories, leave nothing but footprints' kind of gal.

Initially, she hadn't been looking for a boat of such modern design; she had been enamored of traditional vessels like *Vengeance*, the Herreshoff 59 that belonged to her friends, Dani Berger and Liz Chirac. She had learned to sail on *Vengeance* down in the Caribbean, so it was her standard of comparison.

As she had started shopping for boats, she'd been forced to compromise. She needed a private stateroom for her charter guests. The Herreshoff had two double staterooms; there were no other sleeping spaces and she couldn't manage with only two double accommodations. Liz and Dani shared the forward double when they had guests aboard, but she wasn't about to share her sleeping quarters with Paul Russo. She liked him well enough, but she was still off men since her last bad experience.

Paul was her friend, and he was a great cook. She was thrilled that he was going to help her get started with the charter business, but she wasn't ready for romance, and he didn't seem to be, either.

∼

Paul was sitting on the patio at the Miami Yacht Club, sipping a beer and wondering what he had gotten himself into. Connie Barrera was drop-dead gorgeous, not to mention being a pleasant person, but he was still dumbfounded that he had agreed to spend a few months as the first mate and cook on her new charter yacht. Of course, at the time she had asked him, the whole thing had seemed like a pipe-dream. She hadn't even bought *Diamantista* when they were talking about it. They had been in Martinique on *Vengeance*, sailing along without a care in the world after he had helped bring Sam Alfano to justice. The fact that Connie was planning to buy a yacht with the money from diamonds she had found on a beach in the Bahamas had seemed no more real than the notion that she had just ripped off Alfano and his partner for over ten million dollars' worth of those same loose diamonds.

The morality of her 'finders, keepers' attitude didn't bother him; he had been part of her support group as she rationalized keeping the diamonds for herself. Alfano didn't deserve the stones; they were fruit of a tainted tree. If Connie hadn't contrived to end up with them, they would have enriched some undeserving government agency or further corrupted a few bureaucrats somewhere. He liked Connie and wished her well, but he was first and foremost a cop, albeit a retired one. Connie wasn't exactly crooked, but her ideas of right and wrong were much less structured than his.

He'd been granted a little extra time to figure out what to do about the situation because he'd been called back from his early retirement to help prepare a case that he'd been working for almost two years. It was about to come to trial, and the prosecution team asked for Paul's assistance as a consultant because the other members of the task force of which he'd been a part were occupied with ongoing investigations. That had left Connie in a bit of a bind, as she'd planned on Paul's helping her deliver *Diamantista* from Annapolis to the islands in the next week or two. She was up in Annapolis getting the boat ready and looking for temporary crew.

And then there was the question of where this whole thing with Connie would end up. They were attracted to each other;

they had discussed that at length on several occasions, but neither was ready for a romantic relationship. Connie still hadn't gotten over her last bad experience, and Paul clung tenaciously to his hard-won second term as a bachelor. He'd been single since his train-wreck of a marriage had ended in an acrimonious divorce five years ago.

Even with that understood between them, Paul was dubious about the notion of the two of them living on a small boat in such a romantic environment. Despite their agreement, temptation could make a mockery of their intent. He didn't want to see either of them get hurt, and given their fragile emotional states, that seemed to be a strong possibility.

∽

JIMMY DORLAN AND KIRSTEN JONES studied the index cards pinned in random fashion to the cork board outside the Annapolis Harbormaster's office. Kirsten grasped a card in her fingers, the bitten nails of her other hand plucking out the thumbtack that held the card to the board.

"I like the looks of this one," she said, handing it to Jimmy.

He stared at it, squinting, as she read aloud over his shoulder.

"Fifty-six-foot sailing yacht bound for the Virgin Islands in early November seeks two experienced crew members. Expenses and return airfare paid. Apply in person to Connie Barrera aboard *Diamantista,* at anchor in Back Creek, any day after 5 p.m."

"How we gonna find that?"

"Water taxi. Wonder if Connie's got a man aboard?" Kirsten asked.

"Why? You lookin' for a little action on the side?"

"No, stupid. If she's a single woman, it would be even better."

"Connie's a man's name sometimes."

"No, it's not."

"Is, too. I had a roommate named Connie, an' he sure as shit wasn't a woman."

"We'll need to convince her we know what we're doing, Jimmy."

"Yeah. I still bet it's a man, though."

"Doesn't matter, but you'd better let me do the talking, okay?"

"Whatever."

Kirsten slipped the card in her shoulder bag and they turned and walked toward one of the park benches that overlooked the harbor. They were a mismatched couple, physically and intellectually. Kirsten was one of those girls best described as 'cute,' a chipper, five-foot, four-inch-tall blonde. Her short, curly hair framed a round face with rosy cheeks and baby-blue eyes separated by a perfect little upturned nose. She looked like the college cheerleader that she had been until her recent downfall.

In contrast, Jimmy was tall, an inch over six feet, and strong-looking, but in that wiry way of men who did manual labor. His mouse-brown hair was pulled back in a short, unkempt pony-tail, exposing what could have been a handsome face except for the arrogance that was all too obvious in his dark, flashing eyes. He was attractive to women in a dangerous, bad-boy way, and he knew it. Where Kirsten was quiet, well-brought up, and well-educated, he was brash and street-smart. Although only a few years older than Kirsten, he had seen much more of the gritty side of life, and it showed in his dissipated features.

2

Ralph Giannetti sat on the patio of his Star Island mansion, his iPhone pressed to his ear, listening to Mark Murano's bullshit. He put it on speaker phone, turned up the volume, and put the phone on the glass tabletop as Murano babbled. Gazing across the water toward the Miami Beach Marina, he picked up the Cuban cigar that his butler had brought out with his mid-afternoon coffee. He rolled the cigar under his nose, enjoying the rich aroma and thinking about the stories of how the cigars were rolled on the thighs of virgins. He chuckled at the thought, paying more attention to clipping the end from the cigar than he did to Murano's chatter. Striking a wooden match, he lit the cigar. He held the match well away from the tip, drawing the flame, making a ritual of the simple act. He savored the first puff of smoke and then held the cigar a few inches away, studying the ash forming on the tip. He set it down in the ashtray and picked up the phone.

"Mark?"

"Yeah, boss?"

"Never mind all that. I already told you that you can try this, even though we gave it up years before you were born. I know times change and you MBA bastards know stuff about marginal costs and shit. I already said it was okay to try moving the product north on yachts, like we did in the old days. All I want to know is whether it's gonna work and when we'll be back to moving the full volume. You got a boat spotted for the trial run yet?"

"Yeah, we got one picked out. The kids are gonna go see the owner tonight. They'll sign on as crew. Once that's done, I'll get the cash to them and they can stash it aboard. Supposed to leave in a couple days."

"How long to St. Martin?"

"Week, ten days, maybe. It's not like smuggling the shit on an airliner."

"Yeah. So once they make the buy in St. Martin, then what?"

"Then they get another crew gig on a northbound yacht and bring the product in."

"So how's this different from the way we used to do it in the '80s?"

"First off, we're not stealing the yacht. The owner's aboard, and none the wiser, so they handle all the customs clearance. There won't be any of that hassle of trying to slip in past the Coast Guard like you used to do."

"Customs still checks some boats when they come in."

"Yeah, but we're picking boats that won't meet their profile."

"What about random searches with the dogs?"

"This shit's vacuum packed like you wouldn't believe, and we got a perfect new place to hide it."

"How's that gonna work, smart guy? Every damn boat's different. That was one of the big problems when we used to do it back in the '80s."

"They all got these holding tanks, now. It's the law. They didn't used to have to have them, right?"

"Right. You gonna put the shit in the holding tank?"

"That's why it's there, to put shit in. Every boat's got one now. Between the stink and the vacuum pack, the dogs'll never find it, and the customs agents aren't gonna look down in the bottom under two weeks' worth of sewage."

"Maybe. Sounds cobbled together to me, but you're the one's gotta make it happen."

∽

"So how far is it, anyway?" Jimmy asked, slurping the foam from his second beer. He and Kirsten were sitting at an outdoor table at a dockside bar overlooking the anchorage in Back Creek. They had taken one of the water taxis from the dock in front of the Harbormaster's Office and told the driver they just wanted to ride through Back Creek and look at the boats. They spotted *Diamantista* nestled in among all the other boats in the anchorage and decided to wait at the bar until five o'clock, figuring they could hitch a ride in one of the dinghies that were constantly coming and going from the bar to the anchored boats.

"From the Virgin Islands to St. Martin?" Kirsten asked.

"Yeah."

"I don't know. They're both in the Caribbean; it can't be too far."

"You college chicks are supposed to know shit like that."

"Gimme a break; I'm majoring in theater."

"Yeah, well, I hope you can act good," Jimmy said, gulping down the last of his beer and signaling to the waitress for another.

"Well," Kirsten said.

"Well, what?"

"You hope I can act *well*."

"Ain't that what I said?"

"That's enough beer until after we meet with her," Kirsten said as the waitress took his empty glass and replaced it with a full one. "She's not going to take on somebody that shows up drunk for the interview."

"Jesus! It's just beer. I'm not drunk. This is my show, Kirsten, and don't you forget it, hear?"

"I just want to be sure we get this gig; it's the only way we can get square with your scumbag friends."

"You don't think they're such scumbags when you want some blow."

"Yes, I do. I just keep it in perspective and do what I have to do to get what I want. That's what you need to do right now, babe. That's all I'm saying," Kirsten laid her hand on top of his clenched fist and stroked it gently. "Now let's go over our story again -- make sure we got it right, okay?"

Jimmy clenched his teeth and jerked his hand away from her, but he nodded his agreement.

∾

THE YARD CREW had launched *Diamantista* with no problems, and the foreman had insisted that one of the line handlers accompany Connie aboard the boat to help her get anchored. She had been grateful for the assistance; she still found it intimidating to handle the boat by herself, especially in close quarters like the anchorage off the boatyard's dock.

Once she had satisfied herself that the anchor was holding and that *Diamantista* wasn't too close to the neighboring boats, she and the line handler had climbed down into the dinghy. As she took him back to the yard, he had complimented her on how easily she negotiated the crowded anchorage. She had felt her chest swell with pride, even though her cynical side suspected that he was angling for a generous tip.

As he climbed onto the dock, he grinned as he pocketed the folded bills she had given him. Touching the brim of his cap in a quick salute, he had said, "Thanks, Captain Barrera. Give a shout on the radio if we can do anything else for you."

Although she had recently acquired a captain's license, it was the first time that anyone had called her 'Captain.' She liked the sound of that.

Connie took the dinghy around to Ego Alley to check out of the hotel where she had been staying, relieved to be moving back aboard *Diamantista*. After she signed the credit card receipt proffered by the desk clerk and slung her duffle bag over her shoulder, she walked out the front door with a spring in her step. As she wove her way through the throngs of tourists, she felt herself start to swagger; she and *Diamantista* were part of the local color that the tourists came to admire along the waterfront.

Dropping the duffle bag into the dinghy and climbing down to untie the painter, she realized that not too long ago she had carried a purse as big as the duffle bag. In the last few months she had adopted a minimalist's approach to life. Once she would have found the idea of living for a couple of weeks with what she could fit into a small shoulder bag ludicrous, but now she felt a great sense of freedom at being so unencumbered.

Though her physical burden was light, her mind was filled with the things that she had to do before she could set sail for the Caribbean. There was a long list of stuff to buy and stow and enter into her computerized inventory. From toothpaste to fishing tackle, olive oil to engine oil, she had to provision the boat for two or three weeks at sea.

Planning meals and buying groceries were foreign to her; she wished Paul were around. She desperately needed a cook for the trip south. That was more important in her mind than competent crew; she was comfortable with her ability to sail the boat, especially in open water, but putting food on the table was beyond her ken.

She was surprised when she looked up and saw *Diamantista*. Lost in her thoughts, she had negotiated the ten-minute dinghy ride from downtown Annapolis to the anchorage in Back Creek without realizing it.

She tied the dinghy alongside *Diamantista* and set her duffle bag on deck, scrambling up the boarding ladder. She took her key ring with its orange foam float from the pocket of her shorts and unlocked the companionway. She went below and tossed the bag on the double berth in the aft stateroom. She would sleep there until she had to give it up to paying guests.

3

Connie settled in the cockpit with a glass of Shiraz and a plate of fruit with some cheese cubes. The day had been exhausting. First, there had been the helpless anxiety as she watched and waited while the yard crew had launched *Diamantista*. Then, as she pulled away from the boatyard, she had the sudden realization that she was truly on her own.

When she had taken delivery of the boat two months ago, Paul had been with her to sail *Diamantista* from Charleston, South Carolina, to Annapolis. She had been in charge, but she had known she could depend upon his years of sailing experience.

Today, for the first time, she had gotten a sense of the stress that accompanied being the only one responsible for a vessel. The line handler from the yard had provided much-needed muscle power, but no advice. She had been on her own when it came to matters of navigation and seamanship.

She was frustrated to realize how much she had been depending on Paul when they had brought the boat to Annapolis. Determined to be her own woman, she didn't want anyone else, male or female, to make decisions for her. For the first time, she was glad that Paul wouldn't be accompanying her on the offshore voyage to the Virgin Islands. She wouldn't have anyone to rely upon except herself.

By the time he joined her, she would have the assurance of having skippered the vessel without anyone to serve as a crutch. "At the rate I'm going finding crew, I may do the voyage solo," she said, surprising herself when she vocalized her thoughts. She had spent too much time alone, lately. She would have to watch that when she found crew for the trip. It wouldn't do to give voice to every stray thought when she was in the company of strangers.

She had just finished her wine and hors d' oeuvres when she noticed a dinghy approaching. There was a young couple sitting up forward, and the man at the tiller looked familiar. Connie thought she had seen him on one of the neighboring boats. As the helmsman brought the little boat to a smart stop inches from *Diamantista's* rail, the young woman called, "Hello, *Diamantista!*"

"Good afternoon," Connie said, noticing that the couple, if they were a couple, looked mismatched. The woman looked to be in her early twenties. She was well groomed and had an air of assurance about her. Connie pegged her as a college kid. The man was a few years older and looked as if he had made some token effort at cleaning up his appearance. He looked uncomfortable in his obviously new clothes, and she could see from the pale skin around his hairline that the haircut was recent, although his hair was still on the long side.

"Are you Connie Barrera?" the woman asked as the man running the dinghy held onto *Diamantista's* rail.

"Yes."

"I'm Kirsten Jones and this is Jimmy Dorlan. We'd like to talk to you about the crew openings."

"Great. Come on aboard." Connie stood up and stepped to the side deck, offering Kirsten a hand as she negotiated the step up. Jimmy scampered aboard and turned to thank the man who had dropped them off.

"Have a seat in the cockpit," Connie said, motioning for them to precede her. Before she sat down across from them, she paused. "Can I offer you anything to drink?"

"No, thanks," Kirsten said, frowning at Jimmy.

Connie noticed that she shook her head as Jimmy started to open his mouth. After a second passed without his answering, Connie said, "How about for you, Jimmy?"

"No. I'm good," he said.

She saw the smirk that he threw Kirsten's way and wondered what their relationship was. "Did you have any trouble finding *Diamantista*?"

"Not really," Kirsten said. "We just told the water taxi driver. He spotted you not long after you anchored. This is a beautiful boat. What is she?"

"A Taswell 56, built by Ta Shing Yachts."

"Pretty. Are you the owner?"

"Yes, I am. Why do you ask?"

"We checked on a couple of other boats, and they had paid captains. They couldn't really decide anything about when they were leaving; it was kind of up to the owner, and they, like, didn't know yet."

"I see. I'm the owner, and the captain. *Diamantista's* ready to go. We just need to provision for the passage. As soon as I settle on crew, we'll make an overnight shakedown run to Norfolk. Figure we can take care of any last-minute stuff there and leave as soon as we've got a couple of days of decent weather to get across the Gulf Stream."

"But what about for the rest of the trip? It's more than a couple of days, right?" Jimmy spoke for the first time, drawing another angry stare from Kirsten.

"What do you mean, Jimmy?" Connie asked.

"Um," he looked down at his hands. "I, er ... I was wondering about the weather for the rest of the trip. That's all."

"We'll take what we get once we're across the Stream. I want settled conditions and no strong northerlies for the first day or two. After that, it won't matter; we'll have plenty of sea room to ride out whatever weather Mother Nature throws at us."

"How long do you think we'll be at sea," Kirsten asked.

"A couple of weeks, give or take a few days, depending on the wind. Tell me about your sailing experience, Kirsten."

"I grew up sailing weekends and holidays with my family. Dad's got a Cape Dory 36 on Long Island Sound. And I'm on the sailing team in college, but that's mostly dinghy racing."

"Where do you go to college?"

"St. Mary's University."

"And are you on some kind of break? How long is your schedule clear?"

"Oh, I'm taking some time off. I'm thinking I'll go back in the spring. I kinda wanted to kick around a little before my senior year. Once I start interviewing for jobs and all, it'll be tough to do this kind of thing, so I figured now was the time."

"What's the longest sailing trip you've made?"

"We did the Newport to Bermuda race once when I was in high school. Took us six days; we didn't win." She smiled ruefully.

"And how about you, Jimmy?"

"Don't know much about sailing small boats. I was in the Navy for four years, though, right out of high school. I got a lot of sea time, but on ships. I was an Able Bodied Seaman. Deck crew. I can stand watch okay."

"Let me show you around *Diamantista*," Connie said, buying herself a few minutes to think about her decision. She led them below and encouraged them to look around on their own as she watched to see what they did. Kirsten checked out the galley and the staterooms, poking into lockers and opening drawers. Jimmy wandered aimlessly, eventually finding his way to the engine room, where he rummaged a bit while Connie balanced her desperate need for crew against her instinct that something was off about this couple, particularly Jimmy.

"It's really nice, Ms. Barrera," Kirsten said after a few minutes.

"Thanks. Connie will do fine. You think you want to do this?"

"Oh, yes. I surely do. Um ..."

"What?"

"I just wondered if you had any other crew for the trip."

"No. It would just be the three of us. Why?"

"Just curious, that's all."

"I saw you checking out the galley. Can you cook?"

"Pretty well. Basic stuff, though, nothing super fancy. That was my main job on the Bermuda race."

Jimmy emerged from the engine room, wiping grease from his hands onto his new-looking khaki slacks. That made Connie smile.

"And how about you, Jimmy?"

"Me? I can't cook so good. Eggs, maybe. Stuff like that. Mostly I eat sandwiches, or McDonald's."

"No McDonald's in mid-ocean, I'm afraid. I didn't mean could you cook. I wondered if you wanted to do this trip."

"Oh. Well, yeah, I guess. Whatever, you know."

"Do you have references?" Connie asked.

"I thought you'd probably ask," Kirsten said, producing an index card with four neatly printed names with telephone numbers. "The first two are mine; the last two are for Jimmy."

"Thanks." Connie took the card. "We've got a day's work to get ready for the leg to Norfolk. We need to make a grocery run and stow everything for sea. When could you two start?"

Connie watched as they exchanged glances. "Whenever you say," Kirsten offered.

"Eight o'clock tomorrow morning?" Connie suggested.

"Sure."

"One duffle bag each; bring your own foul weather gear. No drugs without a prescription, and U.S. passports. Can you both handle that?"

"Yes, ma'am," Kirsten said.

"Whatever," Jimmy nodded.

"Good. I'll see you in the morning. We'll get you settled and go to the grocery store. Once we get everything stowed, we'll leave for Norfolk. You need a ride ashore?"

"No, that's okay. If we can use the VHF, we'll call the water taxi. We're staying out near the mall; he can take us around to Ego Alley and we can catch the bus," Kirsten said.

∼

AFTER KIRSTEN AND JIMMY LEFT, Connie called the people on the card Kirsten had given her. Kirsten's references were both connected to the sailing team at her university, and Jimmy's were former shipmates. Connie had hired enough people in her life to know that reference checks were meaningless most of the time, and these were no exception. No applicant ever listed a person who would give a bad reference, but it never hurt to call.

She poured another glass of wine and picked up her cell phone, taking both to the cockpit. She set the wine on the fold-out table in front of the steering pedestal and punched in Paul's number.

"Hey, Connie. You back afloat?" Paul answered.

'Yes, and I'm glad of it. I've had enough of being a dirt dweller. How're you doing?"

"Okay. This stupid case is taking just enough time each day to keep me tied down. I'm not sure what it is lawyers do all day, but they keep asking the judge for extra time."

"Don't forget they get paid by the hour."

"Right. So how did the yard do with all the repairs?"

"Great. *Diamantista* looks like new; ten coats of varnish on all the bright work sure changes a boat's appearance. Now I'm scared to touch it, though. After paying the bill, I understand why Dani threatens to kill people who scratch the varnish on *Vengeance*."

"Get yourself an old nail polish bottle and clean it out, especially the brush. Then fill it with good varnish and keep it in your pocket. That way, you can touch up every scratch as soon as you notice it. If you don't, the moisture gets into the wood and lifts the edges of varnish around the scratch. Then you get to start over."

"That's a good idea. It'll have to wait, though. I'm running out of time here. I'm probably off to Norfolk late tomorrow."

"You found crew, then?"

"Yeah, I think so. Two kids -- they wouldn't be my first choice if they weren't my only candidates, but I'll see how they do between here and Norfolk."

"Want me to check 'em out?"

"Sure. Can't hurt. I'll email you with the details late tomorrow after I get their passports. All I've got right now is their names and a couple of references each."

"Did you call them?"

"Sure. Both of them walk on water; they could probably jog to the Virgin Islands and carry the boat. You know how that goes."

"I wish you had more time. It'll take me a day once I get the particulars. How long are you going to stay in Norfolk?"

"No longer than I have to. Right now, the weather's looking good for crossing the Stream any time in the next few days. We'll spend the night there day after tomorrow in the anchorage at Hospital Point. If nothing breaks on the way down, I'll top off the diesel tanks and leave the next morning."

"Think you'll be able to sail to Norfolk?"

"Probably not. The forecast is for a light southwest breeze on the Bay, but that's okay. It'll give me a chance to shake down the engine, just in case."

"Right. Well, send me the details on those two and I'll run them as fast as I can. If I get anything worth knowing, I'll send you a text message on your sat phone; you'll probably be out of cell phone range by the time I've got anything."

"That's fine. I'm sure they're okay. They just seemed to have an odd relationship -- kind of mismatched. Given that there're only three of us and we'll be standing four-hour watches, they won't see much of one another anyway, so it won't matter."

"Okay. Well, be careful, and don't forget to turn the tracker on so I can follow your route. Wish I was coming with you."

"I do, too, Paul. I miss you. I realized this afternoon that I've started talking to myself again."

They both chuckled at that.

~

"She's hot, for an old broad," Jimmy said.

"She didn't look that old to me."

"Thirty, at least. Maybe thirty-five. Them Mexican women, they don't show their age much."

"Your red neck is showing."

"What're you talkin' about? You don't think she's Mexican? She's some kinda beaner, for sure."

Kirsten shook her head and took a deep drag on the joint, holding the smoke in her lungs as she passed it to him. She exhaled with a long sigh. "That's good stuff," she said. "Think we got enough to last us to the Virgin Islands?"

"Yeah. We got plenty, but the *capitán*, she say we can't bring no drugs on her sheep."

In spite of being disgusted by Jimmy's bigotry, Kirsten found that incredibly funny. Encouraged by her fits of dope-induced giggles, Jimmy took another hit and passed the joint back to her. "No drugs without prescriptions," he said in a falsetto voice, pulling at the chest of his T-shirt to make it look as if he had breasts. "Or jou weel be keyholed an' walk on zee plank."

"Keyholed!" Kirsten squealed, laughing until tears ran down her cheeks. "It's keel-hauled, you moron. And she doesn't have an accent."

The ringing of Jimmy's cell phone intruded on their high. He fumbled it out of his pants pocket and looked at the caller i.d.

"Shit. It's him," he said, sitting up straight as he thumbed the green button. "Yeah, what?" he growled.

Kirsten bit down on her right index finger to keep from laughing as he struggled to maintain his tough-guy voice. She could hear the other party, but not well enough to understand the conversation.

Jimmy grunted into the phone several times. "No," he barked. "Can't get there that quick." He listened for a moment, the other person's inflection rising in anger. "An hour. Okay, man. Chill. I'm on my way." He disconnected the call. "Asshole," he muttered as he slipped the phone back in his pocket.

"What's happening?" Kirsten asked.

"He's got it, but he won't bring it here. Gotta play spy games -- meet him on the third bench out on the north side of Ego Alley. He'll have a folded newspaper under his arm. Don't talk to him or nothin'. When he sees us, he'll put the newspaper down and get up and leave. I take his seat and pretend to read the newspaper for five minutes, then if nobody pays me any attention, I pick up the duffle bag under the bench and walk away. Anything's wrong, he's gonna leave and take his friggin' paper and duffle bag with him."

"I'm hungry," Kirsten said. Let's eat a big dinner in one of those restaurants on the water after you meet him."

"Yeah, okay."

"What's the matter?"

"He's just such a dick-head, that's all. One day I'm gonna keyhole that sumbitch."

"It's keel-haul, dumb-ass," Kirsten shrieked, clutching her sides in laughter.

4

Connie felt her fever-like pre-departure anxiety fade as she turned from Back Creek into the main channel of the Severn River. The relatively open water of the Chesapeake beckoned. It was late afternoon and the weather forecast for their trip to Norfolk was benign. The breeze was light and from the southwest, but there was not enough wind to make sailing attractive.

They had 120 nautical miles to cover before they reached the mouth of the Bay at Norfolk, Virginia. A cold front was predicted later in the week; she wanted to get out of the Bay and across the Gulf Stream ahead of it. Then she could take advantage of the strong northerly winds that would follow.

Connie's plan was typical. She would ride the northerly winds from the frontal passage to a point south of Bermuda, around 25 degrees North and 65 degrees West. Then she would turn south to pick up the trade winds. With a steady 15 to 20 knots on the port beam, the remaining thousand miles to the eastern Caribbean would be a fast, easy ride.

The 600 miles in those first few days were the tough ones. Not only was the crew green, not yet into the rhythm of the sea, but they would be crossing the Gulf Stream. The legendary river of warm, tropical water flows north along the east coast of the U.S. at speeds as high as four knots. The width of the Stream could be close to a hundred miles at the latitude where they would enter it.

With a southerly breeze, the crossing was usually a pleasant trip, the crisp fall temperatures moderated by the Gulf Stream's warmth. Conditions in the Stream could deteriorate quickly if the wind shifted to the north and picked up strength as it did with a frontal passage. The strong wind against the current would set up big, square-shaped waves only seconds apart, dreaded by generations of sailors.

Cape Hatteras would be just to the south as they crossed the Stream. The effect of those square waves piling up on the relatively shallow waters that extended far out to sea from the cape was responsible for the area's reputation as the graveyard of ships.

Connie reined in her thoughts before she worked up another bout of anxiety. First, she had to get to Norfolk. Then she could worry about crossing the Gulf Stream.

Right now, her biggest problem was whether she could rely on Kirsten and Jimmy to stand watches. Tonight would give her some idea of their skills and dependability. She was more worried about Jimmy. His lack of sailing experience wouldn't matter tonight. They would be under engine power, following a direct course along the western edge of the well-marked ship channel. With the autopilot preprogrammed to follow a course a few hundred yards outside the channel, the only problems would arise from encountering other vessels doing the same thing.

She would take the first watch, from 8 p.m. until midnight. Kirsten would take the watch from midnight until 4 a.m., leaving Jimmy with 4 a.m. until 8 a.m. Connie had chosen the schedule thinking that as they got farther south from the Baltimore-Annapolis area, the traffic would get progressively lighter and more spread out. Not only that, but the Bay got steadily wider to the south. By the time Jimmy came on watch, they would be out of sight of either shore and their chances of seeing other traffic would be minimal.

She watched Jimmy as he scrubbed the foredeck, washing the mud from the anchor chain over the side. He was giving it a half-hearted effort at best. Connie reminded herself that she needed to check his work. She wasn't worried about the mud, but she had told him to secure the anchor in its chocks by tying a short length of line from the anchor shackle to the nearest cleat.

Trivial as it seemed, she knew what could happen if several hundred pounds of anchor and chain came adrift in unexpectedly rough water. At best, you would have to fight the elements and gravity to try to retrieve the ground tackle; at worst, the anchor could swing back into the hull with enough momentum to put a hole below the waterline, endangering the boat and her crew.

She didn't trust Jimmy; he had a shifty air about him. Also, the way his eyes moved over her body when he thought she wasn't looking annoyed her. She was determined to get the boat to the islands before winter weather made it a tougher trip, so she was going to make this work with Jimmy and Kirsten.

She didn't want a confrontation now; they might jump ship in Norfolk. Once they were at sea, though, she intended to sort Jimmy out; she knew his type. She'd grown up amidst predatory males; he wouldn't be the first one to regret leering at her.

⁓

KIRSTEN HAD her iPhone propped on the galley counter, a pasta recipe on the screen as she picked through the canned goods in the locker above the galley counter looking for tomatoes. She'd been distressed to learn while they were grocery shopping that there was no microwave aboard *Diamantista*. She had a buggy full of TV dinners when Connie caught up with her at the checkout counter. They had spent a few minutes returning all the frozen, single-serving meals to the freezer case as Connie tried to explain about energy budgets and electric power consumption. It reminded Kirsten of the lectures she'd heard from her father back in her teens.

"But don't you have a generator?" she had asked.

"Yes, but we don't want to burn diesel fuel that way, especially early in the trip. We don't carry enough fuel to motor all the way as it is. Conserving it's a safety issue on a long voyage; unless there's an emergency, we'll sail the boat and cook with propane. That way, if something goes wrong, we stand a chance of being able to use the engine to get us out of trouble. Suppose we lost the rig and didn't have enough fuel left to motor to the nearest port? It can happen."

Kirsten nodded, suddenly sober. "Sorry, Connie. I know that from my father, but I thought it would be different on such a big boat."

Connie smiled. "As a friend of mine always says, all ships are small at sea. Don't feel bad; I'm thinking about getting a microwave. It would be handy once we start carrying charter guests and we aren't making long passages. I just ran out of time; I'll probably do it in St. Martin."

"We're going to St. Martin? I thought we were going to the Virgin Islands."

"We are. I'll pick up my first mate and cook there. He and I will go on to St. Martin and finish up the boat preparations before we pick up any charter guests."

"Sorry I messed up. Let me just start over with the shopping, then. I'll need a few minutes to regroup and get a new list together."

"No problem. I'm going to the coffee shop next door and use

their Wi-Fi. Take your time." Connie looked around for a moment. "Where's Jimmy?"

Kirsten shrugged. "I dunno. Said he had to run some last minute errands. If he's not back by the time we're done, he'll meet us at the boat."

Connie had nodded, a frown on her brow, and walked away. Kirsten knew Connie wasn't comfortable with Jimmy; she didn't blame her. He was a condescending bastard. She wished, not for the first time, that she hadn't gotten mixed up with him, but it was too late now. She was committed.

∽

JIMMY COILED the wash-down hose and hung it back in its place on the bow pulpit, stealing a glance at Connie as he did. She was easy on the eyes, no doubt about that. She filled out that red knit shirt in a way that made a man want to see what was there. If she was wearing anything under it, it couldn't be much. And those shorts! Or whatever that garment was called. He'd noticed a lot of women around the yachts wearing the same thing. From the front, it looked like a really short skirt; from the back, it was shorts.

The way Connie wore it put the younger girls he'd seen to shame. She was one hot babe, even if she had some time on the clock. That just meant experience, by his reckoning, especially for a Mexican. Everybody knew about them. Climate, diet, whatever. They were all hot to trot, and he'd seen the way she was checking him out.

Too bad that Kirsten was taking the watch right after Connie. It could be just the opening he needed with Connie to come up on deck and chat her up at the end of her watch while Kirsten was asleep below. Oh, well, there would be plenty of time for him and Captain Connie over the next two or three weeks.

Finished washing the mud off the deck, he dropped the scrub

brush in the bucket and started to take it back to the cockpit when he saw Connie shaking her head and pointing. He looked in the direction of her gesture and saw the anchor. He had forgotten all about tying it in place like she said. Stupid broad. It wasn't going anywhere; the windlass was pulling the chain tight.

She probably just wanted to see him bend over again, check out his butt in the tight jeans. He blew her a kiss and set the bucket down, turning around and dropping to hands and knees to lash the anchor in place. Let her look; what the hell. It would just get her in the mood.

He found the short piece of rope that was already tied to the cleat by the anchor windlass. Passing the end through the anchor shackle, he tied a couple of knots in it, lingering to give Connie her money's worth.

He wondered what Kirsten was cooking for dinner. Silly bitch. She thought she knew it all. College girl, sailed on Daddy's yacht. She wasn't smart enough to avoid his clutches, though. Kirsten had gotten seriously messed up on coke and then she couldn't pay for it after her old man found out and cut off her allowance.

She was out of school now, working off her debt to his employers by helping him with Giannetti's latest scheme. Lucky for her she knew something about boats, otherwise she'd be working it off the old-fashioned way, turning tricks like the others.

He hadn't known she could cook; he'd been surprised when she answered yes to that question. Hell, all broads could cook, probably, but he never thought of her that way.

He snickered to himself, thinking about the things she'd do for a snort. She was probably down there in the galley, high as a kite. They'd be lucky if she didn't set fire to this damn boat. Then Captain Connie would have something to worry about besides his cute ass and the stupid anchor.

Connie -- every time he thought of that name, it reminded

him of his old cell-mate at the Tennessee Correctional Institute. He would have gotten a real kick outa this Mexican babe, that's for sure. He'd even thought Jimmy was hot. Pushed him a little too far, though, and got a shank in the kidney for it. Jimmy's first kill; he'd never forget old Connie, but he'd much rather get it on with this one.

5

"I hope it's good," Kirsten said as she set the three steaming bowls on the cockpit table that Connie had folded out. "I never cooked spaghetti from scratch before."

"I'm sure it'll be fine," Connie said, poker-faced, as she eyed the strange-looking, glutinous mass in her bowl.

"It'll be great as long as there's plenty of beer," Jimmy said. "Beer makes everything better, right, Connie?" He gave her an exaggerated wink.

"Perhaps, but not when we're standing four-hour watches and there're only the three of us. I'm sorry, but the liquor locker's closed until we make port."

Jimmy groaned. "Aw, c'mon, sugar. A beer never hurt nobody. Just one?"

"Sorry," Connie said. "We all need to stay sharp. I'd feel differently if there were more of us, but with just the three, that's the way it has to be. Four hours on and eight off will mess up everybody's sleep rhythms, especially this early in the trip. Alcohol will compound the problem."

"But we're only going to Norfolk," Jimmy said, sprinkling a

heavy layer of grated Parmesan cheese over his bowl and stirring it vigorously.

"I'm watching this cold front that's coming in from the Midwest over the next few days. We'll see what the forecast is once we make the Thimble Shoals channel. If we've got two days clear, I'm going to skip Norfolk and run for the east side of the Gulf Stream."

"But what about resting up for a day?" Kirsten asked.

"If we stop in Norfolk, we won't be able to get across the Stream for several days, once the wind comes out of the north. If we can get across before that, the northerlies will give us a quick ride out to just south of Bermuda, and with any luck we can ride them south from there for a while before they blow out. Then we can catch the trades, and we'll have an easy thousand-mile ride to the Virgins."

"It's a thousand miles?" Jimmy asked, shoveling a fork-full of the vile-looking pasta into his mouth.

"More like 1,600 from here," Connie said, tasting a small bit of the pasta.

"We could use the engine," Jimmy said. "Make some speed."

"I told you it doesn't work that way," Kirsten said. "A displacement hull will only go so fast."

"Yeah, but that engine's turbocharged. It said so right on top," he protested. "Right, Connie?"

"You're right. It's turbocharged, but Kirsten's right, too. *Diamantista* will only make about nine knots, no matter how hard you push her."

"That don't make sense to me."

"It's the physics of a displacement hull. Once the boat begins trying to cross its own bow wave, the fluid friction increases dramatically. You can get a tiny bit more speed by applying a huge amount of extra power at that point, but it's extremely inefficient and it just puts unnecessary stress on the boat. And on the crew, for that matter. It makes for a very uncomfortable ride."

"Then why would they put a turbocharged motor in it, except to go faster? Tell me that, huh?"

"To save weight."

"What?"

"This 75-horsepower turbocharged diesel weights around 60 percent of what a naturally aspirated 75-horsepower engine would. Saving that much weight means we can carry several hundred pounds more fuel or food or water."

"Harrumph," Jimmy grumbled. "Or beer, if we didn't have such a tough captain."

Connie focused on her food, forcing herself to eat the gooey pasta to avoid further debate with Jimmy.

Kirsten noticed. "You like it okay, Connie?"

"It's okay. The flavor's pretty good. The texture's kind of strange, though."

"Yeah. I think I put the spaghetti in too soon. It said eight minutes, but they wanted you to boil it separately. I thought it would be better if it cooked in the sauce, but I guess not. It got all mushy by the time the hamburger was done. I'm out of practice at cooking. I'll get better; I promise."

"It's food. It's hot and nourishing. Don't worry about it," Connie said, feeling sorry for the girl as she choked down the last mouthful from her bowl.

"There's more, if you want seconds," Kirsten said, hopefully.

Connie shook her head. "No, thanks. I'm fine."

"Gimme some," Jimmy said, holding his bowl out. "Man's gotta keep his strength up with two women to keep satisfied."

Kirsten looked at Connie and rolled her eyes.

∼

Two hours later, Connie was alone in the cockpit, gazing at the occasional lights on the distant shoreline. The dark water glistened in the silvery light of the nearly full moon, giving her surroundings an otherworldly look. Over the soft droning of the well-insulated diesel, she could hear heavy metal music from the stereo. She assumed that was Jimmy's doing; she hoped that Kirsten was at least trying to sleep so that she would be alert for her watch. Connie considered going below and suggesting that the music was too loud, but she restrained herself. They were adults; Kirsten could fight her own battles with the jerk.

They were definitely an odd pair. Kirsten seemed like a decent kid, except for her choice in men. Jimmy had little to recommend him, in Connie's view. He was ignorant, arrogant, and condescending, not to mention his slovenly appearance. She thought about putting in at Norfolk and dumping the two of them, but then she remembered the weather forecast. She should take this weather window. This time of year, it didn't pay to dally in the face of opportunity. Once they were at sea and truly in the rhythm of the four-hour watches, there wouldn't be much interaction with either of them.

She had called Paul a few minutes after Kirsten and Jimmy had gone below. Her cell phone had a spotty signal, and they hadn't been able to hear one another until she switched to the satellite phone. She had heard Jimmy complaining to Kirsten that he couldn't get a signal on his phone as she spoke to Paul. She mentioned to Paul that maybe she should offer to let Jimmy use the sat phone, but Paul discouraged her from doing that.

"You should keep that in reserve; sounds like he's a confrontational sort. I wouldn't do him any favors just yet. Having the sat phone as your secret might come in handy if things turn ugly."

"You're such a cop," she teased. "Always suspicious."

He had replied, "And you, why, you're right up there with Mother Teresa. Such a trusting soul."

They had both gotten a good laugh out of that.

"I got some preliminary info on the girl, by the way," he had said. "She's got a record."

"That's a surprise," Connie said. "I would have guessed it

would be the other way around. She seems like a pretty good kid -- maybe overly pampered, but not bad. He's the one I pegged for having a record."

"Yeah, well, you may be right. I've pushed a little on that. Nothing came back on his passport; I mean really nothing. No traffic violations, no driver's license, even. It's a little suspicious. Her record's basically college-kid stuff. Public intoxication, disorderly conduct. She got busted for possession, but it was just a single joint; they didn't prosecute. Her father's a lawyer, a straight-up type, apparently. Can't imagine he'd be very happy about this guy she's with. Even if he's clean, he sounds like a dirt-bag."

"I'm surprised you got so much information on her so quickly."

"Nah. That's the way it usually works. She's probably just a mixed-up spoiled brat. Getting nothing on somebody when your gut tells you he's dirty is a bad sign, though. I don't feel good about this Dorlan character. Keep an eye on him."

"You said you were pushing a little harder on checking him out. What's the story?"

"Well, given the way you described him, a perfectly clean record makes me think the passport's not in his real name. You know how easy it is to build a false identity, *Maria*."

They laughed at the memory of her experience with an assumed name a few months earlier. "Well, I had some ugly people after me, Paul. A girl's gotta look out for herself."

"No argument from me on that score. Just keep your guard up this time, too. I'll let you know the minute I hear anything about him."

"Thanks. Hey, he did say he was in the Navy for four years, if that helps."

"Yeah, good. That should help; I'll pass it along. I guess I'd better let you go for now. You've got a boat to run. Wish I was there."

"Me, too, Paul. I ..." Connie caught herself, surprised by what she had almost said.

"What was that?"

"Oh, nothing. I wish you were here, too. That's all."

"It should only be another three weeks or so."

"Right. Goodnight, and thanks again."

"G'night, captain."

Remembering the conversation with Paul made her feel warm and secure in a way to which she wasn't accustomed. When she was with Paul she could be herself, just like with Dani and Liz. She'd had girlfriends like that from time to time in her life, but she could recall only a few with whom she felt as comfortable as she did with the two of them. Before Paul, she'd never had a man in her life with whom she felt that kind of ease. Her feelings for Paul were alarming; she didn't dare let him know how much she craved his companionship. Men didn't like for women to feel that way -- at least none of the men she'd been around before.

The alarm on her wristwatch beeped softly, saving her from pursuing that thought. It was time for her to check the engine instruments and take a stroll around the deck to make sure all was as it should be. In another 30 minutes, she'd be off watch; the chilly evening air made her warm berth below seem especially inviting tonight. She stood up and stretched, noticing that sometime during her reverie the music from below deck had stopped.

～

KIRSTEN WAS on watch from midnight until 4 a.m., alone with her thoughts. She was past crashing; that had been this afternoon. Jimmy had let her do a couple of lines before they came aboard, but that was 18 hours ago. She'd begged for a hit when they had gone below to rest for their watches, but the bastard had laughed at her.

"Thought you could stop any time you wanted," he had jeered.

She could, too, but this wasn't a good time for her. He should understand that. When her bastard father had cut off her allowance, she'd kept herself going for a while by selling off all her stuff. The money from her car had been good for a couple of months' worth of rent and coke, but when that ran out, Jimmy had threatened to cut her off.

She had begged then; that was when he had told her he could fix her up with a friend of his that ran a string of high-class 'escorts.' Shocked and appalled by the suggestion, she had slapped him. That was the first time he had beaten her, and he had laughed at her the whole time.

"Don't worry, babe. I ain't gonna hit you in the face. Not good to spoil the merchandise," he had said. Afterward, he'd been good to her, bringing her food, fixing ice packs for the sore ribs. She had apologized for slapping him when he shook out a couple of lines for her.

"I'm sorry I lost it, but I'm not gonna be a common whore," she'd protested. "I'll quit snorting first."

"Uh-huh. I heard that before. Ain't nothin' common about Willie's girls, anyways. Most of 'em are college girls, just like you. I mean, he ain't gonna make you sell it on the street or nothin'. You won't have to do nothin' you ain't prob'ly done before. Just that now you'll get paid for it."

"There's gotta be another way, Jimmy. I don't mind working. Can't I help you? Like, keep the books, or carry the stuff, or ... or something?"

He rubbed his jaw, his poorly shaved whiskers making a rasping noise as he moved his callused palm across his chin. "Maybe so. Your old man's got a yacht, don't he?"

"Well, it's just a big sailboat. I wouldn't call it a yacht. Why?"

"You said you'd crossed the ocean on it."

"Yeah, that's true."

"I'm about to become a yachtsman myself. Prob'ly be easier

for a couple to find jobs as crew, 'specially if you got some experience -- speak the language, like. You know what I mean?"

"Yeah, I think so. Would I have to ..."

"Have to what?"

"You said 'couple.'"

"Well, that would be part of the job, but it'd be with me, not some stranger in a hotel room. I ain't such a bad sort. I know how to treat a lady. It'd be like you was my wife, see?"

"Not with Willie, or that other guy you both work for up in Baltimore?"

"Nah, I don't think so. You worried 'cause he's black, ain't-cha?"

"No, that's not it. I'm just not ..."

"Yeah, sure. Bullshit. Look, no guarantees, but if I can make this happen, you 'n' me, we'll be sailin' back and forth to the Caribbean on yachts, see. We'll be hired crew, and we'll carry money down and bring the shit back. Like a paid vacation. You can sample the goods, make sure it's not goin' bad along the way."

She was feeling low; on a rational level, she knew that it was a backlash from the coke. She'd kept herself on a pleasant high for the last few days while they had been looking for crew positions; now Jimmy had cut her off.

He said it was to keep Connie from kicking them off the boat, but she knew he just did it to be mean. She could snort a couple of lines every so often and Connie would be none the wiser. This was going to be a long dry spell. She had to figure something out. She could find his stash; there weren't too many places it could be. If she did, though, she'd have to cover her tracks. She shuddered at the thought of what he would do to her if he caught her sneaking hits.

Maybe she could take half of it; cut what was left with sugar or something so he wouldn't miss it. She could tell he had the hots for Connie. Maybe she could help that along. If he was distracted by trying to get in Connie's pants, he'd be less likely to notice what she was up to.

The problem with that was that she liked Connie; she really didn't want to get her mixed up with him. Connie projected the kind of confidence that Kirsten wished she could muster. If she were strong like Connie, she could kick this coke thing and ditch Jimmy.

She yawned and looked at the time on the GPS display at the top of the steering pedestal. She stood up and scanned the horizon. She saw nothing except the lights from a freighter that had passed going in the opposite direction a few minutes ago.

She'd go below and put on a kettle of water. By the time it was hot, she could wake Jimmy and give him a cup of coffee. She'd make herself a cup of the herbal tea she'd bought when she and Connie were in the grocery store.

6

Jimmy was fighting to stay awake. He'd only had a couple of hours of sleep when that bitch Kirsten stuck a cup of coffee under his nose and woke him up. Who the hell could go to sleep at eight o'clock in the evening, anyway?

This Connie was a real hard-ass. They coulda stopped somewhere for the night, but no, she wanted to go all the way to Norfolk. That's okay. Once they were at sea, she'd be stuck with them. Then he could straighten her ass out, all right. He looked forward to that. He'd never had a Mexican before, and she was one hot babe.

All he had to do was keep that dumb-ass junkie, Kirsten, from messing things up for a couple more days. She had crashed hard yesterday. Served her right; spoiled bitch. "I can quit any time I want to," he mumbled under his breath, mocking her.

He looked around, studying *Diamantista*. He ran his fingertips along the smooth, varnished teak of the cockpit coaming. It felt like he imagined the skin along the inside of Connie's thigh would feel. He smiled as he felt a stirring in his crotch. A few more days, and he could find out. Meanwhile, he'd just keep giving her the look; he knew that would make her hot after a while. It always worked.

This was some kind of fine boat she had. Where the hell would a Mexican girl Connie's age get the money for something like this? He wondered if she was maybe hooked up with one of them Mexican cartel bosses, or something. She looked good enough.

If she was, he'd be better off not messing with her. That gave him pause for a moment. This didn't seem like the kind of thing one of them would let his woman do, though. She'd most likely kept some rich old fart company and inherited his money. That was more likely. If that was how she got her money, she'd probably be ready for a young stud like him to help her make up for lost time.

∼

CONNIE GLANCED at her wristwatch in the gray light that filtered through the porthole over her berth. It was 6 a.m. She'd had six hours of sleep; she might as well get up and see how Jimmy was coping with his first watch.

She stopped in the galley before going up on deck and made herself a cup of coffee. As an afterthought, she made a second cup and put it in a thermal mug. If Jimmy didn't want it, she'd drink it. She was going to be awake for a while.

She took the coffee and climbed into the cockpit, noticing as she came out of the companionway that Jimmy was slumped behind the helm, snoring. Angry, she set the coffee down and made a visual sweep of the horizon. They were well into the lower Chesapeake Bay, out of sight of land. There were no other vessels in sight, and the autopilot had kept them running parallel to the ship channel, just as she had intended.

She considered how to handle this. If she were Dani Berger, she'd give him a vicious chewing out -- maybe even slap him around a bit. Thinking of Dani brought a smile to her face. Her style wasn't Dani's. She could put in at Norfolk and try to find another couple, but then she'd miss the weather window. Besides, Norfolk wasn't as good a spot as Annapolis to find pick-up crew.

She'd checked the weather before she turned in last night and made her decision; she was going to skip Norfolk. She'd talk to Kirsten about it. They could alternate checking on Jimmy every hour or so during their off watches to be sure he stayed awake. Once everybody got into the rhythm of the watches, it would be less of a problem. Also, there wouldn't be much traffic to worry about once they were across the Gulf Stream.

She stepped back behind the helm and reached down, putting a hand on Jimmy's shoulder and shaking him. He jerked awake and rose to his full height, grabbing her upper arms in a painful grip as he tried to wake up. Remembering her self-defense skills, she thrust both hands up between his forearms, every muscle in her upper body and legs behind the movement as she knocked his arms aside and stepped back out of his reach.

"Sorry," he said, shaking his head. "You startled me; I don't like it when somebody touches me when I'm sleeping."

"I don't like it when the man I've trusted with my boat goes to sleep on watch, either, so I guess we're even." She turned and retrieved the coffee, offering him a cup.

He took it, raising it to his lips and sipping carefully. "Sorry I dozed off; I couldn't get to sleep last night. I'll do better."

Connie nodded. "I'm counting on it." She took a sip of her own coffee, inhaling the heady aroma.

"Is it already eight o'clock?" Jimmy asked.

"No. It's around 6:30. You're on duty for a while yet."

"Just checking up on me, huh?"

"Yes, that's right. If you're awake, I'm going back below. I've got to check our position and get an updated forecast."

"Okay. So how long until we hit Norfolk?"

"I've decided to skip Norfolk, unless the forecast has changed.

We've got a perfect shot to make our easting over the next few days. I don't want to miss it."

"What does 'make our easting' mean?"

"It's a phrase from the days of sail. It means getting far enough east in the northern latitudes so that we don't have to fight the trade winds to hold a course to the islands."

"You ain't just pretty to look at, you know? You got some smarts, too."

Connie locked eyes with him and glared until he looked away. She continued to stare at him, watching as his discomfort built. He took another sip of coffee and sat down behind the helm. "Try to stay awake this time," she said, turning and going below.

∼

BY MID-AFTERNOON, they had the seemingly endless span of the Chesapeake Bay Bridge-Tunnel in sight, and a moderate breeze was filling in from the southwest as they got farther away from the protection of the western shore. They had secured the engine and raised the sails an hour ago, enjoying the silence after listening to the rumble of the engine for almost 24 hours straight. Everyone was in the cockpit. Connie had the helm and Kirsten and Jimmy were taking turns studying the 23-mile-long structure through the binoculars.

"That's really somethin'," Jimmy said, as he handed the binoculars to Kirsten. "That break in the bridge where the ships go through ... that's where the tunnel is?"

"That's right," Connie said. "In another hour or so, we'll go through and you can get a close-up look. It's kind of weird to watch the cars and trucks. It looks like they just drive into those big blocks of whatever that mark the beginning of the tunnel and disappear."

"Did you ever drive through the tunnel?" Kirsten asked.

"No," Connie replied. "Did you?"

"No. You can tell we're almost out of the Bay; I feel the ocean swells."

"That'll stop once we get through the bridge, right?" Jimmy asked, looking uncomfortable.

"No, we'll have that motion until we get to the Virgins," Connie said. "You okay? You look a little queasy."

"Me?" Jimmy asked. "Nah, I'm all right. Maybe that lunch didn't set so well with me."

"There's Dramamine, if either of you needs it," Connie said.

"I'm fine," Kirsten remarked. "Once we got the sails up and shut the engine off, I felt right at home. I didn't realize how much I missed this."

"How long since you've sailed?" Connie asked.

"It's been years since I sailed like this. Racing dinghies isn't the same. I mean, it's sailing, but ..."

Jimmy shoved her to the side and hung his head over the downwind lifelines, heaving painfully until there was nothing left in his stomach. He sat back down where Kirsten had been.

"Are you ..." Connie was interrupted as he leapt up and leaned over the side again.

When he was finished, he said, "I'm not feelin' so good. I'm gonna lie down for a minute."

"That's probably not a good idea, Jimmy," Kirsten said.

"Just shut up," he grumbled, staggering to the companionway and disappearing below decks.

Connie shook her head. "He's out for a while. Looks like it'll just be the two of us until he gets his sea legs."

"Big Navy man," Kirsten giggled.

"The motion's a lot different on a big ship, I imagine, but I know people get sick on them, too. I'm surprised he didn't say something about being prone to seasickness. It's too late for Dramamine now. I would have expected that he'd know after his Navy experience. If he's seasick in this, he's going to die once we get offshore."

"Oh, well, he'll get over it in a day or two," Kirsten said. "Meanwhile, we can enjoy sailing without mister macho."

"How long have you been together?" Connie asked.

"Well, um ...,"

"Sorry. I don't mean to pry. I was just making conversation."

"No, that's okay. Really. It's just, I hadn't, like, thought of us being 'together,' like, you know?"

Connie nodded.

"It just kind of happened, I guess," Kirsten said.

"Sometimes it's like that," Connie said. "Were you in school together?"

"Oh, no. Jimmy worked on campus. He was, like, a handyman, kinda. That's where I met him. How about you?"

"Me? What about me?"

"Is there a man in your life?"

"Oh," Connie said, pausing to think about that. "Not really. I ended a bad relationship a few years ago, and I've been on my own since then."

"I can't imagine going without a guy around for *years*," Kirsten said. "I'd climb the walls if I didn't have somebody to, to ..."

Connie laughed. "I used to be the same way when I was your age. I guess I look at it a little differently, now. I'd like to get it right the next time, you know?"

"You mean, like, mate for life?"

"I think so. At least, if I take up with another man, it has to have that possibility. I'm tired of the guys looking for another notch on the bedpost. After I got free of the last jerk, I decided to take it slow. It'll happen, or not. Meanwhile, there's life to live, you know?"

"Yeah. That's cool. I mean, you're, like, really lucky to be able to live like this, with this nice boat and everything."

"I am indeed. I just discovered sailing in the last year. I have two friends who run a charter yacht down in the islands. That's where I got the idea. I'd been just taking it easy since I split up with my ex, and I was bored, so I decided to give it a whirl. I've got a guy lined up to help me who's a first-rate cook and an experienced sailor, too, but he can't join me for a few weeks yet."

"He hot?"

Connie laughed. "Maybe so. He's pretty cute. He's older, though, and he's kind of in the same mode I'm in as far as romance is concerned."

A few minutes passed in comfortable silence as the big boat sliced cleanly through the swells and made her way past the Bridge-Tunnel and into the open water. Connie looked over to see Kirsten with her legs stretched out on the cockpit seat. Her arms were draped along the lifelines behind her; her head was back, eyes closed, a smile on her face as she enjoyed the last bit of warmth from the late-afternoon sun.

"Kirsten?"

"Yes?"

"Why don't you go below? Check on Jimmy and then get some rest. I'll call you in around three hours. We can just trade off until Jimmy gets over his *mal de mer*."

"Okay. You want anything to eat before I crash?"

"Yes, if you don't mind. Just hand me up one of those fruit yogurts that we bought. That'll hold me for a while."

7

Kirsten passed Connie's yogurt up through the companionway. As she dropped back below deck, she held onto the handrail of the ladder for a moment, waiting until she grew accustomed to the difference in the boat's motion. The swells were much larger now than they had been when they passed the Bay Bridge-Tunnel.

Given the course they were steering, the motion wasn't abrupt, but it was constant. The changes in direction as the boat rolled were sudden, and they seemed more violent below deck than in the open. It was enough to make walking through the open space of the main cabin treacherous.

Kirsten was careful to always have a solid handhold before committing to take a step. She worked her way to the forward double stateroom which she had been sharing with Jimmy. He was sprawled across the queen-sized bed, rolling sluggishly from one side to the other as the boat shifted.

She knew from her time sailing with her father that this forward berth was the least stable, most uncomfortable place to sleep at sea, but Jimmy was unconscious. She decided that she didn't care whether he recovered from his seasickness or not.

She was enjoying her one-on-one time with Connie; she hadn't had a female friend since she'd dropped out of college. Jimmy wasn't a stimulating companion; his only attraction was that he had access to coke, which made up for some of his other faults.

Once she established that he was not about to wake up, she began to search through his duffle bag looking for his stash. She found his baggie of grass, complete with a couple of joints already rolled, stuffed inside a dirty sock.

While he smoked marijuana regularly, he wouldn't touch coke; he was vocal in his view that it was a sucker's drug. "I should know," he'd say. "I've sold enough of the shit and seen what it does to people."

As she plundered his bag, he rolled over and groaned. Startled, she shoved the duffle bag behind the door, which was held open by a hook that left about a foot of space behind it. "You okay, babe?" she asked, touching his clammy cheek.

When he didn't respond, she returned to her search. In his shaving kit, she found a Ziploc bag of the white crystals that she sought. She put the duffle bag back together and took her treasure to the galley. Checking over her shoulder to make sure Connie was still at the helm, she opened the clear plastic bag.

Bracing herself against the rolling of the boat, she scooped up a trace of coke with the nail of her right little finger and resealed the bag. She closed her eyes in anticipation and raised the fingernail to her nose, snorting. Her eyes watered and she stifled a violent sneeze.

She put the bag in her pocket and leaned back against the counter, waiting for the rush. When she felt the lift leveling out, she opened her eyes and took a new small Ziploc bag from one of the galley lockers. She took the bag of coke from her pocket and shook about half of the contents into the new bag. She sealed the new bag and put it in her pocket.

Opening one of the canisters that was secured to the galley

bulkhead, she dropped several pinches of sugar into the original bag, shaking it to mix it and settle it. Satisfied that her theft couldn't be detected, she closed the sugar canister and made her way back to the forward stateroom.

Jimmy hadn't moved except for rolling with the motion of the boat. She put the bag of coke back in his shaving kit and returned his duffle bag to the locker where she'd found it. She went back into the main cabin, where she loosened the waistband of her jeans and took off her shoes before stretching out on the settee on the leeward side of the boat.

Jimmy could roll around in the big queen-sized berth by himself. She knew that amidships on the downwind side of the boat would be the place with the least motion. As she drifted off to sleep, she was imagining what it would be like to work charters on *Diamantista* as Connie's cook.

~

CONNIE WAS ENJOYING her early evening watch. She knew she should be tired, but the excitement of the first day at sea was better than any stimulant she'd ever experienced. Her decisions were made; her worry about crew behind her. She was stuck with them now, and they with her. They'd just have to deal with the friction.

She had enjoyed her conversation with Kirsten. Jimmy was a problem, but she knew from years of dealing with people in the business world that working relationships were rarely smooth. She did wonder whether to take his clumsy flirting seriously or whether he was just trying to get under her skin for some reason.

She resolved to bring it up with Kirsten the next time she had a chance; after all, Kirsten was the one he was with at the moment. She should be able to assess his intentions.

Whichever way he intended his remarks, Connie knew she'd have to put a stop to them, and sooner rather than later. Allowing that sort of behavior to go unchecked would inevitably lead to trouble. Maybe Kirsten could help her sort him out.

After steering for a few minutes and getting a feel for the vessel's attitude through the helm, she decided the sails were trimmed well enough. She engaged the autopilot, setting it to steer a course relative to the wind. It wasn't critical to maintain a precise compass course at this stage of the trip; keeping the boat speed up was what mattered now.

She could tell from the change in *Diamantista's* motion and the sudden warmth of the night air that they were into the western edge of the Gulf Stream. The wind was holding steady out of the southwest, and they should be well across the Stream before the strong northerlies came in with the cold front.

She was glad that she'd decided to skip Norfolk; life always looked better with an open horizon off the bow. She studied the behavior of the boat for a few minutes. The sails continued to draw and the autopilot wasn't overcompensating for the motion of the waves. Satisfied, she made a mental note of the heading and speed and stood up to make a 360-degree visual sweep of the horizon. There was nothing in sight but the open sea.

She stepped to the companionway and went below, turning on the red night light over the chart table. She entered the course, speed, time and GPS position in the log book as well as plotting their position on the chart that was spread out on the table. Extending the course line using parallel rules, she smiled when she saw that they were heading straight for 25 degrees North, 65 degrees West.

She reached into the pocket of her shorts, feeling for the single key that would unlock the top drawer under the chart table. Pulling it out, she palmed it and stepped into the main cabin, noticing that Kirsten had been sharp enough to choose the best sea berth on the boat. She smiled again as she saw how young the girl's face appeared in the dim light, her habitual frown gone for the moment.

She crept forward, poking her head into the forward cabin to see Jimmy sprawled awkwardly across the queen-sized berth. She shook her head, wondering again why an ex-Navy man didn't have better sea sense. He'd picked the spot on the boat where the motion was at its worst.

She went back to the chart table and unlocked the top drawer, taking out the satellite phone. It hadn't occurred to her to lock the drawer until she'd talked to Paul the other night. His suspicious nature was rubbing off on her. At his suggestion, she had moved the passports and her wallet into the drawer with her cell phone and the satellite phone in case Kirsten or Jimmy got nosy. She slipped the sat phone in her pocket and locked the drawer, pocketing the key again as she climbed the companionway ladder. Back in the cockpit, she made another check of the horizon before she settled into the cushion behind the helm. She turned the phone on and waited several seconds until it established a link with the satellite. She saw that she had a text message from Paul, but decided to call him before she read it. She missed talking with him.

～

PAUL WAS in his kitchen finishing the dishes after his solo dinner of seafood marinara à la Russo when his cell phone buzzed in his pocket. He dried his hands on the dish towel and slipped the phone out, smiling when he saw the caller i.d. Thumbing the green button, he raised the phone to his ear.

"Good evening, *Diamantista*. Where are you?"

"Hi! I'm so glad you answered. I was afraid I'd get your voicemail," Connie said.

"Something wrong?" Paul was worried by the relief in Connie's tone.

"No, everything's fine. It's a beautiful night out here. We're well into the Stream; it's warm for a change, and there are a bazillion stars. It's easy to see why they call it the Milky Way when you see it like this."

"Great. You're making me jealous. I'm glad everything's okay. How's the crew? Can you talk?"

"Yes. Kirsten's off watch and sleeping like a baby. Jimmy's been seasick ever since we hit the mouth of the Bay. He's out of it, so Kirsten and I are just trading off when we get tired. She's a good kid; I really like her."

"Did you get my text?"

"Yes, but I haven't read it yet. I wanted to hear your voice. Want to tell me what's in it?"

"Sure. We pretty much had Kirsten calibrated, but she's been in a little more trouble than we thought at first. She was caught doing lines of coke in the library and got kicked out of school. Her dad gave her an ultimatum; either go through a detox program, or hit the road. She hit the road."

Connie swallowed hard. "That's pretty rough. She still seems like a good kid; I'm sorry for her now, hearing that."

"Yeah, well, it doesn't mean she's a bad kid, but she's got a coke habit. That's bad; I gotta figure her old man knew what he was doing. Let's just hope she sees the light and takes him up on his offer before it's too late for her."

"Think I should try to talk to her about that?"

"I wouldn't, unless she brings it up. Coke heads are pretty squirrelly. If you caught her in a paranoid moment, she might really go off on you. On the other hand, if she's in a downer, you'd have a basket case on your hands. Any sign she's using now?"

"No. I told them no drugs aboard without a prescription, but I couldn't very well search their stuff. She seems okay, but I'll keep an eye on her. What do you think I should do if I catch them using drugs?"

"Don't say anything to them; just quietly head for the nearest port and call me. I'll arrange for a reception committee. Don't ignore it, though. You know it could get *Diamantista* impounded."

"Yes. Damn, I was just feeling like everything was going to be okay."

"Well, don't borrow trouble. Let's hope she's clean."

"Yes, that would be best. How's the case?"

"It's not much different. I'm still looking at being in the Virgins in three weeks, but Connie?"

"Yes?"

"I hate to give you more to worry about, but ..."

"But what?"

"There's no record of a James Henry Dorlan serving in the Navy, or any other armed service."

"Damn it! I'm not surprised. Any more on him?"

"No. My gut says that's a false identity. I don't think we're gonna find anything."

"Kirsten said she met him at the school. He was handyman or janitor, or something, if that helps."

"It might. I'll get on it first thing in the morning, but I wouldn't bet on learning anything. Look, be careful, but don't get all nervous about this. They're probably just two screwed up kids on a lark, running away to sea. I wouldn't trust them too far, but there's no reason to think they're looking for anything more than a ride to the islands."

"I know, but it's kind of like picking up hitchhikers, isn't it?"

8

It was a clear night, and the full moon bathed the seascape in silvery light. Conditions were moderating as they worked their way through the eastern edge of the Gulf Stream, and Kirsten was in a great mood. She had been on watch for about an hour.

With Jimmy out of the rotation, she and Connie had agreed to just wake the other person when the one on watch started to fade. Kirsten had slept soundly for several hours, waking with a start and worrying that she had overslept. That had been at two o'clock according to her watch. She had slept for six hours, so she got dressed and relieved Connie, who was now asleep in her aft cabin. That had been about an hour ago.

Before Connie had gone to sleep, she had made Kirsten a cup of coffee and passed it to her through the companionway. Once she had been sure that Connie was asleep, she had helped herself to another hit of coke, so she was feeling fine. The beauty of the ghostly sea around her was stunning; she thought she would never tire of sailing like this. She worried about what would happen when Jimmy got over his seasickness, but it was only a fleeting thought, and then her imagination took hold.

She was sure she could figure out how to ditch Jimmy; she was pondering how to get Connie to take her on as full-time crew. Her earlier notion of getting rid of Jimmy and becoming Connie's first mate and cook had taken root. She was excited at the prospect. His only value to her was that he could keep her supplied with coke, but she had realized that she didn't need him for that anymore.

She could make the buy in St. Martin without Jimmy. She would have to find where he'd hidden the money, but how hard could that be? It was somewhere on the boat. Once she made the buy, she and Connie could disappear and run charters.

She could just hang onto the coke; she wouldn't need to sell it. Connie's charter business would support them. Fifteen kilos of the good stuff would last her a long time, and it was like money in the bank if she needed to part ways with Connie for some reason. The only problem was getting rid of Jimmy.

She didn't know much about the people he worked for. They smuggled the drugs into Florida; she'd picked that up from listening to Jimmy's side of several phone calls. The guy he sold for was in Baltimore. She had gathered from Jimmy's comments that they had a network of small dealers like Jimmy all up and down the coast.

Jimmy couldn't get in touch with them now; *Diamantista* was out of cell phone range. She had a couple of weeks to figure out how to help him fall overboard. She would make sure she had his cell phone so that she could call his contacts and set up the buy in St. Martin. Once she had the coke, she'd disappear. If he fell off the boat, it would solve all her problems and it wouldn't leave any tracks.

She knew that Connie wouldn't go for that. Losing a crewman would be a reflection on Connie's seamanship, if nothing else. She would come up with something, though; she had time, and Jimmy didn't see her as a threat. All she had to do was wait until he was on watch and Connie was asleep.

She could sneak up behind him and knock him out with something. Then it would just be a matter of rolling him over the lifelines, and she'd be free. She could go back below and go to sleep once he was gone, leaving the autopilot to steer. She would let Connie come up on deck and discover that he was missing. Her plan made, she was eager for him to get over this seasickness so she could execute it.

~

Connie sipped her coffee and admired the golden light playing across the surface of the indigo water. Nothing was more beautiful than the open sea on a nice day during the first hour after sunrise. Like Kirsten, she had slept until she woke up; she felt well-rested and alert. She and Kirsten seemed to have fallen into an ideal rhythm of watch-keeping without any particular effort. As long as the weather stayed benign, they didn't need Jimmy in the rotation, which was just as well, since he had not moved from the forward berth for over 24 hours.

As if summoned by her thoughts, he appeared. He stood on the companionway ladder, gazing at her. His sudden, quiet arrival startled her when she looked over and saw him staring at her. He was freshly shaved, his long hair combed neatly and pulled back into a short ponytail. She smiled at the memory of what Dani had once said about men with ponytails. "You know what you always find under a horse's tail, don't you?" She suppressed the smile as she saw that he was leering at her.

"Morning, gorgeous," he said as he climbed up into the cockpit. "Lookin' at you first thing makes a man's whole day."

"You seem to have recovered. Did you find yourself something for breakfast?"

"Nah, not yet. I got other things on my mind right now. I'll get Kirsten to fix me somethin' in a while. Right now, I want to spend some of what they call 'quality time' with the mistress of the ship."

"Okay, since you want to talk, I guess this is as good a time as any."

"Oh, I didn't have talkin' in mind."

"Yeah, well maybe you need a cold shower, because talk is all you're going to get from me, and you're probably not going to like it much."

"Aw, now, don't be that-a-way, baby. You don't have to put on no airs with me. See, I got no problem at all with you bein' Mexican and all. Fact, I had me some purty good friends was Mexican, when I was in the Navy. Lotsa them wetbacks enlisted to get citizenship, you know. Some of the fellas didn't like 'em very much, but I figured they was sailors, just like me, see?"

"Uh-huh. There're just two problems with your bullshit. You know what they are?"

"I reckon I'm gonna find out here purty quick, but first, can I ask you somethin'?"

"What?"

"You ever done it with a white man?"

She stared him down. When he finally swallowed hard and looked away, she said, "Right. First, I'm not Mexican. I was born in the U.S. and so were my parents and grandparents, so just cut the condescending shit out, okay?"

He grinned at her. "You're a fine lookin' woman, and mad sure puts a nice rosy color in them purty cheeks of yours. Bet you was really somethin' when you were younger ..." His voice trailed off as he caught the look in her eyes. "Sorry. You just do somethin' to me. What was the other thing you wanted to tell me?"

"You were never in the Navy."

"No. That's not so. I was ..."

"Look," Connie interrupted. "I've had a friend who's a cop check you out, so don't bother with any more of your bullshit. James Henry Dorlan was never in the service -- Navy, or any other. In fact, my friend's pretty sure that's not even your real name."

"Um, Connie, I can ..."

"Shut up and listen for a minute. I've done some things I'm not proud of; I've even used a forged passport a few times, so I'm not judging you for that." She paused, watching him.

"I hear a 'but ... ' coming," he said.

She nodded. "But I've listened to all the crap from you that I'm going to listen to. I don't really give a damn who you are or what you've done up until now, but this is my boat. There's one person in charge, and that's me. If you can deal with that and pull your own weight, I'm happy enough to have you sail to the islands with me. If you keep up your bullshit, you and I are going to have trouble. Don't forget for a minute that I've got a friend ashore who knows all about you and Kirsten."

Jimmy looked at her for a moment, a sober expression on his face for once. He nodded. "Reckon maybe I ought to go get me some breakfast," he said, standing up.

"Jimmy?"

"Yeah?"

"Get it yourself. Don't wake Kirsten up. She needs her sleep. We've been covering for you while you were seasick."

"Yeah, okay."

"One other thing," she said, as he started to turn away.

"Any time you feel like testing me, feel free, but don't expect any mercy from me. We clear on that?"

He nodded and stepped below. Connie could hear him rummaging in the lockers and the refrigerator. A few minutes later, he returned to the cockpit. "If you meant what you said about me sailin' to the islands with you, I reckon it's about time I stood watch, assumin' you trust me, of course."

Connie held his eye for a few beats. Then she nodded and stood up, stepping from behind the helm. She reached in her pocket and handed him an orange plastic whistle on a lanyard.

"If you need me for anything, just blow this. I'm going to get some sleep. Wake Kirsten up when you get too tired; she's up next."

As she stepped onto the companionway ladder, he said, "Connie?"

"Yes?"

"Reckon I owe you an apology."

"Thanks, Jimmy. Have a good watch."

"Yes'm, and thank *you*."

∼

CONNIE MADE herself a cup of herbal tea and was about to retire to her aft stateroom when she heard Kirsten's soft call.

"Is that herbal tea?"

"Yes, would you like some?"

"If it's not too much trouble."

"No trouble at all." Connie dropped a teabag in another mug and poured boiling water over it. She took the two mugs into the saloon and Kirsten joined her at the table.

"I heard you talking with Jimmy."

"Sorry. Did we wake you?"

"No, I was up. I woke up when I heard him cleaning himself up in the head. Is everything okay between you two?"

"Maybe. We'll see, I guess. Why do you ask?"

"Oh, I can tell he's got the hots for you. Jerk. He thinks he's such a stud."

"Yes. That's what we were talking about. I was pretty blunt with him. Maybe it sunk in; maybe it didn't."

"Watch him. You can't trust him, and he can turn violent in a heartbeat."

"I figured that. It'll be okay; I can handle him. Don't worry about it."

Kirsten looked doubtful. "I'm sorry he woke up. We were

having a good time, just the two of us. At least I was. I hope you were, too."

"I was. I've missed having another woman around."

"Yeah. Me, too. Maybe ..."

"Maybe what?" Connie asked.

Kirsten shook her head. "It was a dumb thought."

"What?" Connie encouraged her.

"I was just thinking how cool it would be if we could ditch him. You know, just the two of us take *Diamantista* to the islands."

Connie smiled. "It's a little late for that. We're 200 miles offshore; we're kind of stuck with him, at least until we make landfall somewhere. Then maybe we could talk about it."

"Really?" Kirsten's tone was filled with wonder. "You'd do that? With me?"

"You're good people, Kirsten. Just hold that thought. We'll have to see what happens, okay?"

Connie drained her mug and rinsed it at the galley sink. "Wake me when it's time," she said, as she stepped through the door to her cabin.

~

KIRSTEN MADE herself a sandwich and ate it in the galley, right outside Connie's door. She listened until she heard Connie settle into her berth, and then helped herself to a snort of coke to celebrate her progress.

She was pleased that she had laid the groundwork with Connie already. That went much more smoothly than she had expected. Of course, she really did like Connie, and she did wish that it was just the two of them aboard. Now all she needed was a clear shot at Jimmy.

She went to the forward head and took a shower, careful to conserve water as her father had taught her. She dried her hair with a towel, glad that she had recently had it cut shorter. As an afterthought, she applied some makeup. Wrapping the towel around her torso, she stepped into the forward cabin and dug a skimpy bikini out of her duffle bag.

She dropped the towel and slipped on the bathing suit, studying her reflection in the small mirror on the bulkhead. She had in mind distracting Jimmy; she wanted to make the most of the weapons at her disposal.

She hung the towel up to dry and fetched her hairbrush. She would sit in the cockpit and brush out her hair in the breeze, giving Jimmy a bit of a show. If she didn't get a chance to do him in today, she could at least keep his guard down.

9

Connie awakened with a start to the sound of a piercing scream followed by several thumps and muttered curses. As she rubbed the sleep from her eyes, she realized that the ruckus was coming from the cockpit, which was directly over her berth. She rolled out of bed, fastening the waistband of her shorts as her feet hit the deck. As she opened the door, she saw Kirsten staggering forward from the companionway ladder. Her first thought was that the girl was naked, but then she saw the bikini bottoms and the torn top clutched to her chest.

"Kirsten?"

The girl turned toward her and Connie saw her battered, bloody face. Her lips were split and one eye was swollen shut. She reached toward the sobbing girl and took a step, but Kirsten shook her head. "No, please. Just leave me alone," she blubbered, turning and stumbling into the forward head.

Opening the tool locker behind the companionway ladder, Connie grabbed the heaviest thing that was close at hand, a 15-inch adjustable wrench that she had used to tighten the propeller nut before *Diamantista* was launched. She hefted it, deciding it would do, and grabbed an aerosol can of insect spray.

As she mounted the ladder, she saw Jimmy sitting behind the helm, his feet propped up on its rim. He took a deep drag on a small, twisted-looking joint, leaning back with his eyes closed. He held the smoke in his lungs, unaware of Connie's approach until she was almost within arm's reach.

She held the wrench out of sight behind her right thigh as he rose to an erect sitting position. He gave her a bleary-eyed grin, running his bloodshot eyes over her body and whistling.

"Hey, hot stuff," he greeted her. "Come to Papa." He patted the seat cushion beside him.

"I told you, no drugs," Connie said, glaring at him. "Toss it over the side now, and stand up."

"Uh-uh, babe, I don't think so. Kirsten and me, we had a little discussion, see. We kinda broke up, so I'm all yours, now."

"One last time, lose the joint and get on your feet."

He put the joint in his mouth, holding it between his teeth as he casually stood up. "Sure you don't want a hit? Put you in the mood, like? We gonna party, you and me."

Still holding the wrench out of sight, she aimed the aerosol can at him and pressed the button on top. Gagging on the spray, he slapped the can from her hand.

"You bitch! I'm gonna make you scream for mercy before I even do it to you the first time."

She watched as he drew back his right fist, stepping toward her with his left leg, his weight back on his fully extended right leg. She sidestepped to her left and shot her right leg out, the side of her foot landing just above his right kneecap as he started his swing. She put all of her one hundred twenty-five pounds behind her foot, popping his kneecap out of place and forcing his right knee to bend the wrong way. His weight did the rest, his right leg collapsing beneath him with a tearing sound as he screamed.

Mindful of Dani's advice to never leave an adversary conscious, she brought the wrench around, landing it on the side of his head just above his left ear. He collapsed in a heap, his screaming silenced. She picked up the smoldering joint and flipped it over the side, watching him to see if he was still breathing. She worried briefly that she had hit him too hard, but then she saw his chest rise and fall. She kept her eye on him for a few breaths, making sure he was out, and then she went below.

Opening the tool locker again, she grabbed a handful of twelve-inch cable ties and a roll of duct tape. Back in the cockpit, she set her supplies on the seat and dragged him from behind the helm. Rolling him into a face-down position on the cockpit seat, she cable-tied his wrists together behind his back. She tightened the cable ties until they cut into his flesh, and then repeated the process with his ankles.

She grabbed a short piece of line that she kept draped over one of the engine controls; she normally used it to tie odds and ends in place when the going got rough. It was about three feet long, with an eye spliced in one end. She passed the end without the eye between his ankles and brought it back between his wrists, tucking it through the eye splice in the other end. She tugged the end of the line, putting her weight into it as she pulled his ankles up behind his back until his feet were touching his hands. Even though he was still unconscious, he groaned as his broken knee bent.

Connie reminded herself of what he had done to Kirsten as she tied off the line. She felt badly about the knee; he'd never walk normally again. She had nothing but contempt for a man who would abuse a woman the way he had Kirsten, but she hadn't intended to inflict permanent damage. He was beginning to stir, no doubt because of the pain. She tore off a three-foot length of duct tape and wrapped it around the lower part of his face, closing his mouth securely. She was tired of listening to his crap, and at this point, there was no need.

∽

About a half-hour later, Kirsten appeared at the companionway dressed in a sweatshirt and cutoffs. She stood on the ladder, arms crossed beneath her breasts as she took in the sight of Jimmy, hog-tied and moaning, while Connie sat behind the helm sipping coffee.

"What happened?"

"Jimmy and I had a little disagreement. Are you okay?"

"Yeah, I'll be all right. He's beat me worse than this before."

"You shouldn't put up with that, you know?"

"Yeah, I know. I just ... I dunno ..." She shook her head and came up into the cockpit.

"Where'd that come from?" Connie asked, startled by the sight of a semiautomatic pistol in Kirsten's right hand, dangling down by her thigh. Kirsten looked down at the gun, frowning, almost as if she'd forgotten she had it.

"It's Jimmy's. He didn't know I knew about it."

"What are you doing with it?"

"I ..., um, I wasn't sure what I'd find up here. I kind of passed out, I guess." She put the pistol down on the cockpit seat.

"You know how to use it?"

"I guess. Maybe not." She looked at the pistol and shivered. "I just thought I might need it, if he had ... well, you know?"

Connie nodded. "Guns are dangerous, especially if you don't know what you're doing."

"Yeah, I know, but ... How'd you do that to him, anyway?"

"I learned to fight dirty. Men like Jimmy never expect a woman to put up much of a fight, so I had the element of surprise in my favor. I blinded him with bug spray and hit him in the head with a wrench."

Kirsten noticed his right knee, now looking like a purple basketball. "What about his knee?"

"Broken, I think. I kicked it out and he fell on it. I'm sorry; I didn't mean to do permanent damage."

"Don't be sorry. That miserable bastard had it coming. I wish you'd killed the son of a bitch."

"Well, I'm glad I didn't. That would be hard to live with, even if he had it coming."

"He does have it coming. You don't know half of what he's done. He deserves to die."

"Maybe so, but not by my hand. Not on purpose, anyway."

"We can't take him all the way to the islands like that," Kirsten said.

"No, we can't."

"We could just toss him overboard -- say he fell."

"I'm not comfortable with that, Kirsten."

"You could have killed him when you hit him with the wrench."

"I could have; for a minute, I was afraid I had. But I didn't."

"So what are we gonna do?"

Connie eyed the girl, not trusting her for a moment. The pistol didn't worry her, but the fact that Kirsten was sitting there calmly discussing cold-blooded murder troubled her. Until now, she had intended to tell Kirsten what she planned, but she changed her mind. She realized that she didn't know much about Kirsten, and that she'd been favorably disposed toward her for reasons that stemmed from her own past. "I'm kind of shaken right now, Kirsten. I need a little time to chill out and think my way through this; it's not a situation that I anticipated. Okay?"

Kirsten nodded. "What should I do with the gun?"

"I'd feel more comfortable if you gave it to me so that I can lock it up. Do you know how to unload it?"

Kirsten shook her head.

"Let me do it, then."

Kirsten nodded. "Okay."

Connie held out her hand, and Kirsten passed her the gun. Connie popped the magazine out and pulled the slide back, ejecting a round from the chamber. She collected it and slipped the others out of the magazine, handing the loose ammunition to Kirsten. "Put those somewhere. I'll lock up the pistol."

Kirsten held the bullets in her cupped hand, looking at them. She glanced up at Connie. "Where'd you learn to do that?"

"Like I told Jimmy the other day, I'm not proud of some of the things I've done. I learned to shoot because I thought it was important at the time."

Kirsten nodded.

"Look, I'm settled in up here; I feel pretty good. Why don't I take this watch? You go recover from your beating. You could use a little extra rest."

"Okay," Kirsten said. "Can I get you anything before I sack out?"

"No, thanks. I'm okay. I've got some ibuprofen in the first aid kit. You want some?"

"No, thanks. I had some in my purse; I already took it."

∽

Kirsten was stretched out on the settee in the main cabin, a light blanket providing enough warmth for comfort. She was too wired to sleep, between the excitement and the coke. There was something different about Connie; she sensed a change in Connie's attitude toward her. She considered whether it might have something to do with Jimmy's pistol, but she rejected that idea.

She hadn't known what to expect when she had poked her head up a little while ago, but she had been surprised to see Jimmy hog-tied and semi-conscious. She had been prepared for almost anything but that. She had taken the pistol thinking that she could shoot him and say that she'd done it to save Connie. She had heard them when she was washing up after he beat her. She had assumed that he would have his way with Connie, one way or another. She had been in no rush, thinking that if he had time to ravage Connie, she'd be more grateful when Kirsten came to her rescue.

Now Connie seemed all righteous and suspicious. She thought about how she could win Connie over. She'd thought she was making progress, but now she wasn't sure. The two of them could make short work of Jimmy, but she needed to find a way to motivate Connie and bring her around to her own point of view.

If Jimmy escaped his bonds, or partially escaped, so that he was a threat again, that could work. She'd have to be sure that they could kill him before she'd be willing to let him loose. She would have to manage it so that Connie thought he'd gotten free by himself and was taking his anger out on Kirsten. It had to be a setup that left no alternative but to kill him. She was thinking about how to stage something like that when she dropped off to sleep.

10

Connie was stretched out in her berth, trying to slow the racing of her thoughts. Kirsten had relieved her at about 3 a.m. She had come below and made herself a cup of tea and spent a few minutes studying the approach charts for Beaufort, North Carolina. *Diamantista* had been about 200 miles east of Cape Hatteras when she'd sent Kirsten below earlier.

Once she was sure Kirsten was asleep, Connie had gone below and locked the pistol in the drawer below the chart table, taking out the satellite phone while she was there. Back up on deck, she had checked on Jimmy. He had recovered consciousness, although he seemed groggy. She had rolled him onto his side in an effort to make him a bit more comfortable. She would have preferred to have him out of the way below deck, but he was too heavy for her and Kirsten to move him. She checked the autopilot and the sails and took the phone up to the bow. She wanted to call Paul, but she didn't want either of her shipmates to know about the sat phone.

Paul had been groggy when she called. She heard him fumbling with the phone and pictured him asleep, reaching for it on the nightstand. He had grunted something unintelligible.

"Paul?"

"Yeah. Who's this? What the hell ... time is it, anyway?"

"It's Connie. Sorry to wake you, but I've ..."

"Connie?"

"Yes. I've got a ..."

"What's wrong? Where are you? Are you ..."

"Paul, let me talk, okay? I'll answer all your questions in a minute. I may not have much time alone, here."

"Yeah. Sorry. Talk to me."

"Jimmy beat up Kirsten while I was off watch. She came below all bloody, and I went up to confront him and found him smoking a joint. He attacked me, but I subdued him. He's got a broken leg and he's bound and gagged. I'm not sure I trust Kirsten, either, so I'm up on the foredeck for a little privacy. She's below, asleep right now, and he's in the cockpit."

"Where are you?"

"I've just altered course. I'm headed for Beaufort, a little less than 200 miles out. We're making nine knots on a beam reach in a nice southeast breeze. It's blowing maybe 12 knots, so it shouldn't be too rough crossing the stream, you think?"

"No, you should be okay as long as it's less than 15 or 20 knots. Might get bumpy if it pipes up. You figure you'll be approaching Beaufort this evening, then?"

"Yes, if the wind holds."

"Okay. Are you okay, or do you need help?"

"I think I'm okay. Like I said, I'm not sure about Kirsten, but ..."

"She know you've turned around?"

"No, but she might notice. Probably not until this evening, though. She's not been paying any attention to the course. If she notices, I'll just tell her there was a wind shift, or something. Once it gets dark, she'll see the lights from ashore, I guess, so I'll have to deal with that then."

"Okay. I'll make some arrangements with the Coast Guard to meet you at the Beaufort entrance tonight. I'll send you a text with the details, but you'll probably end up needing to call them on the VHF when you're a few miles out. They can escort you in and put somebody aboard to give you a hand bringing her in."

"That sounds good. I'll call if I ..."

"Connie?"

"Yes?"

"You sure you don't want me to arrange for them to send a chopper out to you? They could drop a couple of rescue swimmers to help you bring the boat in."

"I feel like that's crying wolf; they might need those people for somebody that's in trouble. Everything's under control here for the moment, anyway."

"Okay, but it's an option; don't forget it if something happens. Meanwhile, I'll give them the password to your satellite tracker so they can monitor your progress."

"Hey, I'd forgotten about that. I mean, I knew you'd be watching, but I hadn't thought about being able to share that."

"Right. So let me get to work on this. I'll send a text or leave a voicemail; you probably should keep the phone out of sight."

"Paul?"

"Yes?"

"Thanks. You can't imagine what a comfort you are to me."

"Sorry I'm not there with you. It won't be too long. I'd better get moving, okay?"

"Yes. 'Bye."

"Good-bye."

∼

WHEN KIRSTEN WOKE UP, she sensed that something was different. As she looked around, she realized that she was on the high side of the main cabin. Since they left Norfolk, they had been on a starboard tack with the wind on their quarter. The port settee where she had been sleeping had been on the downhill side of the boat. That was why she had chosen it, so that she wouldn't get rolled out of bed by the boat's motion.

The boat was heeling to the starboard now; the wind was on the opposite side. She concluded that they must be on the port tack; the wind must have shifted. She remembered Connie saying something about expecting it to back, or clock or whatever. She shrugged that off; she had more important things on her mind, but first, she needed a pick-me-up.

She swung to a sitting position and put her feet on the deck, peering out the companionway. She could just see that Connie was behind the helm. The motion of the boat was a little more erratic than it had been when she went to sleep; it must be because of the change in the wind. She swung from handhold to handhold as she made her way into the forward head. She closed the door and helped herself to a snort of coke before she relieved herself and washed her face.

Closing the lid on the commode, she sat for a moment, savoring the rush. Feeling better, she opened the second door of the head, the one that opened into the forward stateroom where she and Jimmy had stowed their stuff. She opened a locker and took out her duffle bag, dropping it on the berth where Jimmy had been sleeping off his seasickness.

She wrinkled her nose at the sour stench emanating from the bedding as she felt around in the duffle bag. She soon found her own pistol, smiling at the memory of the way she'd played Connie earlier with Jimmy's gun. She'd gotten something out of three years as a theater major; she could fool most people most of the time.

She unloaded the little .25 caliber semiautomatic, dropping the bullets into the pocket of her cutoff jeans. She might want to load it again before this was over, but she had no intention of giving Jimmy a loaded gun.

She stuck the pistol in the other front pocket and realized that the cutoffs were not going to work; they were too tight. The outline of the tiny pistol was all too obvious. She took a pair of sweat pants from the duffle bag, thankful that the weather was cool enough so that they wouldn't be remarkable. She stepped into them and pulled them up over the cutoffs.

Replacing the duffle bag in the locker, she went back to the galley and put on a kettle of water. She enjoyed the ritual of sharing a hot drink with Connie when they changed watch. She looked forward to a chance to chat with her; she would focus on winning back her confidence.

∽

"SHUT UP," Kirsten hissed, prodding Jimmy with her foot. "She'll hear you." With Connie's concurrence, she had cut a small hole in the duct tape over his mouth so that they could give him some water through a straw. Since Connie had gone off watch an hour ago, he had tried to converse with Kirsten, but she had not encouraged him. Besides, with the tape still drawn tightly over his lips all he could do was mumble. She was enjoying his discomfort and making no secret of the pleasure she found in his plight.

Once she was sure that Connie was settled, she had taken the sweat pants off and folded them neatly on the cockpit seat not far from his head. Making sure that Jimmy was able to see what she was doing, she took the pistol from her pocket and slipped it under the folded sweats. Amused by the quizzical look in his eyes, she shook her head and wagged her index finger back and forth. "Uh, uh, uh," she said softly smiling. Now she was waiting until she was sure Connie had fallen into a deep sleep; she wanted her groggy for the next act in her little performance.

She had noticed that the autopilot was holding *Diamantista* on a southwesterly course, and the wind had not shifted as she had originally assumed. It was clear to her that Connie had changed course during her last watch. Kirsten's mental picture of the East Coast wasn't all that clear, but she was guessing Connie was headed for somewhere in the Carolinas. More than the course change, the fact that Connie had done it on the sly disturbed Kirsten. It would have been natural for Connie to have mentioned the new course to her when they changed watch; that was the usual way of such things. Kirsten interpreted that as a confirmation of her earlier suspicion that she had lost Connie's trust; maybe what she was planning would put her back in Connie's good graces.

When they had dealt with Jimmy, there would be no reason not to head back out to sea and resume their earlier course. Since Connie would either be responsible for his death or at least complicit in it, she would not want to make a landfall in the States, according to Kirsten's thinking. The water out here must be thousands of feet deep; with a little weight to help him sink, Jimmy would be fish food in no time. She smiled at the thought and blew him a kiss, checking her watch. It was almost time to raise the curtain on the final act of the Jimmy Dorlan show.

∼

CONNIE AWAKENED with a start when she heard Kirsten screaming her name. "Connie! Connie, come quick! Hurry!" She shook her head and rubbed her eyes as she rolled out of bed. She could hear hurried footsteps on the deck above her stateroom as she staggered to the door, surprised by how erratic the boat's motion had become while she slept.

"He's got a gun!" Kirsten screeched as Connie swung onto the companionway ladder and looked out into the cockpit. She saw Kirsten standing with her hands up, her back to the companionway. Jimmy was in a sitting position, a small pistol held loosely in one hand as he tore at the duct tape around his jaw with the other.

Before he spotted Connie, she dropped off the ladder and

opened the tool locker, grabbing her trusty adjustable wrench. In a crouch, she held onto the ladder and peered cautiously over the threshold of the companionway. Kirsten had backed away from Jimmy; she was standing on one of the cockpit seats. Jimmy was facing Kirsten, oblivious to Connie's presence.

Connie leapt into the cockpit and was on top of Jimmy before he saw her coming. She dropped the wrench, grabbing the pistol in her left hand and his right wrist in her right hand. Before he could resist, she twisted the pistol out and away from the three of them, hearing the click as the hammer dropped and registering that it had misfired. She continued to twist the pistol as she held Jimmy's wrist; forcing his right hand back at an unnatural angle as his fingers gave way. He screamed in pain as she wrenched the pistol from his grasp, dislocating his index finger, which was caught in the trigger guard.

She dropped the pistol behind her and took a half-step back. As she groped for the wrench with her right hand, she saw Kirsten step behind Jimmy. Her eyes still on Jimmy, Connie found the wrench, gripped it, and started to swing at his head. She checked her swing when Jimmy gasped in mid-scream and arched his back, groaning.

Kirsten, a wild look in her eyes, heaved her body to the side, her hands still out of Connie's sight behind Jimmy's back. Kirsten rose to her knees, as Jimmy fell to the side, shuddering. Connie saw the razor sharp, eight-inch chef's knife from the galley gripped in both of Kirsten's blood-covered hands. Jimmy curled into a fetal position, moaning softly.

Connie was nauseated when she saw the blood pouring from the wound where Kirsten had driven the knife in just above his kidney. She had torn the blade out to the side, and blood gushed from the long, deep gash.

Kirsten dropped the knife and leaned over the lifeline, throwing up violently. Connie suppressed her nausea and gathered up the pistol and the knife, moving to where she could get a better look at Jimmy's wound. She saw that there was no hope of stopping the bleeding. Without an emergency room, he would be dead in minutes, no matter what she did.

Although she knew it was pointless, her instincts drove her to grab one of the beach towels from the locker behind her. She dropped the knife and the pistol in the locker before she closed it. Folding the towel, she pressed it to the wound, attempting to control the bleeding. Jimmy stopped moaning as he slipped into shock, and soon she felt him go limp. Still holding the sodden towel in place with her left hand, she touched his throat with the index and middle fingers of her right hand. There was no pulse. She sat back, drained, and looked up to see Kirsten watching her.

"He's dead?" Kirsten asked in a tentative tone of voice.

Numb, Connie stared at her for a moment. "What?"

"Is he dead?"

Connie nodded. She went below and came back with a sheet, which she spread over the corpse. "Give me a hand, Kirsten. Let's move him to the side deck so that he won't be in the way."

11

An hour later, Kirsten and Connie were sitting in the cockpit. Connie had washed the area with liberal quantities of seawater and detergent, removing most of the blood from the unfinished teak decking. She thought that periodic rinses with salt water and exposure to the tropical sun would take care of the rest of the stains in a few weeks. Otherwise, she would have to sand the teak down.

They had both showered, and if she ignored the sheet-draped form on the side deck, Connie thought things looked reasonably normal. Unfortunately, it wasn't that easy to rid her memory of what had happened. Kirsten, however, seemed untroubled.

"Connie?"
"Yes?"
"I noticed that you changed course, before ... um ..."
"Yes, I did."
"Where are we headed?"
"Beaufort."
"Where's that?"
"North Carolina. Probably make landfall not long after dark."
"Why?"

"Why what?"

"Why did you decide to go there?"

"I wasn't about to keep him tied up on deck all the way to the islands, and I knew better than to trust him if we untied him."

"Oh. Well, I guess that's not an issue now."

"No, I suppose it isn't."

"So we might as well resume our original course, huh?"

"Kirsten?"

"Yeah?"

"Tell me what happened, okay?"

Kirsten nodded, collecting her thoughts. "After you'd been below for a while, he wanted more water. He was kinda making this slurping sound, you know? I finally figured it out. I asked him if that was it, and he nodded, so I went below and filled that cup with the straw thing that we used before."

"Uh-huh. Then what?"

"When I came back up, he was sitting upright, pointing the gun at me. That's when I started screaming for you. You came up and ..."

"Kirsten, you killed him. I know you wanted him dead, and I think I understand why. Maybe you thought there was no other choice, given what was going on. I'm not making any judgment about that right now, but I want some straight answers, please."

"I don't understand, Connie. What are you asking?"

"Let's start with how his hands got free."

Kirsten locked eyes with Connie, holding her gaze for a moment. "He must have broken those plastic thingies, I guess."

"Those were twelve-inch cable ties; they'll hold hundreds of pounds. The Incredible Hulk couldn't break them, let alone a skinny jerk like Jimmy. They had to be cut."

"Then I guess he cut them ..."

"Bullshit! There was no way he could cut them. He was hogtied, and there was nothing sharp he could have rubbed them against."

Kirsten shook her head, her eyes tearing up. She sniffled. "You think I cut him loose? After what he did to me?" She sobbed. "You're not going to believe me no matter what I say, so just think what you want, I guess."

Connie waited until the blubbering subsided. "The next thing is, where did he get that pistol?"

"I forgot about it," Kirsten said, sniffling.

"Forgot about it? I don't ..."

"I mean I forgot he had it; he kept it taped to his leg, like, under his jeans. Maybe he could reach it and he used it to break the cable tie somehow."

"Why would he carry an unloaded gun taped to his leg, Kirsten? That doesn't make sense."

"No. No, it doesn't. But he's kinda crazy, like. Not all there, sometimes."

"Uh-huh. One more question."

"What's that?"

"Why'd you have that butcher knife up in the cockpit?"

Kirsten broke down sobbing again. "You think I killed him!"

"That's not even in question. We both know you killed him."

"Then what are you driving at, Connie? Why are you tormenting me like this?"

"I think you set this up, Kirsten. I know you wanted him dead; now he's dead. You happy?"

"No."

"What do you want, Kirsten. What is it that you think we should do now?"

"I just wanted us to be free of him."

"Us?"

"You. Me. We can sail to the islands now, just the two of us. I'll learn to cook; I know I'm not great at that. But I'm a good sailor. What do you say?"

"I don't know; I ..."

"Connie?"

"What?"

"I need to level with you, okay?"

"Okay."

"I'm in trouble."

Connie waited, letting the silence drag on. Finally, she nodded.

"I lied about taking time off from school. I got caught doing drugs and got kicked out. My father cut me off. Jimmy was good to me at first. He helped me when no one else would. Then he tried to blackmail me into working for a friend of his who's a pimp, but I convinced him we should head for the islands, both of us, and get a fresh start. He agreed, but then the other day, he told me he wanted to, like, set himself up as my pimp in St. Thomas and get some more girls. That's what we quarreled about when he beat me. I saw you and this charter thing as a way out of all that."

Connie nodded, studying the abject girl, until Kirsten said, "Well?"

"That's kind of a lot to take in," Connie said. "I need a little time alone to think it over. Why don't you go get some rest; I know you must be drained."

Kirsten nodded, a hopeful look on her face as she got to her feet. "Thanks, Connie," she murmured, stepping toward the companionway.

"Thanks for telling me," Connie said. "I know that can't have been easy for you. Get some sleep, and we'll talk again."

~

THE LONGER CONNIE considered Kirsten's story, the less sense the girl's explanation made. She had not denied that she set Jimmy up, but Connie wasn't sure of her motive. Kirsten's cold-bloodedness frightened Connie; she wasn't about to take off to the islands with the girl.

When Connie was scrubbing the cockpit earlier, she had found the cable ties. They had been cut cleanly. After Kirsten left, Connie had retrieved the gun and discovered that it was not loaded. Except for those things, the girl might have argued that she killed him to save Connie, but it was obvious to Connie that Kirsten had set Jimmy free and put the gun in his hand. Kirsten's acts spoke of premeditation, and that made Connie nervous.

Kirsten was probably high on something. Looking back over the last couple of days, Connie recalled that there were times when the girl seemed much more enthusiastic than others. She could well have a stash of cocaine aboard, given that Jimmy had marijuana.

She had hidden the sat phone in one of the small lockers in the cockpit coaming the last time she'd used it. She took it out and turned it on, holding it down in her lap, out of sight if Kirsten decided to come back on deck. Using her thumbs, she keyed in a brief text message to Paul and sent it. A few minutes later, she felt the phone vibrate against her thigh. She looked at the screen and read Paul's response.

∽

KIRSTEN WAS IN THE HEAD; she needed a little extra focus to work her way through this. She was going through the coke much more quickly than she had thought she would; she had worried earlier today that she might run out. Then she remembered the rest of the stash in Jimmy's duffle bag. She didn't have to worry about his finding out anymore. She relaxed and took a little extra to celebrate. As the rush faded, she thought about the situation with Connie.

She was frustrated that Connie had seen through her plan. Although Connie professed not to judge her, she could tell that Connie was repulsed by her actions. She couldn't think of a way to persuade Connie to team up with her at the moment, but she couldn't let Connie take them back to the States. She could imagine that arriving with a dead body aboard would attract attention.

Depending on how Connie decided to present her side of the story, Kirsten might escape prosecution, but the thought of the frenzy of activity alarmed her. She'd certainly end up in jail, even if just for a brief period, and that would mean no coke. Then there was the question of her family and whether they would help her or not. She'd be better off in the islands, surely, whether or not she was working with Connie.

She needed to find the money; $250,000 would go a long way toward solving her problems. Maybe she'd make that buy and sell some of the dope after all. That was an option, especially if things didn't work out with Connie. But before that could happen, she needed Connie to take her to the islands. She briefly considered offering Connie some of the money, but then rejected that idea. She would need the money, and besides, Connie seemed to have plenty; this boat alone must have cost her more than $250,000.

Anyway, Connie was playing Miss Righteous; she'd hardly accept what she'd probably see as a bribe. Kirsten remembered a remark Connie had made about having 'done things she wasn't proud of.' That might be a key to changing her mind; maybe she could play on Connie's sympathy.

And then there was always the pistol. She had the bullets from both of the pistols, but she didn't know where her little one was. She'd lost track of it in the confusion. Connie probably had it. She had mentioned that it wasn't loaded, so she'd examined it after they killed Jimmy. Maybe she locked it in that drawer with Jimmy's. Kirsten decided to go have a look at that drawer under the chart table. However things worked out with Connie, a pistol was always a good thing to have if you were carrying cash and dealing drugs.

She stepped in to the forward stateroom where her duffle bag was stored and unzipped it. Opening one of the side pouches, she took out a selection of hairpins and a nail file. She palmed her makeshift lock-picks and made her way back to the chart table.

Checking to be sure she was out of Connie's line of sight, she slipped into the seat at the table and examined the drawer. The lock was just like the one on her dad's desk at home, which she learned to pick as a child. She stuck the tip of the nail file into the bottom part of the keyhole and twisted it slightly as she probed for the tumblers with one of the hairpins.

In a moment, she was examining the contents of the drawer. She found both pistols, as well as the passports and the ship's papers. There was an iPhone, presumably Connie's, and an envelope with a few hundred dollars in it. She decided to leave everything but the guns, at least for now. She pondered the guns.

If Connie went into the drawer for any reason, she was bound to notice that the guns were missing. That would end any chance of Kirsten gaining her trust. On the other hand, she wasn't doing very well at gaining Connie's trust anyway. She took both of the pistols and locked the drawer. There was no reason for Connie to open it, so she was probably safe enough from discovery.

She went back to the forward cabin and loaded both guns, smiling again at the memory of how she had deceived Connie about her knowledge of guns. She slipped her little .25 caliber pistol into the pocket of the loose-fitting shorts she'd put on after showering to rinse off Jimmy's blood. She put Jimmy's .40 caliber in her duffle bag and returned the bag to the locker where it had been. She went back to the main cabin and stretched out on the settee, closing her eyes and drifting off to sleep.

12

Less than an hour later, Connie was surprised when Kirsten stepped into the cockpit. She raised her eyebrows and said, "What's wrong? Too rough below to sleep?"

"Guess I'm just too wound up; I keep replaying everything, and I'm kind of on pins and needles until you make a decision."

"What do you think I should do, Kirsten?" Connie asked, mindful of Paul's advice to humor the girl for the time being.

"It's your decision, but I wish you'd resume our course for the islands."

Connie nodded. "Okay, then. We might as well, I guess. You know how to jibe the boat?"

"Sure. You want me to tend the mainsheet; haul it in while you steer to bring the stern through the wind, right?"

"You got it. Ready?"

Kirsten nodded, crouching at the mainsheet winch, both hands gripping the winch handle. She nodded at Connie.

"Here goes," Connie said. She swung the helm and watched as Kirsten cranked madly on the sheet winch, at first meeting heavy resistance as she pulled the big sail against the force of the wind. She had almost brought the mainsail to the centerline when the boat rolled with a wave and the sail filled on the opposite tack with a loud crack, Connie fought the helm as the boat tried to round up and put her bow into the wind. Kirsten released the mainsheet, easing the sail out on the opposite side. The boat came up on a more even keel, and the pressure on the helm fell off as *Diamantista* settled on the new course, once again headed for that waypoint south of Bermuda.

"Well done," Connie said, smiling. Nothing like actively sailing the boat to take your mind off your troubles, she thought, pleased with the way the boat had come through the maneuver. "Happier now?"

"Yeah," Kirsten replied, "But ..."

"But what?"

"Couldn't we just roll him over the side? I mean, every time I look over there and see him ..."

Connie's thoughts were racing; she'd anticipated this, but had hoped that the timing would preclude dealing with it just yet. "Um ... this really isn't a good place. We're still on the continental shelf."

"I don't understand," Kirsten said. "We're way out of sight of land."

"Yes, but this part of the ocean is shallow and it's heavily fished; if we dump the body here, there's a good chance it'll foul somebody's nets. Then the authorities will start looking for boats in the area."

"Oh. So what do we do?"

"Give it a hundred miles on this course -- say another 12 hours. We'll be in thousands of feet of water then, and we'll put a weight belt on him and dump him, okay?"

"You think of everything," Kirsten said.

"It's important to consider all the possibilities when you do something like this. I have zero interest in getting caught, and that means thinking everything through."

"Okay. You want to try to get some sleep while I take her for a while? One of us might as well get some rest."

"Sure. I think I can drop off without any trouble. If you feel yourself crashing, thought, wake me. There's too much traffic in this area to chance falling asleep on watch, okay?"

Kirsten nodded, and Connie stepped toward the companionway.

"Connie?"

She turned as she was about to step below. "Yes?"

Thanks," Kirsten said in a soft, sincere tone.

Connie nodded and went below.

∼

KIRSTEN WAS SO EXCITED that she could barely contain herself. She forced herself to wait for a few minutes before she took a snort to celebrate. She was leaning back with her eyes closed, enjoying the feel of the fresh breeze in her short hair when she became aware of the low-pitched noise. Startled, she sat up and looked around, expecting to see another boat in the vicinity. She swept the horizon, but saw nothing as the sound continued to increase. So quickly that she thought she was hallucinating, a big, white helicopter with an orange stripe appeared off the starboard side, dropping to hover just a few feet above the waves. She saw that there was a man wearing body armor sitting in the open door with a machine gun aimed at her. Before she could think of what to do, a deafening voice, distorted by the high level of amplification, boomed out.

"*Diamantista,* this is the United States Coast Guard. Heave to immediately!"

Kirsten froze, gripping the helm. She was trying to think of what to do when the machine gun barked, raising plumes of frothy spray 50 yards off the bow.

"Turn your bow into the wind, NOW!" the mechanical voice boomed over the thumping sound of the helicopter's blades.

Connie scrambled from the companionway and shoved her aside, swinging the helm to bring the boat's bow through the wind. *Diamantista* coasted to a stop, and the sails filled on the wrong side, back-winded, holding the vessel steady against the motion of the sea but providing no forward movement.

"Everyone step to the side deck facing the helicopter, hands in the air. Wave both arms if anyone is below deck." There was a pause of several seconds as Connie and Kirsten complied. "We will be boarding. Do not leave your current positions until you are told to do so."

Two figures in bulky orange suits appeared in the door beside the machine-gunner and plummeted into the water, surfacing a few yards from *Diamantista's* starboard side. They swam to the boat and clambered over the side with practiced ease, pistols appearing in their hands as soon as they were aboard.

"Is there anyone else aboard?" one of them asked.

Connie was surprised to hear a woman's voice. "No," she replied.

"Are there any weapons aboard?"

"There are two unloaded pistols locked in the drawer below the chart table," Connie said.

"Are you Connie Barrera?"

"Yes."

"I'm Chief Boatswain's Mate Simmons. Where are your passports?"

"They're in that same locked drawer."

"Okay. I need to see them and your ship's papers. You and I will go below in just a second. Don't open any drawers or lockers until I tell you to. Clear?"

"Yes."

Simmons nodded. "You," she said, looking at Kirsten, "don't move."

Kirsten jerked her head up and down in nervous agreement, her hands still in the air. "Let's go, Ms. Barrera. You first, please." When the two of them were standing in front of the chart table, Simmons said, "I only see the one drawer with a lock. Is that the one?"

"Yes."

"You have the key?"

"In the right front pocket of my shorts."

"Take it out slowly and unlock the drawer. Don't open it."

Connie did as instructed.

Simmons said, "Step over there, and stay in my line of sight, please," gesturing with her pistol. When Connie was in position, Simmons opened the drawer. Keeping her eyes on Connie, she reached into the drawer, a look of puzzlement spreading over her face as she withdrew three passports held together by a rubber band.

"You said there were two pistols ..." she was interrupted by a man's voice yelling, "Gun!" A flat, popping sound was followed by a piercing scream.

Connie noticed that Simmons eyes never wavered. "Kevin?" she yelled.

"It's all under control," the man's voice replied.

Simmons tossed the passports to Connie. "Pull yours out and show me the page with your picture, please."

Connie held her passport open so that Simmons could see it. The woman studied it for a moment, her eyes flicking between the passport and Connie's face. "Okay," she said. "Thanks for your co-operation. I'm to tell you that Lt. Russo sends his best." She holstered her gun.

"Thank you," Connie said. "I guess she must have picked the lock."

Simmons nodded. "Junkies can be resourceful; it's just a question of motivation, Ms. Barrera."

"Connie will do, Chief."

"Good. Connie, call me Sally. You and Kevin and I are going to be shipmates; we're supposed to help you sail *Diamantista* to Beaufort."

"That's great. Sure you don't want to sail to the Virgins instead?"

"I wish. You've got a dead body aboard. Is that right?"

"Yes."

"That the bundle on the port-side deck?"

"That's right."

"Okay. Kevin and I need to get it into a basket stretcher so they can hoist it into the chopper. Then we'll secure the prisoner, and we can get under way. Let's go topside, Connie."

~

"I'VE NEVER BEEN SO happy to see anyone in my life," Connie said, putting a fresh pot of decaffeinated coffee on *Diamantista's* dining table. She took a seat opposite Paul and poured them each a cup.

Diamantista was tied securely along the face dock at Beaufort's Town Dock marina. They had arrived a couple of hours ago, and the time since was a blur for Connie. She had answered interminable questions, signed a seemingly endless series of forms, and tried to stay out of the way as a team of investigators and crime scene technicians swarmed over every inch of her boat.

Paul smiled at her as he stirred sugar and non-dairy creamer into his coffee. "There's a break of a couple of days in the trial prep; I thought you could maybe, um, use a little friendly company."

"You can't imagine what it meant to me for you to be on that dock when we brought her in, Paul. Thank you seems so ... inadequate, I guess. But thank you again."

"I feel like it's kind of my fault, you know?"

"That's nonsense. You couldn't very well bail out on that case after all the work you put into it over the last few years. Besides, I'm the one who decided she could do the trip with pick-up crew. Hah! Fine judge of character I am."

"Don't be so hard on yourself. You weren't totally comfortable with them, remember?"

"No, but I let my sense of desperation overcome my better judgment."

"You're not the first skipper who tried to make do with the crew she could find. Let it go."

"Oh, I am. I'm resigned to sitting here until spring now. Maybe I'll lay the boat up and come to Miami; I kind of liked South Beach when I spent time there a few years ago."

"Well, I don't think you should make any big decisions tonight, but I do have a message for you from Phillip."

"Phillip Davis?" There was surprise in Connie's voice. She sat up straight and looked at Paul, eyebrows raised.

"None other. He heard from Dani a few days ago that you were looking for crew. He wanted to get in touch with you, but Dani and Liz were off by then, running a charter, and he didn't know how to reach you. By the time he figured out to call me, you'd already left Norfolk."

"He wanted to crew on *Diamantista*? I'm ... I don't know what to say."

"He has a love for sail, and Sandrine's off in some kind of training thing in France for a few weeks. He was thinking he'd drag Sharktooth up to Annapolis and the three of you could make the trip."

"Wow. I wish he had gotten in touch with me."

"Well, I talked to him while I was waiting for you guys to bring *Diamantista* in. He's still willing, if that's what you want to do. Eager, I'd say. Sharktooth, too. But I don't think you should decide right now."

"No, but that's not a tough decision. I'm pretty beat, though."

"I can imagine that you are. I should get out of here and let you get some rest."

"Paul?"

"What?"

"I know we agreed ... not to .... um, but ..."

"What is it?" Paul asked, worry in his voice and in the lines on his brow.

"Could you just hold me? Just ... hold me for a minute? That's all. I need you ..."

He shifted in his seat, making room for her to slide in beside him and spreading his arms. She snuggled against him, dropping her head on his shoulder and returning his gentle hug. Within seconds, she was sound asleep. Paul twisted on the settee until he could stretch out, settling her on his chest, her head still on his shoulder. He reached over with his free hand and switched off the light over the dinette.

13

Connie was in that pleasant state between sleep and wakefulness that only came after a full, stress-free night's sleep. It was something that she couldn't remember ever experiencing until after she split up with Rick and left for the Bahamas. Even then, it was a rare thing. She imagined it was the kind of sleep that an infant had, untroubled by any intrusions from life's uncertainties. She felt a smile spread over her face and decided it was time to get up. She was craving a cup of coffee. She forced an eye open and was disoriented; the first thing she saw was a man's unshaven chin, inches from her eyes, too close to focus. She fought her instinct to jump out of bed, taking a moment to figure out where she was. Her surroundings were familiar; she cut her eyes to look straight up, and saw the ceiling of *Diamantista's* main cabin. The man beneath her took a deep breath; she waited, thinking he was waking up. Then he exhaled and shifted his position slightly. She moved her head a little and shifted her focus again, recognizing Paul Russo's face.

She was mortified as she realized that she slept the entire night in his arms. She reached a hand out to the edge of the dining table a few inches in front of her face, stretching her right arm across the sleeping Paul. Grasping the table to support her weight, she rolled slowly until she got her feet on the floor. She managed to slip out of the space between Paul, stretched out on the settee on his back, and the table. He didn't stir; she was relieved that she had extricated herself without waking him, but still a bit worried about how she had come to pass the night in his arms. Pleasant though it had been, it ran counter to all their discussions about maintaining some distance in their relationship until they were both ready.

She stood for a moment, gazing at him; he was a handsome man and surprisingly gentle, given his career as a homicide detective -- or maybe it was because of that; she really couldn't say. She felt a warmth spreading through her body as she studied his sleeping form. She shook her head, snapping herself out of her dangerous trance. She padded into the galley and filled her stove-top espresso maker with water and finely ground, espresso-roast coffee, careful not to make any noise. As she lit the burner under the pot, she glanced at the clock on the bulkhead, surprised to see that it was 10 a.m. Of course, they had been awake almost until dawn; they both needed the sleep.

She had been far too excited to drop off after the investigators had finally left, and Paul had seemed willing enough to sit up with her, rehashing her aborted voyage and discussing her plans from here. She still couldn't figure out how they'd ended up passing the night with her curled up on his chest, though. She felt her face flush again at the recollection of how natural that had seemed.

Hearing the coffee burble into the top of the pot, she cut off the burner and waited until the soft gurgle told her the coffee was ready. She took two espresso cups from the locker by the stove and filled one for herself, raising it until it was almost touching her nose. She inhaled, savoring the rich aroma and anticipating the way it would feel on her tongue. Lost in her favorite morning ritual, she was startled when Paul spoke.

"Any more of that, or did I miss my chance?"

"Good morning. You surprised me."

"Sorry. Guess we kinda fell asleep, huh?"

"Yes, we did. And yes, there's more," she said, pouring a cup for him.

She stepped back into the saloon with the coffee to find him sitting up at the table. She set one of the cups in front of him and sat down across from him.

"Thanks." He lifted the cup, gazing down into it for a moment. He set it down and raised his eyes, looking into hers. "Um, about last night, did we ..."

Connie swallowed hard, dreading the question that she knew was coming. She waited, watching as he took a sip of coffee.

"Did we talk about how Kirsten's wrist got hurt?"

Connie didn't know whether to be relieved or angry. She took a sip of coffee while she got her emotions under control. "She took a shot at the Coast Guard helicopter and then turned the gun on Kevin, the guy who was on deck with her. He didn't want to shoot her, so he smacked her wrist with his pistol."

Paul shook his head. "Typical coke-head. Gonna shoot down a chopper with a .25 caliber pistol. She's lucky he didn't blow her away."

"Yes. What do you think's going to happen to her?"

"Oh, she's bound to be charged with murder; there's no way around it. She admitted killing him; you confirmed it. There was premeditation. What happens after that is anybody's guess, though. I think a good lawyer could spin that whole situation in her favor."

"You don't think she'll get off?" There was worry in Connie's voice.

"Hard to say, but probably not. She'll end up doing some time; maybe she'll plead to a lesser charge, but I doubt any prosecutor will let her skate. Why do you sound so worried? I thought you agreed that he was a scumbag."

"Oh, no doubt about that. It's not that he was killed; he probably had that coming. He beat her like you wouldn't believe just a couple of days before."

"What's the problem, then?"

"She ended up scaring me more than he did. I mean, I understand jerks; I've been around enough of them. But she was something else. She was so cold and calculating. Clumsy and stupid when it came to executing her plan, but she intended to kill him. I told you how she tried to persuade me to just roll him over the side."

"Yes. Yes, you did." Paul shook his head. "It's over; you're fine. Try to let it go."

Connie nodded. "Think I'll have to come back and testify?"

"My bet is they're going to let her plead to something, maybe in exchange for her telling them what she knew about his connections in Baltimore. It'll be interesting to see what turns up now that they've got some prints for him. They'll find out who he really was; could be that she's got some important information to trade and doesn't even know it."

"Well, I hope it comes out that way. I'll have trouble putting it behind me if I know I have to come back for a trial."

"Not to change the subject, but can I buy you a late breakfast? I'm starving," Paul said.

"Sure, that would be great. Can you wait long enough for me to take a quick shower? I'm still salty from our bash into the wind getting back here."

"Yeah. In fact, I'd like to swing by the B&B and freshen up myself. Pick you up in half an hour?"

"Good. See you then."

∽

BUSTER DANIELS SAT on the bench along the waterfront and watched as the tall, fit-looking middle-aged man stepped from

Diamantista onto the dock. He raised his smart phone, pretending to key in a number as he snapped a picture. Studying it for a moment, he cropped it and applied a filter to enhance the man's features. Satisfied, he emailed it to his boss with a note indicating that this guy had apparently spent the night on the boat. When he had relieved Vinnie a couple of hours ago, Vinnie had reported that one guy had remained aboard with the Barrera woman after all the Feds had left last night. Vinnie hadn't been able to get a picture; there was too much activity, and too many people, not to mention that it had been dark.

The two of them had driven down from Baltimore yesterday evening. Tony Ferranti, their boss, had discovered that the boat that shithead Jimmy Dorlan was on had altered course and was about to enter Beaufort Inlet. Tony didn't trust Jimmy even a little bit; that's why he'd had Buster put the satellite tracker on the boat. Tony wanted him and Vinnie on hand when the boat came in, just in case Jimmy was up to something. By the time the two of them got to the town dock, the boat had been tied up and was swarming with cops. Some had been in Coast Guard uniforms, and others had been wearing FBI windbreakers. There were a couple that had DEA jackets and a drug dog, and one with U.S. Customs stenciled across his back.

He and Vinnie had watched as they led one ratty-looking girl in handcuffs to an unmarked car. There had been no sign of Jimmy, and calls to his cell phone went to voicemail. Vinnie, dumb shit that he was, argued that Jimmy was shacked up with the woman on the boat, but the departure of this last guy this morning made that seem unlikely. Buster figured that guy for the woman's boyfriend. The girl in handcuffs had to be the junkie that Jimmy had been hanging with, but where the hell could Jimmy be?

He pried open the plastic cover on his takeout coffee and took a careful sip, surprised that it was decent. As he set the cup down, the guy who had left about thirty minutes ago walked back down the dock toward the boat, *Diamantista*. Strange name, Buster thought. He wondered what it meant; it made him think of diamonds. Maybe it was some foreign word for diamond.

The man leaned over and knocked on the deck with his knuckles. A woman's head popped out of the opening into the cockpit. She gave the guy a big smile as she climbed up and out. She was a knockout, Buster noted. Tight white T-shirt, short khaki skirt, and man, what legs. He bet Jimmy couldn't leave that one alone. Buster watched with interest as she fluffed her wavy, shoulder length black hair in the breeze like she was drying it; probably just got out of the shower, he thought. She ran her fingers through it, flipping it one way and then the other, while the guy stood there grinning at the show. With her head back and her elbows pointed at the sky, that T-shirt was a real eyeful. Buster caught his breath as she turned and bent over to lock the hatch. He recovered in time to snap a series of shots when she stepped across to the dock, that skirt riding up to show how long those legs really were.

As the couple walked into town, he sent off another email, but only including a shot of her face; he was saving the rest of those pictures. He thought briefly about breaking into the boat, but there were too many people around, and it was sitting right out there in plain view of half the town. Besides, it was clear at this point that Jimmy wasn't aboard; he'd watched the woman lock the boat. Chances of finding anything worthwhile were slim after all those Feds had gone over it last night. He stifled a yawn and took another sip of coffee. Vinnie would be showing up in another hour, and it would be Buster's turn to sack out for a while.

∼

RALPH GIANNETTI SAVORED a mouthful of the freshly grilled mahi-mahi. He had caught the fish just a few hours earlier, trolling along the near edge of the Gulf Stream just north of the Government Cut channel. He took a sip of the crisp, cold sauvignon blanc as he listened to Mark Murano's report on the Jimmy Dorlan debacle. They were sitting on his patio, looking out across the water on another glorious fall day in Miami.

"Which one of 'em killed the dumb bastard?" he interrupted as Mark began to speculate about where the money was.

"That junkie college girl he took up with. She confessed. The other woman backed her story up."

"Yeah, of course she did. What makes you and Tony so damn sure the two broads didn't find out about the money and off him? They could be gonna split it, once the dust clears."

"I don't think so, Ralph. That wouldn't make sense."

"Makes perfect sense. $125,000 each, and he probably pissed 'em both off in the bargain. But either the women got the money, or the Feds got it. Your boys said they had a regular army searchin' that boat."

"The Feds didn't get it. Our guy in the Carteret County Sheriff's office woulda known."

"So the women got it."

"I don't think ..."

"Yeah, I noticed that. Never mind what you don't think. You get a lawyer to go talk to that junkie? See what she's got to say for herself. And keep an eye on the other one, that Barrera woman."

"We can't grab her and beat it out of her, Ralph; it would ..."

"Did I say anything about grabbin' her? I said keep an eye on her. If we want to grab her, the time would be later; she's probably gonna take that boat back offshore. That would be the time and place, but my money's on the junkie givin' up the game. You get somebody in to talk to her; fix her up, kick her ass, whatever. She'll talk."

"Okay. That's a good suggestion."

"Damn right it is. Now here's my next good suggestion. You get somebody to work checkin' up on this Barrera broad. She came from somewhere; she's got some history. Let's find out who the hell she is before we go jumpin' in her shit, okay?"

"Yes. I'll get right on it."

"Good."

"I'll call you when I ..."

"I'll call you. Meanwhile, college boy, you got a quarter mil of my money, and I ..."

"Relax, Ralph. I'll make it good. I ..."

"Don't tell me to relax. I'm not the one with the stress; you're the one with the problem. The only way you can make it good is with 20 kilos, you understand? Not money -- product, and delivered on time. You got that?"

"Yes."

"Good. Now get outta my house and go make some shit happen."

∽

MARK MURANO WAS deep in thought as he sat in the traffic on the MacArthur Causeway. He was headed back to his office in Coconut Grove. As he was passing the turnoff for Watson Island and the Miami Yacht Club, he saw a Coast Guard 40-footer in the ship channel to his left, and that reminded him of the point he'd been about to make when Ralph had cut him off. If the two women had been plotting to kill Jimmy and keep the money, why would they have come back to Beaufort? They would have kept going, wouldn't they? And how did so many Federal agencies get involved in what should have been a simple case of murder? Granted, the murder had taken place on a yacht in international waters, but the reception the yacht received didn't make sense. He picked up his phone and touched a speed dial button. In a few seconds, he had Tony Ferranti on the line.

"Hey, Tony?"

"Yeah, Mark?"

"Your guy in the sheriff's department down there in North Carolina?"

"Yeah, what about her?"

"Her?"

"Yeah, her. You got a problem with that, Murano?"

"No. I just didn't know. Did she say how all the Feds got involved?"

"No. You want me to ask her?"

"Yeah. Something's not making sense about that mess."

"I'll call ya right back."

Five minutes later, as traffic crept across the high bridge over the Intracoastal Waterway, Mark's phone rang.

"Yeah?"

"Yeah, Mark. I talked to her. She said the call came from the Coast Guard to begin with. Somebody on some drug task force in Miami called it in. Said somethin' about Greco?"

The name Greco sent a chill down Mark's spine. That was too close to home; no way could that be a coincidence. He suppressed his concern; Tony didn't know about Greco. "Okay, thanks. Good work. You got a lawyer we can trust down there in North Carolina?"

"I can find somebody quick. Why?"

"I want somebody to talk to the junkie girl; see what the hell she's got to say for herself. Somebody's got that damn money, and we got a business to run. You know what I'm sayin', Tony?"

"Yeah. No problem. I'll get somebody in this evening or first thing tomorrow."

"Great. Let me know, okay?"

"You bet. Hey, Mark?"

"What?"

"I got pictures of the gal that owns the boat, and the guy who spent the night with her last night. You want I should send 'em to ya?"

"Yes, please. I'm gonna put an investigator on her soon as I get to the office. Email me those pictures; good thinking."

"Okay. They're on the way. Unless you say different, I'm gonna keep Vinnie and Buster watchin' her. Too much goin' on for them to check out the boat or question her, but I figure, you know, might as well watch. No tellin' what we'll see."

"Yeah, okay. I gotta go. Call me if anything happens."

14

Connie sat on the outdoor balcony of the restaurant that occupied the second floor of the marina building. She had a perfect view of *Diamantista* as she ate the last of her broiled seafood platter. She took a sip of her wine and leaned back, propping her feet on the chair across the table from her.

Before Paul left to catch his flight, they had called Phillip Davis; he and Sharktooth would be arriving late tomorrow afternoon, so she had some time to rest. That suited her; she was drained from the tension of the last few days. The prospect of sailing with her two friends lifted her spirits somewhat, but as much as she tried to ignore it, she was missing Paul terribly.

She felt her face flush as she remembered the feeling of waking up in his arms this morning; she gave herself a mental slap in the face. She had to get over that. Neither of them had mentioned it, and Paul had given no indication that it was worth a second thought. She told herself that they had both been exhausted and had just fallen asleep.

While that was true, it didn't explain the warm flush she got every time she thought about it. As a distraction, she forced herself to think about Phillip and Sharktooth. She had met them both while she was sailing on *Vengeance* with Dani and Liz.

Phillip was in his forties. He had been a business partner of Dani's father; Dani looked up to him as a much older brother. Phillip and his wife, Sandrine, lived in Martinique and hosted Dani and Liz and their charter guests when *Vengeance* passed that way.

Sharktooth was another partner of J.-P. Berger's; he lived in Dominica and was even more of an enigma than Phillip. Both men had an air of danger about them, yet neither was at all threatening. Sharktooth was married, and she understood from Liz that his wife owned a successful art gallery in Dominica.

She was excited at the prospect of getting to know both men better, realizing that their contacts in the islands could be of great help to her in establishing her business. Connie was a little anxious about what they would expect of her as captain and hostess. Although she was comfortable with the two of them, she worried that they would expect her to cook.

Of course, she had met them at the same time she'd met Paul, so she found herself having come full circle back to Paul. In spite of what he had told her when they had discussed their mutual worries about a romantic relationship, she sensed that Paul was more secure emotionally than she was. His marriage had ended in an ugly divorce a few years ago, but he seemed at ease with that now.

She, on the other hand, was still wary of beginning a new affair. Her one long-term relationship had left her with an overwhelming sense of guilt when it ended with the death of her paramour.

She'd had a ten-year relationship with a married doctor from the time she was 19. His marriage had been of little consequence to Connie, as she had no inclinations that way herself. Initially, she had been impressed by him, but over time, he had become a burden.

His increasing dependence on her had gone beyond their romantic relationship. His failure at the practice of medicine and Connie's entrepreneurial skills had led the two of them into a business partnership. The business had been doing well until his drinking got him in trouble. By then, Connie was fed up with him and wanted out.

As she tried to extricate herself, he was murdered by one of their investors. Connie had escaped to the Bahamas, and only recently had she begun to get over her sense that her departure had led to the doctor's death.

During an extended stay in the Bahamas, she'd literally stumbled into a fortune. She chartered *Vengeance* to flee from Nassau to the eastern Caribbean and in the process developed a boundless love for sail. She decided to go into the charter business herself.

She and Paul had met when he joined them for a few days on *Vengeance*; he was a friend of Dani's godfather and was visiting Martinique. She had learned that he was recently retired and was passionate about cooking and sailing, and they had quickly become close friends.

The decision for him to help her start her charter business had seemed obvious, but then there was this matter of Connie feeling all squishy inside when she was around him. She wasn't sure what to do about that, and she wasn't ready to share it with anybody, especially Paul.

∼

KIRSTEN, her manacled wrists chained to the table in the small visitor's room at the Carteret County jail, studied the gray-haired man sitting across from her. The guard had come for her a few minutes ago, telling her that her lawyer was here to see her.

"Ms. Jones, I'm David Clinton. I'm an attorney."

"You from the public defender's office? They said they'd get somebody."

"The cops?"

"Yeah, and that district attorney woman, or whatever she was. She said I didn't have to talk to anybody without my lawyer present."

"And did you?"

"Did I what?"

"Talk to anybody."

"No, of course not. My father's a lawyer; I grew up with the right to remain silent."

"I see. Does he know you're in trouble?"

"He doesn't give a rat's ass about me now. You didn't answer me."

"Sorry. No. I'm not from the public defender's office. Those folks are stretched so thin they'll probably have somebody come running in out of breath just in time for your arraignment in the morning."

"Well, whoever the hell you are, I can't pay you, so what are you doing here?"

"My fee has been taken care of. I'll represent you at the arraignment tomorrow, if you'd like."

"Did my father send you?"

"No, I don't think I know him. Tony Ferranti asked me to help you."

"Tony Ferranti? You mean Tony, Jimmy's boss?"

"That's right."

"Why would he do that? I killed Jimmy, the piece of shit."

"You and Tony seem to agree on that, anyway."

"Jimmy?"

"Yes. Not one of Tony's favorite people, it seems."

Kirsten thought about that for a moment, the silence hanging between them. She studied her bitten down, grubby fingernails, remembering when she used to pay for a weekly manicure. The handcuffs chafed on her swollen wrist. She looked up at Clinton. "So what's going to happen?"

"We'll appear before a judge in the morning, where you'll be formally charged and asked to enter a plea."

"They said premeditated murder, or something like that."

"That's right."

"I killed him; Connie watched me do it, and I already said I did, so I guess that makes me guilty, right?"

"Jimmy was an abusive man, from what I know. He ever beat you?"

"Yeah."

"Were you afraid of him?"

"I was tired of him beating me. Yeah, I was afraid of him."

"Did you kill him so he couldn't beat you again?"

"I see where you're going."

"You had some provocation. I think we can make a case that his death wasn't premeditated murder."

"So I'll get off?"

"I doubt that, but we'll make a case that you aren't a cold-blooded killer. We might plea-bargain this down to manslaughter. You could get a pretty light sentence, compared to the possibility of death or a life sentence."

"I see."

"You have any questions, Kirsten? It's okay if I call you Kirsten?"

"Yeah, sure. That's my name."

"Good. Call me Dave. Now, did you have a question?"

"Yeah. About this Tony."

He nodded his encouragement.

"He's not doing this because he's a nice guy. What does he want?"

"You're a smart young woman, Kirsten. What do you think he wants?"

"Me to keep my mouth shut about the drugs?"

"I'm not sure what you mean, 'about the drugs,' but certainly, he wouldn't want you making his business with Jimmy public."

Kirsten nodded. "I get it."

"Good. There's something else you might be able to help him with."

"What's that?"

"I gather Jimmy was carrying some cash to make a payment of some sort for Tony. Tony would like to know where the money is; he figures Jimmy probably stashed it somewhere on that boat."

Kirsten shook her head. "I don't know about any money. Sorry."

Clinton gazed at her until she looked down at the table. "Well, if you think of anything like that, let me know. Here's my card; my cell phone number is on here. Call me any time, okay?"

She nodded. "Yeah, okay."

"I'll see you in court in the morning; try to get a good night's rest, and think about that money. That seems important to Tony."

∽

PAUL SUMMONED the waitress to remove the remains of his unappetizing dinner. He was killing time between flights in the Atlanta airport.

"You didn't like it?" she asked as she picked up the plate.

"Not very hungry after all, I guess," he said with a smile.

"Get you some coffee or dessert?"

"Coffee, please."

She looked over her shoulder, balancing the plate. "I'll make you a fresh pot; it'll be just a few minutes. You're not in a rush to catch your flight, are you?"

"No, I have time."

"Good. I mean, I could make you some instant if you're in a hurry."

"No, there's no rush. I've got an hour."

She smiled and gave him a big wink. "Too bad I've gotta work, handsome. But the coffee's good, anyway."

Paul chuckled as she sashayed back to the double doors into the kitchen. She wasn't bad looking, but lately, Connie had spoiled him for girl-watching. Ever since he woke up and found her curled on his chest early this morning, he hadn't been able to get her off his mind. He had kept still all night, although he didn't sleep much. He had told himself that she was exhausted and that he didn't want to disturb her much needed rest. Deep down, though, the truth was gnawing at him. He feigned sleep because he liked the way she felt, curled up on his chest like that.

He had studied her face, beautiful in repose, for several minutes at a time in the gray light that was filtering in the portholes. The creamy, porcelain-smooth skin of her cheeks set off by that dark, dark hair took his breath away. He had felt guilty, like he was spying on her. Guilty, too, because he knew his feelings for her had moved beyond mere friendship, and he dared not share them with her. He wasn't willing to risk scaring her off.

She'd been honest with him early on; she wasn't looking for romance. She needed a friend. Beyond that, she needed a cook and a dependable crewman to help her get the business going. Over his objections, she'd insisted that she would split the proceeds with him for each charter that he worked. He had tried to argue that the two things he most liked to do were sailing and cooking, but to no avail. She wanted to keep things on a professional level.

He could tell from the subtle clues in her behavior that she'd been mortified to wake up in his arms. She hadn't mentioned it; he had pretended that he didn't even know it had happened, but he still felt her warmth against his shoulder, even now. She'd die if she knew he faked waking up when she made the espresso. And then there was that business with her hair in the cockpit this morning -- pure torment.

He glanced down and saw that sometime during his reverie

the waitress had brought his coffee and a check. He glanced around, looking for her to thank her, but she wasn't in sight. He shook his head, laughing at himself. He was beginning to feel like an awkward teenager where Connie was concerned; he had to get over it. She needed him, but not that way; he had to be man enough to deal with that if he wanted to keep enjoying her company. He finished his coffee and picked up the check as he stood. He had just enough time to walk to his gate before they called his flight.

15

"What did the lawyer get out of that girl?" Ralph Giannetti asked.

Murano took a sip of the strong, syrup-like, Cuban coffee from his thimble-sized cup, thinking about his answer. "She claims to know nothing about the money, but ..."

"You believe that shit?"

"No. She was with Jimmy when Tony's guy made the drop. He saw her. Tony said she damned well had to know about the money; she unzipped the duffle bag when Jimmy picked it up."

"What'd I tell ya?"

"I know. You called it, Ralph." Murano didn't buy that for a second; it still didn't make sense that the women would have brought Jimmy's body back. Besides, there was the matter of that phone call from the Greco task force to the Coast Guard. "There's more to it, though."

"What more? Wait a minute ... that girl, what's her name, again?"

"Kirsten Jones."

"Yeah, Kirsten. She could screw you over pretty bad if she decides to talk to the cops."

"It'll be taken care of, Ralph."

"It better be."

"Listen, we've got a bigger problem than ..."

"We, my ass," Ralph interrupted. "You got a problem, not me."

"I got to wondering why the women bothered to come back to shore and call the Coast Guard after they killed Jimmy. I would have dumped him over the side and kept going," Mark said.

"Yeah, well, who knows why women do the shit they do?"

"It turns out that they didn't call the Coast Guard."

"Then who the hell did? Why'd they come back?"

"Somebody on the Greco task force tipped the Coast Guard about drugs on the boat."

Ralph sat bolt upright. "You better be shittin' me, Murano."

"I wish, but that's what happened."

"But how the hell ..." Ralph paused.

"I've got the P.I. firm checking on this Barrera woman. So far, she looks clean."

"Where's she from? She from down here somewhere?"

"I don't know yet. All I've got besides her name so far is a picture one of Tony's guys took, but we'll have something before the day's out, I ..."

"Lemme see the picture."

Murano pulled up the shot of Connie on his cell phone and handed it over.

"She's a looker, that's for damn sure." Giannetti scrolled with his thumb. "Wait a second! I know this guy."

"What guy?"

Giannetti returned the phone, Paul's picture on the screen. Glancing at it, Murano said, "We think he's her boyfriend. He spent the night on the boat. You know him?"

"You dumb-ass! Yeah. His name's Russo. He's a Miami cop -- retired, but I heard he's been helpin' on the task force, like some kinda consultant. He was still workin' when they busted Joe Greco, though. He put the damn cuffs on him."

"You think ..."

"Shut up for a minute."

Murano held his peace, taking the last sip of coffee from his tiny cup.

"Want another cup?" Giannetti asked.

Murano shook his head. "No, thanks."

"What were you gonna ask me?"

"You think Joe Greco or one of his people gave us up?"

"None of them even know who I am, except Joe. He ain't gonna talk."

Murano waited.

"Nobody but you and me knows Greco was workin' for me. You didn't tell Tony or Willie or somebody?"

"Ralph, you know me better ..."

"I'll tell you what I know, college boy. I know you better straighten this mess out -- and quick." Giannetti stared at Murano until Murano nodded and dropped his eyes.

"Get outta here and get your business under control."

∼

CONNIE LET her eyes roam over the shelf of cookbooks in the quaint little bookshop in downtown Beaufort. She was in a mild state of panic, having realized that she was going to be the only woman aboard *Diamantista* for a two-week voyage with two strapping men. Phillip, although handsome enough, was an average sized man, but Sharktooth was a giant. They would doubtless expect to be fed, and most men just assumed that women could cook. In her experience, men thought culinary ability was some kind of secondary sexual characteristic, like breasts.

She had taken one of the cars that the marina kept as loaners for their guests and driven to the nearest grocery store. She stocked up on canned soups and stews, as well as several dozen eggs and two cases of Ramen noodles. She loaded the buggy with sandwich meats and packages of sliced cheese, proud of herself for remembering mustard and mayonnaise. Recalling how good a peanut butter and jelly sandwich tasted in the middle of a night watch, she rolled the cart through the aisles until she found peanut butter.

As she put six huge jars in the cart and reached for the jelly, it struck her that bread would be a problem. It wouldn't keep for the length of the voyage unless she froze it. She made a quick estimate of how many loaves would fit in the tiny freezer compartment and clenched her jaw in frustration. She had learned to service the diesel and maintain the house battery bank, but baking bread was as big a mystery to her now as the Immaculate Conception had been when she had found herself briefly attending a parochial school at the age of thirteen. She had tossed several bags of flour into the cart and checked out. Back at the boat, she had stowed everything in the galley lockers and resolved that she would damned well learn to cook -- and fast, too. She skipped lunch in favor of a trip to the bookstore

She jumped, startled that someone was tugging on her shirt-sleeve. She spun on her heel, raising her hands in a defensive posture to confront a short, round, gray-haired woman with a worried look on a face that looked better suited to smiling.

"I'm so sorry, ma'am," the woman said. "I didn't mean to startle you, but when you didn't answer, I thought maybe you were hard of hearing or something. I just wanted to know if I could ..."

Connie put a reassuring hand on the little woman's shoulder, shaking her head and smiling. "No, I'm the one who should apologize. I'm completely freaked out, and yes, I'd love your help."

The woman nodded uncertainly. "With a book, I meant, but anything I can do, I'd ..."

Connie giggled. "Yes, with a book. I'm looking for a cookbook."

The woman gave her an encouraging nod, smiling again. "Tell

me what you like to eat," she said. "Then I'll be able to recommend something."

Connie explained her predicament to the woman, who then led her to another shelf that displayed several books that were written for someone planning to feed a hungry crew on an offshore voyage. She picked one up and thumbed through it with Connie, pausing to discuss the dishes that she had tried. Taking a pad of note paper from the pocket of her apron, she tore off small strips and inserted them into the book, marking her recommendations for Connie's reference. She flipped to the back of the book and then backed up a few pages. "Here. This is what I was looking for; it's kind of a shopping list, to help you figure out how to provision for a trip like yours."

"Great," Connie said. "Just what I need; I'll take it. Thanks."

∽

"BEAUTIFUL BOAT," Phillip said as the three of them walked down the dock toward *Diamantista* later that afternoon.

"Thanks."

"*Diamantista*," Sharktooth said, running an appraising eye over the rig as they approached the boat. "Good name. '*Diamond-cutter*,' right?"

"That's right. You speak Spanish?"

"Speak everyt'ing. Mos' people dungda islan's speak some Spanish, little of the French. Depends on the islan'. Some place more one, someplace the other. Got some Dutch mix in, too, 'long with buncha African words. You speak the Spanish, Connie?"

"Not much; I picked up a little when I was growing up, but it was kind of corrupt. Border Spanish, I guess. I had to look up *Diamantista*."

"Mm-hmm. I guess at the cutter part, 'cause of she be cutter-rigged. The 'diamante' I know. The 'tista' part I guess at."

"Sometimes, it means diamond merchant, too," Phillip added.

"I guess either one could fit, depending on whether it means you or the boat."

"I didn't know that," Connie said. "I wanted something to do with diamonds in her name, and like Sharktooth said, she's a cutter, so ..."

Scrambling over the lifelines, Connie made a welcoming gesture. "Come on aboard, and thanks so much for bailing me out."

"I'd never pass up a chance for a sail like this," Phillip said.

"Yeah, me, too. Maureen, she the mos' beautiful woman in the worl', but she decide I been eatin' too good. She put me on the diet; I come sailin' so I can get my strengt' back."

Connie swallowed nervously, looking at the size of Sharktooth and trying to remember all that she'd read in her new cookbook. "I thought I'd treat you to a big dinner ashore tonight, if that's all right."

"You don't have to do that," Phillip protested.

"But I'd like to, please."

"Le's do that, Phillip. Give me a little time to find my way 'roun' the new galley befo' I go to work." Sharktooth misinterpreted the look of surprise on Connie's face. "Sorry, Connie. Your boat; you the captain. I love to cook, an' Maureen, she doan let me so much, 'cause she like to cook, an' she rule the kitchen. So I hope you let me cook some; when you doan feel like it, mebbe? Jus' sometime?"

Connie doubled over, laughing uncontrollably. Sharktooth cast a worried glance at Phillip, who shrugged. Connie stood up, her eyes running with tears of mirth, and threw her arms around Sharktooth. Feeling his muscles stiffen with shock, she backed away. "Sorry, Sharktooth, I just got carried away."

"It's okay -- all right," he said, looking perplexed.

"I'll explain over dinner," Connie said, beginning to laugh again.

16

"She was a partner in this bogus diet clinic; it was really a money-laundering scheme."

Giannetti's eyebrows went up at that. "Musta been a scam."

Murano looked surprised. "Yeah. They claimed to make up special diets for people where the color of the food had to match the palette of their skin tones, or some shit like that. How'd you know?"

"Know what?"

"About this chromatic nutrition bullshit."

"I don't give a damn about that."

"But you said it was a scam, Ralph."

"Yeah. Had to be a scam the Feds were runnin', don't you see? If she was dirty, she wouldn't be workin' with the Greco task force now. She musta been undercover then. That bitch is some kinda cop."

"I don't get what you mean." Mark frowned.

"I mean the money-laundering. She musta been setting somebody up for the cops."

Murano shook his head, thinking. "I dunno. The thing went to shit, and the cops shut it down, all right."

"See. What did I tell ya?"

"It was pretty complicated, Ralph. What actually got the cops in to begin with was her partner's murder."

"She kill him?"

"No. No, a guy named Taglio's doin' life for that," Mark said.

"Taglio? Never heard of him. Where'd this happen, anyway?"

"Up in Savannah."

"Georgia?" Giannetti asked.

"Yeah, that's right."

"I did some business for a while with a guy that came from there. He was laundering money for a bunch of us, but he was down here. He had this deal goin' with diamonds, but he got busted."

Murano thought for a minute. He wanted to get Giannetti back on track. He tried to think of a way to steer the conversation back to the Barrera woman.

"Sam Alfano," Giannetti said.

"What?" Murano snapped to attention.

"Nothin'. Just thinkin' out loud. Sam Alfano was the guy's name."

"How'd you know that?" Murano asked.

"Because, dumb-ass, I just told you that he laundered money for me for a while."

"You laundered money through that clinic?"

"Pay attention, college boy. Sam Alfano had a money laundering scheme that used smuggled diamonds, but he got busted. Some shit with his partner in the Bahamas, I think."

"He was the guy that Taglio ratted out for the murder up in Savannah, Ralph."

Giannetti took a puff on his cigar and then held it out, studying the ash for a moment. "So this broad was hooked up with him?"

"Apparently. She had a piece of the clinic until it all came apart when Alfano had Taglio kill her partner. Some crooked doctor, it was."

"Alfano's doin' life in some federal pen. Find out where and get somebody in to talk to him. Let's see what he knows about Barrera."

"All right. I can do that," Murano agreed. "So you think she's a cop?"

"Must be. What I want to know is how she got onto your guys up in Baltimore. Find out everything Alfano knows about her. Then I want every damn detail of her life from the time she was born. Before we kill her, we need to pick her brain good. You need to know everything she knows."

"We can't waste her, Ralph. Not if she's a cop."

"Bitch set you up; she killed your boy, Jimmy, and she stole my damn $250,000. She's dirty; dirty cops are fair game. We just gotta have all the goods on her so we can get a good story out there, keep the cops from turning up the heat on us."

"Okay," Murano said. "She's gonna take the boat back out to sea, headed for the Virgin Islands again, based on what she told the cops up there in Beaufort. They want her for a witness when they try Jimmy's girl for the murder."

"When's she leaving?"

"I don't know, but we still have the tracker left on the boat. Tony says it'll work for around a month. Last time he looked, it was sitting still in Beaufort, so we got a little time."

"Yeah, but don't waste it. I want that boat hit while she's at sea; we can take it apart and find the money while somebody works on Barrera, and then just sink the whole mess. It's a perfect setup, Murano."

"Okay."

"Okay, my ass. I want to know who you're gonna send out to question her, and when and where. It's gotta be far out to sea. You got that?"

"I got it, Ralph."

PAUL SAT on the pool deck at the Miami Yacht Club, nursing an after-dinner drink and admiring the pastel colors of a reflected sunset. He was facing east, looking out over the Venetian Islands toward Miami Beach. The reddish-gold light came over his shoulder and gave a wonderful, soft glow to the vista in front of him. He glanced at his watch and decided that it was late enough to call Connie. Phillip and Sharktooth should have been there long enough to get settled, and they should have finished dinner by now. He slipped his phone out of his pocket and hit the speed dial number for her cell phone, assuming she'd be using it rather than the sat phone.

"Hi, Paul." He felt a smile spread across his face.

"Hi, yourself. Your crew get there okay?"

"Yes. We just got back from dinner. Phillip's checking over the boat, getting familiar with everything. He's so thorough; I'm feeling really good about this. Thanks for lining them up for me."

"No big deal; all I did was mention it. What's Sharktooth up to?"

Connie laughed. "Did you know?"

"Know what?"

She laughed harder this time. "You did, you rascal. You let me worry for nothing."

"Connie?"

"What?"

"I'm glad you're happy, but I have no idea what you're talking about."

"Cooking."

"Cooking? What about it?"

"You didn't tell me he'd cook for us."

"Sharktooth?"

"Yes, Mr. 'Butter Wouldn't Melt in His Mouth,' Sharktooth."

"He's going to cook for you? I didn't know he could cook."

"Well, it turns out that he loves to cook, and his wife doesn't let him."

"I see," Paul said, frowning.

"Yes. He's going through all the provisions now, making a list of things we need to pick up before we leave tomorrow."

"Okay. Connie?"

"Yes?"

"I'm glad you're okay with that, if that's what he wants. I mean, I know how women are about their kitchens. I hope ..."

"You ninny! You know I can't cook, damn it! I was worried about how I was going to feed the two of them."

"Oh. I didn't realize you couldn't ..."

"Why did you think I wanted you to be the cook?"

"I just thought you knew I loved to cook and you figured it was a way to entice me to be your crew."

"You're such a tease, Paul. You knew I couldn't cook, didn't you?"

"No. No, I didn't. Honestly, I thought all women could cook."

He held the phone away from his ear until her laughter subsided. After a second, he put it back to his ear. "Connie?"

"I swear, Paul, sometimes you can be such a, a ... man!"

Taken aback, Paul thought for a second. He sensed from her tone of voice that he had screwed up somehow. Searching for a neutral topic, he asked, "So when are you thinking about leaving Beaufort?"

"We've got a great weather window for the next several days. We're heading for the grocery store first thing tomorrow morning. Once we get everything stowed, we're out of here."

"Great. So I'll call on the sat phone tomorrow, then. Have a great sail, and stay safe."

"Paul?"

"Yes."

"I wish you were coming. It was great to see you yesterday."

"Even if I'm a man sometimes?"

"I know you can't help it. Call me tomorrow, please?"

"I wouldn't miss it for anything. Give Sharktooth and Phillip my best."

～

TONY FERRANTI SAT BACK in the shadows of the dim, smoky bar in Morehead City, just across the river from Beaufort. He studied the hard, coarse features of the rough-looking, bleached-blonde across the table. He was certain that she thought she was dressed to kill, with the tight, black sequined dress that hugged her overly generous curves and squeezed her big, blotchy breasts until they threatened to ooze out over the low-cut neckline.

He had suggested that she shouldn't wear her uniform to their meeting, worried at the time about somebody noticing him in her company. Now he was more worried that she had misconstrued his intent, given the way she was coming on to him. He realized that she was talking, tuning in just in time to catch the end of whatever she'd said.

"... my place. All night, if you want."

His thoughts raced as he sought an answer that wouldn't offend her. He had thought she was a dyke from talking to her on the phone. He'd kill Willie for this when he got back to Baltimore. That bastard knew; he'd let Tony walk right into this. Still, the woman was a deputy, the head matron at the county lockup.

She'd sent a lot of young meat to Willie over the last few years, and she'd assured Tony that she could deal with Kirsten. He'd been reluctant to make the arrangements over the phone, fearful that she might record their conversation. Now he thought taking that chance might have been preferable to the risk of having to go home with her.

"I'd love to, but I'll have to take a rain check. I need to catch the flight back to Baltimore here pretty quick. You understand, I'm just trying to take care of her, right?"

"No problem. You just call me anytime you're in the neighborhood. That Kirsten, she's a lucky girl -- got a fine man like you lookin' out for her. Don't worry, hon. I'll see to her for you."

"Willie talked to you about the money, right."

"Yeah. We're square. He'll take care of it -- no problem." She closed one heavily shadowed eyelid in a parody of a wink.

"Myrtle, I know Kirsten's gotta be jonesin' real bad by now. So ..."

"Poor little thing, she's clawing the damn concrete walls. She's desperate for a fix, all right. Don't you worry 'bout her. Just give me the shit and I'll slip it to her."

Tony nodded as he passed the plastic bag under the table. "Myrtle?"

"Hmm?"

"When can you do it?"

"Aw, sugar, don't you worry. Tell you what -- I'll just slip by the jail on my way home and fix your little missy right up."

Tony nodded. "That'd be great. Thanks."

With another reptilian wink, she slithered out of the booth, all back sequins and quivering pink flesh. Tony watched, relieved, as she sashayed out the door.

17

Connie was completely relaxed for the first time since she had left Annapolis. Phillip had just relieved her; she'd taken the first four-hour watch out of Beaufort. They'd been holding a steady nine knots on a course just south of east ever since they made sail leaving the channel. She sat with her back against the coachroof, her legs stretched out on the cockpit seat, watching the white froth of their wake slowly disappear into the indigo swells. They'd made excellent time; they were well into the Gulf Stream, having lost sight of land a couple of hours ago.

"She feel okay to you?" she asked, noticing that Phillip had disengaged the autopilot and was steering by hand.

"Perfect. I just wanted to get a feel for her while there was still daylight and I could see the sails. She's balanced well, but she responds to the helm way more quickly than my old Carriacou sloop."

"*Kayak Spirit*, right?"

"That's right."

"I noticed the same thing, after learning to sail *Vengeance*. It's the difference in not having a full keel, right?"

"Yes. That, and *Diamantista's* a lot lighter in proportion to her waterline length. You'll be using this autopilot a lot more than you were accustomed to when you were sailing with Dani and Liz."

Connie nodded. "I noticed. I couldn't find a full-keeled boat this size that had the kind of guest accommodations I wanted, though."

"No matter. Boats are always a compromise. *Diamantista's* solid. She'll take you anywhere you want to go. You tried the wind vane on the autopilot yet?"

"Yes. It does well, except for dead downwind."

"Nothing does well dead downwind, except a good helmsman."

They were silent for a while, listening to Sharktooth singing as he worked in the galley, conjuring up a West Indian chicken curry of some sort for their evening meal. Connie was surprised at his singing voice; he was belting out Bob Marley's 'Three Little Birds' in a perfectly pitched falsetto. His normal speaking voice was deep and rich, rumbling up from his massive chest.

"I'm glad Sharktooth likes to cook," she remarked.

Phillip laughed. "Sharktooth likes to eat; cooking's just his way of making sure he gets enough food."

"He said his wife had him on a diet. He's a big man, but I wouldn't have thought he was overweight."

"Oh, it's not his weight. Maureen just thinks he needs to eat more fresh vegetables."

"He bought a whole cart full this morning."

"Yeah, but wait until you see how he cooks them -- lots of fat added. His cooking does taste good, though."

"Sounds like southern cooking," Connie said.

"Similar. When I was growing up, all the vegetables were seasoned with bacon grease."

"That's like the local food I used to get around Savannah."

"Yep. A lot of the same influences, if you think about it."

"Is Maureen from Dominica?"

"Yes. They were childhood sweethearts. Why?"

"Just curious. I didn't get to meet her."

"Oh, you will. They're quite a pair. She's a fine artist; got her own gallery in Portsmouth."

"Liz told me."

They sailed along in easy silence, listening as Sharktooth moved on to "Don't Worry, Be Happy." Connie's thoughts turned to her conversation with him while they were grocery shopping. She had asked if his visa for entering the U.S. would work to get into the U.S. Virgin Islands. Sharktooth had responded that he was traveling on a U.S. passport.

"You're American?" she had asked, surprised.

"No." He grinned for a moment. "Is very complicated to get a visa with my Dominican passport. Mus' go to Barbados to apply, then wait a long time. No good when you need to travel in a hurry. Easier jus' to get a U.S. passport from a frien' of mine in the business."

Connie refrained from asking what business that might be, amused at how natural Sharktooth's practical approach to travel documents seemed to him.

∼

"Alfano says she's connected all right, but not to the cops. He's got her figured for being hooked up with some west coast mob; maybe even one of the Mexican cartels."

"That sounds like bullshit to me. What made him think that?"

"I don't know, Ralph, but Clinton said he was adamant that she was mobbed up."

"Who's Clinton?"

"The lawyer Tony uses for shit like this."

"Alfano's full of shit. No mob got women doin' stuff like that. Especially not the Mexicans. She's gotta be a cop of some kind. Crooked, but a cop."

"Alfano said she took his operation in Savannah down and disappeared. Next thing he knew about her was when he got busted for the diamond deal you were talkin' about; she was right in the middle of that."

"Shit, Mark, I think Alfano just can't admit that his whole operation got taken down twice in a row by a broad. He's makin' that mob shit up to make himself feel good."

"You're the boss, Ralph. You said to ask him; we asked him. That's what he told us."

"Yeah, yeah. I know that's what he told you. He probably believes it, too, but I ain't buyin' it."

"So what do you want to do, then?"

"Same as before. Send somebody out to board that boat and search it. Get my money. Question her; then we'll find out who the hell she really is. West coast mob, my ass. She still in North Carolina?"

"No. They left about midday."

"They?"

"Her and two guys."

"Russo one of 'em?"

"No. Tony's guys saw him head out with a suitcase yesterday. These two guys showed up late yesterday afternoon. A white guy looks to be in his forties, nothin' special, and a big black dude, bald-headed, with dreadlocks down to his waist. They said he looked like a damn giant -- close to seven feet tall, they figured."

"Good. Long as Russo's not there. I don't want to waste a Miami cop -- too close to home."

~

CONNIE HAD WEDGED herself in the corner by the galley sink, bracing her hips against the rail in front of the stove to hold her steady against the boat's motion as she washed the dishes. She passed them to Phillip, who was propped in the opposite corner with a towel as he dried them and put them away. Sharktooth was on watch, alone in the cockpit.

"So how long is Sandrine going to be in France?" Connie asked.

"She just left a couple of days ago. It's a three-week training course, and she may stay a few days extra to visit some relatives."

"But I thought she was from Martinique."

"She is; she was born in Martinique, but she's got a bunch of cousins in France. That's not unusual, really."

"I always thought it would be nice to have a lot of family like that. I was an only child of two only children."

"Yeah, me too. Your folks still alive?"

"No. They've been dead for a long time. Yours?"

"Same."

"It's nice that you've got Sandrine, then."

"Yes. Until I retired, I was too busy to notice how lonely I was. It was kind of funny the way we ended up together, though."

"How so?" Connie raised her eyebrows, her interest piqued.

"Well, I thought we were just friends; I'd met Sandrine from time to time when I was arranging for shipments from France through Martinique to the western Caribbean and South America. You know, back when I was still working with Dani's father."

"She's worked for Customs for a good while then?"

"Yes, close to ten years."

"But you discovered you were more than just friends after you retired. That's nice, that you started out like that, though."

"Well, like I was saying, it was funny. My other friends like Sharktooth and Dani, even J.-P., they all started making jokes about when we were going to get married. I thought they were just pulling my chain but damned if they weren't right."

"So, if you don't mind me asking, when did you decide to ask her to marry you?"

"I'm not sure."

"You don't remember?"

Phillip smiled, shaking his head, "Did you meet J.-P. yet?"

"Dani's father? No, I haven't met him -- only talked to him on the phone a time or two. Why?"

"In some ways, he's like a surrogate father to me. Anyway, when I told J.-P. that Sandrine and I were getting married, he said he knew that already. I asked him how he knew, thinking Dani had told him, or something. He gave one of those Gallic shrugs that only the French can do. I guess I looked puzzled, so he said, 'No, but you see, Phillip, I have been married many times, now, and I still don't know how it happens. Somehow, I just find myself with a wonderful wife.' He was right. It just happens, I guess."

"That's a nice story, Phillip. Thank you."

Phillip smiled, stifling a yawn as he put the last dish in its place in the locker and hung the towel up to dry. "Guess I'm still jet-lagged. I think I'll crash for a while. You going to catch a nap before you relieve Sharktooth?"

"Maybe. I've had a couple of days of rest; I'm not too sleepy yet. I get really wired the first day out. You go ahead. I'll be fine. I'll see you in the morning."

18

At midnight, Connie made herself a thermos of coffee to see her through her watch. She enjoyed the watches from midnight until dawn. The moon was going into its last quarter, but this far out to sea, there was no ambient light. As the moon faded, the profusion of stars took over the sky. She was looking forward to Nature's show. It was a cool night, but not chilly, and they had a nice, steady 15-knot breeze on their port quarter, making for a fast, comfortable sail.

She stepped onto the companionway ladder, reaching out to put the thermos on the cockpit seat. "Hey, Sharktooth. How was your watch?"

"Everyt'ing good. Beautiful sailin'. It's midnight already?"

"Yes. Can I make you some coffee? Or decaf? Tea, maybe? Water's still hot."

"No, thank you. I'm already too awake; got to get in the rhythm."

Connie climbed into the cockpit, and Sharktooth shifted his bulk around to the seat on the downwind side, making room for her to slip in behind the helm.

"That was a wonderful chicken curry you made us."

"Glad you like it. It's pretty easy. You want the recipe?"

Connie smiled. "I can't boil water without burning it, but thanks for offering. Maybe Paul would like the recipe, though?"

"Paul, he cook some good food, that mon. He say he learn from he father, cause the Italian men, they like to still eat good when they off away from their wives."

"Was Paul's father from Italy?"

"No, I doan t'ink so. He grandfather, mebbe. Paul's father was p'lice, like Paul, he say."

"How about you, Sharktooth? When did you learn to cook?"

"Always cook. In Dominica, everybody know how to cook. Jus' the way t'ings are."

"But Maureen won't let you cook?"

"She let me, sometime. But Maureen, she go to these classes that the government have, 'bout 'heart-healthy diet.' They worry 'cause so many people got the sugar, and the high blood pressure. Come from the old days. People used to eatin' lots of fat an' sugar from when they have to work hard; they need it then, but now ..."

"Most people don't get enough exercise to eat like that without health problems? Is that what you're saying?"

"I t'ink so. Not mos' people, but anyhow a lot of the people, they doan get the exercise. I t'ink then, the old way of cookin' not so good."

"You don't look overweight."

"No. Not me. Not now, at leas', cause Maureen she cook the low fat, low sugar food."

"Well, it must work, whatever she's doing."

"Yeah, but it doan tas'e as good."

"Does she know you're cooking on this trip? You going to get in trouble when you get home for going off your diet?"

"She knows. She let me cook sometime. I jus' like to tease her 'bout her low-fat food."

"I'm looking forward to meeting her."

"She say the same 'bout you. She know 'bout you from Liz an' Dani."

"Liz told me she's an artist. She owns a gallery, right?"

"Yes. She help the others 'roun' Portsmouth sell they t'ings to the tourists, mostly. She make some little bit of money from it, too, though."

"And you run the water taxi and do tours, is that right?"

"Some. I still do some t'ings wit' Dani's father, sometime. You know 'bout J.-P., right?"

"Not much. I know Phillip worked with him until he retired."

"Yes. Business not so exciting now like when Phillip aroun'. Times change. I t'ink Phillip, he more bored than retired."

"I see. I thought maybe you'd retired too, and gotten married, like Phillip."

"Oh, no. I been married long time. Maureen my wife fo' 25 years, now. Good years. She my bes' frien' since we chirruns."

"That must be nice, to be married to your best friend."

"Yes, I t'ink so. If she not my best frien' she never put up wit' me, fo' sure."

"Aw, come on, Sharktooth. You're easy to get along with."

He chuckled. "You tell Maureen that, okay? See what she t'ink."

"I will, but I'm sure she'll agree with me."

∽

RALPH GIANNETTI WAS FINISHING his breakfast on his patio when his butler announced, "Señor Murano, he is here to see you."

"Bring him out here, José. Ask if he wants anything to eat."

"Sí, señor."

Pushing his plate aside, Giannetti lit his first cigar of the day, mostly because he knew the smoke annoyed Murano.

"Good morning, Ralph."

"Morning, Mark. José take your breakfast order?"

"Nah. I ate earlier. I been on the phone with Tony all morning."

"Yeah? So what's happenin'? You guys got your shit together yet?"

"Yes. Everything's under control. He's sending the two guys he used in Beaufort down to ..."

"I don't want to hear all that. These guys, are they any good?"

"Yes. They're ..."

"Just tell about their skills; I don't want any names."

"One of them's got shit for brains, but he's as mean as a rattlesnake. Big redneck son of a bitch, and he's got the hots for the Barrera woman. He's pumped up about questioning her. The other one's got enough sense to make it all happen. They're going to ..."

"That's enough. When?"

"That depends on how fast they sail; probably a few days yet. We're tracking the boat, and when they get to ..."

"What about the two guys on the boat with her?"

"You said to ..."

"I know what I said. Who the hell are they?"

"We don't know, I thought it didn't matter if we were gonna ..."

"Find out who the hell they are, dumb-ass. They're probably cops of some kind. If we goin' to burn them, we might want to know something about them, so we can do some damage control. Besides, they might be worth questioning, too, if your shit-for-brains rattlesnake can handle more than just a girl."

"That's a good point. I'll ..."

"Get outta my house and do some damn work. I'm tired of having to explain everything to you."

∼

DIAMANTISTA WAS SLICING along through the two-meter high, long-period swells, leaving a straight, creamy wake on the indigo surface. The color of the sea seemed to get darker with distance, until a thin, almost black band marked the point where the blue began to fade to clear sky. There were only a few fluffy white cumulus clouds to punctuate the endless expanse of brilliant blue sky.

"That was great, Sharktooth," Connie said, wiping butter from her chin with a paper napkin. "Thank you."

"Thank Phillip. He catch the fish. Me, I jus' put in the pan wit' a little nice brown butter an' some spices."

"Thanks, Phillip."

Phillip smiled. "Fish is always best when it's right out of ..."

They were interrupted by the chirping of the satellite phone. Connie lifted it, shading the display with her hand to see the caller i.d. screen. She flipped it to hands-free and set the phone on the cockpit table. "Good afternoon, Paul. You just missed grilled mahi-mahi sandwiches on warm French bread. Phillip caught the fish about an hour ago, and Sharktooth had just baked baguettes."

"I'm jealous. From what I got on NOAA's website this morning, you're probably having a perfect sail, too."

"Absolutely. It just doesn't get much better. I'm glad I was delayed; it worked out for the best. I could have done without Kirsten and Jimmy, though."

"Yeah. No kidding. That's what I'm calling about."

"Oh? There's news?"

"Yes. First off, Kirsten was found dead in her cell this morning. She had a syringe hanging out of her arm."

"That's horrible. I ..."

"I know you had sort of mixed feelings about her. Anyway, they're writing it off as an accidental overdose. Her record makes that sort of credible."

"Sort of? I hear some question there," Phillip said.

"Yeah. Jails are full of drugs, but her gear was first-class stuff. The syringe and the needle were brand new, and the coke was the purest stuff the coroner's ever seen -- he didn't think it had been cut."

"So what do you think, then?" Connie asked.

"Well, when I put that together with what they got back on Jimmy when they ran his prints, I think somebody didn't want her cutting any deals that might involve her talking about who Jimmy knew."

"What about him?"

"James Henry Dorlan was an alias, like we thought. His real name was John Henry -- no middle initial. He's got a record as long as my arm, for nearly everything you can think of. The Maryland State Police were closing in on him when he and Kirsten took off. He was a second-tier distributor of all sorts of illegal drugs; he was selling through some kids at the school where Kirsten got in trouble, but he was also dealing around the Patuxent River Naval Air Station. They were pretty sure he was getting his stuff from a guy up in Baltimore, but they didn't manage to pin down who it was before he took off."

Connie related the story that Kirsten had told her about Jimmy trying to hook her up with a friend of his who was a pimp to work off her drug debts. "I don't know any more than that, but ..."

"I'll pass it along to the people in Maryland. It might make some kind of connection for them."

"So what's going to happen with Kirsten's death?"

"I don't know. Carteret County would be happy just to let it be an accidental overdose and hush it up, but the Feds are in the driver's seat. It's hard to say; it'll probably get political before it's over. The coroner didn't sound like he bought accidental death, but there's local politics to consider there, too."

"It's just so sad. Sometimes she seemed like a nice kid who was in over her head."

"Yeah. She probably was, at some point, but don't forget, you thought she set Jimmy up and killed him in cold blood."

"I know, but ..."

"Try to let it go, Connie. You're out of it, now. You're having a great sail with two of the best crew you could ask for, and the fish are biting. Focus on how good things are; I can hardly wait to join you. It's not long, now."

"You're right. Thanks, Paul. You're the best friend a girl could want, and I wish you were with us to enjoy all this."

"Thanks. I'm looking forward to seeing you all soon. I need to get back to my meeting; I just slipped out to call you."

19

E*ight days later...*

THE ALARM on Connie's wristwatch beeped, reminding her that it was time to scan the horizon for other vessels. They were only a couple of hundred miles north of the Virgin Islands, and the shipping traffic had been increasing over the last few days. Right after they had turned to the south when they passed Bermuda, they had gone for three days without seeing another sign of human life, except for the odd plastic grocery bag or soft-drink bottle that drifted past. This morning, she'd already crossed paths with two cruise ships and a freighter, although not closely enough to be of concern. Still, she knew she had become a little too casual about looking for other traffic, so she'd set a recurring 15-minute alarm to remind her.

Given that most ships covered a mile in two or three minutes and that the distance to the visual horizon was about twelve miles, a 360-degree sweep every 15 minutes was a good way to avoid surprises. She picked up the binoculars and stood, bracing herself against the steering pedestal as she scanned the sea. There was no sign of another vessel, so she set the glasses down and settled back into her seat.

As she and the others had gotten more accustomed to the rhythms of life at sea on a small, short-handed boat, the amount of time spent in idle conversation had decreased. They were all a bit weary, and they shared the same immediate experiences. After a while, there wasn't a lot to talk about. That was all right with Connie; it gave her time to sort through her feelings about Paul.

Her earlier conversations about married life with Phillip and Sharktooth provided grist for the mill of her thoughts. As she picked through their passing comments about their wives, she realized that they were the first people she had gotten to know who had normal marriages. Her one serious, long-term relationship had been with a married man, but that didn't give her any useful reference points. She'd never had the luxury of forming close relationships with other women until she spent a couple of months aboard *Vengeance* with Dani and Liz, but they were both young and single. Besides, they were committed to making their charter business successful, and neither had much time for romance.

Connie understood that; she had been driven to succeed when she was their age, too. It was only over the last couple of years, when she had some leisure time, that she felt a yearning for someone with whom to share life. She knew she was ill-equipped to evaluate the attraction that she felt for Paul, since her best friend, the one person with whom she might otherwise feel comfortable talking over her feelings, was the object of her affection.

She had picked up some insights from listening to Sharktooth and Phillip that were new to her. She'd often wondered over the years how a person could commit to spend a lifetime in the company of one other person. It hadn't occurred to her that it might be easy to do if the person happened to be your best friend. That came across clearly from both of the men, although neither was particularly articulate on the subject.

She wasn't normally given to such introspection; she'd achieved what she had by virtue of being decisive and trusting her intuition. She wanted to open up to Paul, but she was reluctant because of the discussions they'd had about moving slowly. They'd been physically attracted to each other from first sight, and the attraction had grown as they spent more time together.

Connie thought something might have happened early in their relationship, but they'd been aboard *Vengeance,* in close company with Dani and Liz, as well as Phillip and Sandrine for much of the time. There hadn't been enough privacy for them to act on their feelings then, and they had since agreed to keep their relationship platonic. Except, she reminded herself, for the night in Beaufort, when they had passed the night, innocently enough, in each other's arms. She felt a tingle at the memory, but she suppressed it.

While they were on *Vengeance,* she had shared her plans to start her own charter business with Paul, and based on his reaction, she'd asked if he might be interested in helping her. Having recently retired, he had the time, and he was an avid sailor as well as a good cook. He had found the prospect appealing.

After their time on *Vengeance* ended, they had begun an almost daily series of telephone calls as they discussed her plans and progress. Paul had confessed to her then that he was a bit worried about his decision. Connie vividly remembered the conversation they'd had after she had bought *Diamantista.*

The boat had been in Charleston, South Carolina, and Connie had made arrangements with a boat yard in Annapolis to do a refit. The boat was ten years old and well cared-for, but Connie wanted to start her business with everything in like-new condition.

She had asked Paul to help her get the boat to Annapolis, and he had agreed. Given that it was an unfamiliar vessel to them both and that the rigging needed to be replaced, they had decided to take it up the Intracoastal Waterway rather than making the coastal passage in the ocean. The trip had taken several days, traveling during the day and stopping in the evenings at transient marinas.

"Connie," Paul had said that night on the telephone, "there's just one thing ..."

"Okay? What's that?"

"Um, you know I find you awfully attractive."

"Well, I ..."

"No. Please, I'm having a tough enough time. I just need to say this, straight out. It's the only way I'll feel like I'm being fair to you. Let me get it done, then we can talk it over, okay?"

"Okay."

"Thanks. You're beautiful, and you're still young. I'm not ancient, but I've got some hard miles behind me, and I don't want to rush into a relationship that's going to hurt either of us. I know we touched on this before, but I just need it out in the open. I like being in your company, and I'm excited about the notion of sailing with you, but I'm not ready for a romantic relationship. I've still got too much unresolved guilt from my divorce."

"I'm sorry, Paul; I've been so wrapped up in buying the boat that I put all that out of my mind, I guess. I hadn't thought about how it would be for us to be living together on the boat."

"Well, yeah. And Connie?"

"Yes?"

"I mean, if that other, um, well if it ... damn."

"I think I know what you want to say, Paul. I'm not in such great shape myself when it comes to romance. I like your company, but I agree that we should stick to being friends for a while and just see where it ends up, if that's what you're thinking."

"Whew. Thanks. You can't imagine how much better you just made me feel about this. When should I come to Charleston?"

~

It had become the ship's custom for the three of them to have a midday meal together, and today it marked the end of Connie's watch. She had been more tired than usual, and had gone below and gone to sleep, leaving Phillip and Sharktooth to pick over the remains of their lunch.

"Connie, she good people," Sharktooth volunteered after she was out of earshot.

"She's good company at sea," Phillip agreed.

"You t'ink Paul know how lucky he be?"

"You think they're ..."

"Well, I doan know 'bout Paul. You know he better. But I t'ink she see him be part of her crew for the long time."

"I don't know. I hadn't thought too much about it. What makes you think that?"

"Jus' the way she ask 'bout Maureen, mos'ly."

"I don't get it, Sharktooth. What did she ask you that made you think she's after Paul that way?"

Sharktooth shook his head. "More jus' the way she listen, an' the t'ings she pay mos' attention to when I talk about Maureen. I see it when she hear you talk about Sandrine, too.

"Really? Sometimes you amaze me."

"Come from bein' one wit' everyt'ing, I t'ink."

"You sound like a Buddhist."

"Mebbe so. Might not be Paul at all, but I t'ink she studyin' 'bout marry up to some fella."

"Well, that wouldn't be a big surprise. She'd make somebody a good wife, if that's what she wants. She's a nice lady."

"Mm-hmm. Pretty, too. I doan mean jus' to look at."

"No. I know what you mean."

"You ask Sandrine when you get a chance. See what she t'ink."

"What about Maureen? You ask her?"

"No, Phillip. Maureen never meet Connie yet. Or Paul. She could tell right quick, though, if she spend a few minutes wit' them. She tell me 'bout you an' Sandrine long time befo' it happen."

"You two are hopeless romantics, aren't you?"

"Love make the worl' go 'roun', they say."

Phillip nodded. "Well, if you're right, it couldn't happen to two nicer people. You okay for a while?"

Sharktooth nodded.

"Good. I'm going to try to nap for a bit."

~

ABOUT AN HOUR after Phillip went below, Sharktooth noticed the smudge on the horizon out to the west. It vanished from sight as he watched it, and he decided his eyes were deceiving him. A few minutes later he saw it again. He picked up the binoculars and got to his feet, bending so that he could rest his elbows on the stern rail to steady the glasses. He decided it might be another vessel, but it was too far away to be sure.

He went below to the chart table and turned on the radar, mostly to amuse himself. He had just managed to pick up an echo in the direction of the suspected boat when Phillip, who had been asleep on one of the settees, woke up. He rolled to his feet and joined Sharktooth.

"What do you have?" he whispered, not wanting to disturb Connie, who was in the aft stateroom a few feet from them.

Sharktooth touched the screen with a banana-sized finger. Phillip nodded, and they stood there watching the display for a couple of minutes.

"Moving fast, and coming straight this way," Phillip murmured.

Sharktooth punched a couple of buttons, and an information box popped up on the screen next to the target. Phillip whistled softly. "Forty-five knots, and headed this way."

"Not a ship," Sharktooth said. "Echo too small."

"He's going to be on top of us in a couple of minutes. I don't like this. Probably some jerk in a big sport fishing boat with his autopilot on, oblivious to everything out here."

"I doan t'ink so." Sharktooth traced the other vessel's track, displayed as history on the screen from the time he'd first designated it as a radar target. "He makin' a curve, keep he bow aim right at us. He comin' to see us."

"That can't be good," Phillip said.

"T'ink mebbe he see us eyeball now. He speed up some."

"Over there, I'd guess he came from Puerto Rico or the D.R.," Phillip said.

"Or Turks and Caicos, mebbe,"

"What's going on?" Connie asked, emerging from the aft cabin.

"Company's coming, it looks like," Phillip said.

"Comin' fas', too. He speed up. Sixty knots, now."

"You don't have any weapons aboard, do you?" Phillip asked.

"No." There was tension in Connie's voice. "Why? Do you ..."

"There aren't a lot of things that move that fast on the water. Unless it's military, it's probably a go-fast boat, and this far offshore in this part of the world, that most likely means drugs,"

"But why would they be coming at us?"

"They think we're somebody else, maybe. They could be picking up something, or delivering it, expecting a ship out this way."

"No ships," Sharktooth said. "Nobody even close. He 'bout two, mebbe t'ree minutes out. Still come straight at us."

"What can we do?" Connie squeaked. "You're scaring me."

"Scared is good; that'll keep you alive. I'm scared too."

Sharktooth cackled, a demented sound. "Me, too. But doan' worry. Every little t'ing goan be all right, jus' like the song."

"You got something in mind?" Phillip asked.

"Mm-hmm. Like they say, been there, done that."

"What? Done what?" Connie asked

"Been in a boat like that, try to stop some big boat like this. We do the ambush. Jus' do what we doin', fo' right now. You see what happen in a minute. Stay hidden below deck."

"But what if they sink us."

"They want somethin'. They doan come way out here to sink us. Besides we be sunk by now, if tha's what they want."

The roar of powerful engines filled the cabin as the boat made a close pass, and the ripping chatter of an AK-47 was barely audible above the engine noise. Connie and the two men watched through a porthole as the oversized, brightly painted speedboat veered at the last minute, throwing a wall of spray against *Diamantista's* side.

"He's leaving," Connie said.

"He be back. He jus' checkin' us out up close that time."

"Be cool. We got the mojo on, but he doan know."

20

The speedboat pulled alongside *Diamantista,* its engines rumbling as the man at the helm held a position a few feet from their port side. Besides the helmsman, there were two armed men in the cockpit, one clutching a pistol, and the other pointing an AK-47 in their general direction.

"Doan let 'em see us lookin' out," Sharktooth said, his gentle hand on Connie's shoulder moving her out of sight. "Connie, go back in yo' cabin. I take the port side; Phillip, you take the starboard. We let 'em come down the companionway an' then take 'em."

As they got into position, Phillip was able to see the boat edging closer. He caught Sharktooth's eye and indicated the distance away by holding his hands apart, gradually bringing them together. When they were about three feet apart, they heard a thud, followed by a soft curse and a second impact as the two men jumped aboard. Phillip and Sharktooth both backed against the bulkhead, one on each side of the companionway ladder. Sharktooth raised a single finger and pointed to his chest. Phillip nodded. As he registered from the corner of his eye that the boat had moved farther away, the man with the pistol jumped like a cat, landing at the foot of the ladder and sweeping the cabin with his pistol, first to the right, then to the left.

"Amateur," Phillip thought. As the man began to turn to his left, Sharktooth grabbed him by the back of his shirt with his right hand, jerking him backwards as he reached around with his left and grasped his forearm, twisting it until a bone snapped and the pistol dropped from his hand. At that point, Sharktooth put his left hand over the man's face and stepped from behind him, turning as he extended his left arm and smashed the man's head into the ladder, knocking him senseless.

The other man crouched in the companionway, his rifle pointed at Sharktooth. "Freeze or you're dead," he barked.

Sharktooth grinned and nodded. "Okay, mon. You win." He raised his big hands in surrender as the man extended his right leg, placing his foot on the top rung of the ladder. As he shifted his weight to the foot, Phillip swept his ankle from beneath him and he tumbled down the ladder, firing an uncontrolled burst into the cabin overhead as he fell. Before he could recover, Phillip was on him, deflecting the muzzle of the weapon as he drove his fist into the man's solar plexus. As he doubled over, gasping and retching, Phillip tore the AK-47 from his grasp and Sharktooth smashed him in the face with the heel of his hand, knocking him over backward and chuckling. "Now we sink the boat," he said grinning at Phillip and reaching for the weapon.

There was a popping sound from behind him, and a pained look spread across Sharktooth's face as he and Phillip turned to see the first man getting to his feet, a tiny pistol in his left hand. Blood began to blossom from Sharktooth's shoulder.

"Next one will be in your head. Both of you, face down on the deck. Right now."

Sharktooth and Phillip complied, barely finding room in the cramped space.

"Hands behind your heads," he ordered. "Either one of you

moves, you both die, but one very slowly. Now where's the woman?"

At that moment, the woman was one step behind him, beginning a fluid motion that ended with a full wine bottle shattering across the top of his head. His eyes rolled up into his head and his knees buckled. As he collapsed to the deck, Connie took the pistol from his limp fingers. Phillip had turned his attention to the other man, who was coming around, shaking his head as he got to his feet, also brandishing a small handgun. Before Phillip got to him, Connie shot him in the gut. As he swung the gun toward her, she put another round in his right knee. He screamed and collapsed to the deck, dropping his pistol.

"Cable ties are in the second drawer below the chart table," she said. "If you want to keep them alive, you'd better tie their wrists and ankles before they come to."

Phillip had already immobilized the man Connie shot by the time she finished her statement. He noticed, as he moved to bind the other man, that Sharktooth had braced himself with the AK-47's muzzle resting on the lip of an open porthole. The weapon barked twice, spitting brass into the cabin as Phillip finished.

"Thanks, Connie," Phillip said, as she handed him the pistol.

"No problem."

"Who teach you to shoot like that?" Sharktooth asked.

"Dani. She also taught me not to leave a live adversary behind me unless he was disabled."

"What about the guy in the boat?" Phillip asked.

"Dead. Two in the head."

"Is it in gear?"

Sharktooth shook his head. "I wait 'til he put in neutral. Still, we bes' go get it, jus' to be sure."

∼

TEN MINUTES LATER, the go-fast boat was in tow, riding easily about 75 feet behind them. Connie was at *Diamantista's* helm and Phillip and Sharktooth were below, questioning their two prisoners. She was still shaken from having shot the one man, but it had been a clear-cut matter of self-defense. She knew that this far out at sea, the stomach wound was a death sentence, even though it hadn't immediately disabled him. With the strange-to-her, small caliber pistol, she hadn't wanted to risk a disabling shot while he had the wherewithal to shoot back, so she'd taken the center of mass shot first and then gone for finesse, hoping he'd be able to answer some questions before he died. Of course, there was always the other one -- he'd be waking up soon.

She flinched as she heard a scream from below, not wanting to think about Sharktooth and his beloved filet knife. She heard muttered discussion, but she couldn't make out the words. After what seemed an eternity, Phillip joined her in the cockpit. He shook his head as he sat down a few feet from her.

"Well?" she asked.

"The one you hit was the one with the answers, unfortunately. The one you shot was just local muscle that the other two picked up in Puerto Rico, along with the boat."

"Who screamed?"

"The one you shot."

"Did Sharktooth have to ..."

"No. He just waved the filet knife around and did his demented routine. The guy screamed before Sharktooth even touched him."

"I don't blame him."

"Me, either. Just so you know, I've never seen Sharktooth actually use that knife. Just the threat is enough. Works every time."

"That's a relief. I'm already upset that I had to shoot the jerk. He's going to die, isn't he?"

"He's the one who's responsible, Connie. Don't beat yourself up. He said they were going to kill us -- me and Sharktooth. You, they were going to amuse themselves with until you told them where the money was."

"Money?"

"I was going to ask you. Apparently, those two you picked up in Annapolis were carrying a quarter of a million dollars in cash. They were supposed to buy coke in St. Martin and hitch a ride back to the States with it on another yacht."

"I don't know where it could be. I mean, they practically took the boat apart in Beaufort. That much money wouldn't be that easy to hide."

"No. With drug runners, there's no telling. Could have been some kind of double cross going on."

"Maybe the guy I hit with the wine bottle will know. You try to rouse him yet?"

Phillip nodded. "He's gone, Connie. Now don't go blaming yourself for him, too. He was the leader; he'd promised you to the other two. He got what he deserved."

Connie felt a tear roll down her cheek. She sniffled and wiped it away.

"Lucky for me you had that bottle of wine handy, or I'd be the one dead," Phillip said, trying to make her feel better.

"It was Paul's favorite," she said, realizing as she did how callous that sounded. "Barolo. It was going to be a welcome aboard gift, and now I killed a man with it."

"Paul will understand, Connie."

Sharktooth appeared in the companionway. "It's time," he said softly. "We heave to and bring the boat alongside, now."

"How's your shoulder, Sharktooth?" Connie asked.

"Jus' a scratch. Bleed a lot, but Phillip fix wit' yo' firs' aid kit. No problem."

"We should bring them on deck first," Phillip said.

Sharktooth nodded and bent at the waist, heaving one of the bodies onto the bridge deck. Phillip dragged it aside as Sharktooth lifted the other one. Connie swung the helm, bringing

Diamantista onto the opposite tack with the headsails back-winded. As they came to a stop, Sharktooth pulled the towline in, bringing the speedboat alongside.

Sharktooth climbed down into the boat and went below into the small, enclosed cabin as Phillip sat on *Diamantista's* side deck with his legs extended to keep the speedboat from bumping them as the wave motion shifted the two boats. In a moment, Sharktooth emerged from the cabin and handed Phillip a vinyl envelope as he climbed back aboard. Within two minutes, he had dumped both bodies in the speedboat. He and Phillip cast it off and waved to Connie.

She eased the sheet that held the jib back winded and sheeted it in on the other side. As *Diamantista* pulled away, Phillip raised the AK-47 and emptied the magazine into the speedboat, opening a large, gaping hole just below the waterline. Sharktooth handed him another magazine which he had retrieved from his search of the speedboat's cabin and Phillip put a short burst into the bow deck of the speedboat, to prevent any trapped air from keeping it afloat. Five minutes later, there was no sign of their encounter, except for the vinyl envelope and the AK-47.

"Souvenirs?" Connie asked.

Phillip shook his head. "We'll get Paul to check out the registration and the passports."

"What about the gun?"

"We'll hang on to it in case somebody follows up. We'll ditch it before we get to the Virgins."

∼

"Heard from your boys?" Giannetti asked, as he fondled his after-dinner cigar. He sat on his patio, enjoying the pastel hues of another glorious Miami sunset. His iPhone was on the table next to his snifter of brandy, the volume turned up so that he could hear Murano over the soft strains of the jazz combo from next door. His neighbor on the other side of the privacy hedge always had some kind of party going.

"Nothing yet, Ralph."

"Shoulda heard by now," Giannetti said.

"They left Puerto Rico about lunch time. Figure it took them a few hours to catch up with her. They're probably working on her right now. We should hear soon."

"You need to train your people better, Murano. They can mess with that broad on their own time. Call 'em on that satellite phone. I want to know where my damn money is."

"They're not answering, Ralph. I'll call you as soon as I hear, okay?"

"Not okay. Somethin's wrong. You shoulda heard hours ago. Get your pansy ass down there to the islands, and get my money, college boy. No more of this delegating shit, you hear?"

"Yes, Ralph."

21

Diamantista swung to a gentle breeze, bobbing in the small waves reflected from the white-sand beach on Saloman Bay. Tethered to the northernmost of the U.S. National Park Service moorings, the boat was in sight of the resort in Caneel Bay, St. John. Connie sat in the cockpit, savoring the last of her morning coffee.

Phillip's friend had left only a few minutes earlier, taking Phillip and Sharktooth away in his high-speed dinghy. The three of them were off for a few days of sport-fishing on the friend's boat, and Paul was due to arrive in the late afternoon on the ferry from St. Thomas, so she had most of the day to herself. Her only planned activity was a trip into town to pick up some prepared food and a nice bottle of wine or two for Paul's welcome dinner. Phillip had told her about a grocery store where she could find a broad selection of prepared, gourmet-quality entrées ready to heat and serve -- just her kind of place, she thought.

Alone for the first time in almost three weeks, Connie was eager for Paul's company. He had finished his stint as a consultant to the team that was readying the prosecution of some big-time Florida mobster, although he had warned that he would have to stay close to shore side Internet service for a few days to be available for video conferences. Still, it would be nice to have him aboard. This was an easy place to while away time as they sorted out a routine for running the boat. While St. John was almost entirely National Park land, there were a number of high-end resorts, and most things that Paul might want to buy in the way of gourmet provisions and kitchen utensils to equip the galley for his future culinary feats should be readily available.

A short dinghy ride into the town of Cruz Bay was all it took to return to an offbeat, funky version of civilization. Connie had been charmed by the quaint village when she and Phillip and Sharktooth had gone ashore yesterday to clear in with Customs and Immigration. She had picked up a few tourist brochures and had intended to look them over while she had her coffee, but she realized she had emptied the thermos while gazing idly at the shoreline a hundred yards away. Her reverie had been interrupted by the simultaneous arrival of several excursion boats that anchored close inshore and began disgorging crowds of pale tourists in snorkeling gear.

The woman at the Park Service office in Cruz Bay had warned her to expect that when she was doing the paperwork for the mooring yesterday. Connie had remarked on the serenity of the spot where they were moored; the woman had said, "Except when they show up with a few hundred people from the cruise ships in St. Thomas. Your mooring is at ground zero for the day trippers, but that can be fun to watch, too. They turn hot pink right before your eyes, and they don't stay very long. Got to hustle them back to the duty-free shopping in Charlotte Amalie -- take their money before the ships leave."

Putting her coffee cup down, she picked up the brochures and began to page through them, imagining what it would be like to explore St. John with Paul. She reminded herself that the outings were a necessary part of learning her way around so that she would be a better hostess for her charter guests, but she still felt a frisson of excitement at the thought of being with Paul, like a couple on holiday. She did her best to tamp down the absurd enthusiasm she felt at the prospect of seeing him as she gathered her things and went below. When she saw the big grin on her face in the mirror in the main cabin, she realized that she had failed to convince herself that her relationship with him was strictly business.

She ran a brush through her sun-dried hair and pulled it back into a ponytail, applied a little sun-block lipstick, and grabbed her purse. She closed and locked the boat and climbed down into the dinghy, starting the outboard and heading to Cruz Bay. She noticed that the tour boats were already leaving and that the mooring field was empty except for *Diamantista*. The woman at the Park Service had mentioned that the moorings would be empty by mid-morning, in case they wanted to move to one more convenient to town. Most of the boats carried people who were on vacation, and they tended to visit a new spot every day, sailing in the morning and exploring ashore in the late afternoons.

She caught herself thinking that she and Paul were lucky; they could enjoy this pristine spot in privacy for a few hours every day, with no schedule to worry about. She felt her cheeks flush and realized that she was doing it again. She had to focus on the charter business -- otherwise, she'd scare Paul off and have to find another cook.

~

PAUL AWAKENED with a start to the sound of a chime and the announcement from the stewardess that the captain had turned off the 'fasten seatbelt' sign. He had a habit of falling asleep every time he buckled himself into an airplane seat. As the stewardess prattled on, he sat up, hunching over so that he could look out the window on his left side. He watched the shoreline recede as the plane gained altitude, and within a few minutes, he could see

Bimini on the horizon. The captain promised a smooth flight to San Juan, Puerto Rico, and Paul's thoughts turned to what he had learned about the men who attacked *Diamantista* the day before yesterday.

The boat that carried the attackers had been reported as stolen from the Puerto Del Rey Marina in Fajardo, Puerto Rico, although based on the timing of the report, Paul suspected that the reported theft was a ruse. The boat was registered to a shady character who managed to stay one step ahead of the DEA, and he had made the report late yesterday, more than 24 hours after the attack. One of the attackers had a Puerto Rican driver's license identifying him as Rodrigo Jimenez. Jimenez had a record of arrests and a few convictions for assault, armed robbery, and theft. He was a small time crook, well known to the local authorities in Fajardo. He was also suspected to be an employee of the boat's registered owner. The other two men had criminal records as well. John 'Buster' Daniels and Vincent Luciano were from Baltimore. They were muscle for hire, working at various times for suspected pimps, bookies, and drug dealers.

Paul was alarmed at this information; it led nowhere, but it was obvious that the three thugs had been working for somebody else. A quarter of a million dollars was enough money for someone to go to such lengths to get it back, and he worried that they would not give up easily. He shook his head and chuckled to himself. Connie just seemed to fall into these situations. If he didn't know her, he would find that suspicious, but he'd had occasion to check her out thoroughly before he ever met her.

She had come to his attention a little over a year ago, when she had chartered *Vengeance* and gotten his friend's goddaughter, Dani Berger, involved in a running battle with some mobsters laundering money by trading in diamonds. He had learned back then that she had been instrumental in helping the police up in Georgia shut down a drug-smuggling and money-laundering ring. The cop who had run that investigation had nothing but good things to say about her; his opinion was corroborated by Dani and her partner, Liz Chirac.

Paul had met her in the aftermath of their troubles, when he had gone down island to serve an arrest warrant on the man behind it all. He had been captivated by Connie; she was a stunningly beautiful and charming woman, for all that she seemed to attract trouble. She had emerged from that escapade unscathed and in possession of several million dollars' worth of diamonds, to boot.

He had spent an idyllic two weeks with Connie and Dani and Liz, sailing through the Windward Islands on *Vengeance*. He had known at the time that he was in trouble; when she turned those big, brown eyes on him, all of his resolve to stay single melted away. As it had turned out, the lack of privacy on *Vengeance* had saved them both; they had each confessed to the other that, while the attraction was undeniable, neither was ready for a relationship. Both were trying to reconcile wounds from the past, so they had opted for friendship rather than romance.

By the time they parted, Connie had asked Paul to help her start a charter business of her own; under the spell of the islands and those eyes, he had readily agreed. Now, here he was, about to join her on *Diamantista* in one of the most romantic spots in the islands, and she was once again the target of some unknown criminals. He shrugged; he was no stranger to dealing with crooks, and he was eager to fall under the spell of those eyes again.

∼

CONNIE BROUGHT the dinghy alongside *Diamantista* and tied the painter to the cleat on the big boat's starboard quarter. As she bent to pick up her groceries, she registered that she had just looked through the companionway doors; that couldn't be right. She looked again, confirming that the doors stood open. She was sure she had locked them. She glanced around, checking the mooring field and the beach. There was no one in sight; *Diamantista* was the only boat in the area.

The outboard engine on the dinghy was still running; she hadn't shut it off. She thought for a moment, and untied the painter from the cleat, leaving it looped loosely as she held the end, ready to cast off in a hurry.

"Hello! Who's there?" she bellowed.

There was no answer. She retied the painter and shut off the outboard, climbing cautiously aboard *Diamantista*. She armed herself with one of the heavy bronze winch handles from the cockpit and peered below through the open doors, surprised at the shambles below deck. She noticed then that the wood on the starboard door was splintered where someone had pried loose the staple that still held the locked padlock.

Angry at the damage, ready to seek retribution, she went below. There was no one there. Everything had been thrown into the middle of the cabins; all the lockers were empty, the doors banging as they swung to and fro with the rolling of the boat. Her anger fading to anxiety, she decided that she probably shouldn't stay aboard by herself, especially since there were no other boats nearby.

She fastened the locker doors to avoid damage and stowed the food that she had bought. Within two minutes, she was in the dinghy, headed back to Cruz Bay. She would stop in at the Park Service office and report the break-in; then she'd have a leisurely lunch in one of the little restaurants near the ferry dock. Paul would arrive in a couple of hours, and they could sort out *Diamantista* together.

∽

PAUL SAW her as soon as he stepped onto the gangway from the ferry's deck, his duffle bag hanging behind him from a shoulder strap. He waved, but she didn't see him. As he shouldered his way through the crowd, he saw her face light up when she spotted him, her frown replaced by a glowing smile. He stopped a pace in front of her, grinning. "It's good ..."

His greeting was interrupted as she wrapped both arms around his chest, squeezing him so tightly he couldn't breathe. As he returned the hug, he heard and felt her sob. Patting her on the back, he asked, "What's wrong?"

"Scared," she sobbed.

"It'll be all right. It's all behind ..."

"No. No, I thought so, too, but they, they ..."

"Okay," he said, running a hand up and down her shoulder blade. "Take it easy. We'll get it all straightened out. What's happened since I talked with you and Phillip last night?"

She blubbered through an explanation, still clutching him, the side of her face pressed against his chest. As she finished the story, he felt her grip relax. She took a half step back and rubbed at her eyes, sniffling. "God, I'm sorry, Paul. I hate acting like a helpless female. I'm just ..."

"Look, no way are you a helpless female. A hell of a lot has happened since you left Annapolis; you've probably been on an adrenalin high since those bastards attacked you guys the other day. You're just crashing; roll with it. It's okay."

"Thanks." She gave him a sheepish smile. "The boat's a real mess; I got us a nice dinner, and a couple of bottles of your favorite Barolo, but ..."

"That's great. Let's go find a quiet spot to sit down. I could use something cold to drink while we regroup."

"Okay. There's this place close by; I had lunch there."

"Good. Let's go, and don't worry about the boat. With both of us, we'll have it back right in no time, and we can enjoy that dinner and the wine in the cockpit after we finish."

22

It was a lovely evening; the moon rose over the island as they were getting ready for dinner, bathing the glassy water in a silver glow. Connie had set the table in the cockpit while Paul busied himself in the galley, warming, tasting, tweaking the spices, and doing those things that people who love to cook do. He had been right; it had taken them less than an hour to stow everything and clean up the mess.

Satisfied with her arrangements, Connie lit the hurricane lantern that was hanging over the table and adjusted the wick so that it gave off a soft, orange glow. Between that and the moonlight, they would be able to see well enough to eat without attracting flying insects or spoiling the moonlit vistas that surrounded the boat in every direction. She sat down and took a sip of the wine that Paul had passed up to her a few minutes earlier. Before she set her glass down, Paul appeared in the companionway, silhouetted in the light from the galley. He held a steaming plate in each hand.

"Take these, please?" He stepped back below, switching off the bright lights, and returned, taking the seat across from her.

"Here's to *Diamantista's* first successful season, coming up!" He raised his glass toward hers and they clicked the rims.

After she took a sip of the wine, Connie said, "A belated welcome aboard."

"Thanks." Paul smiled at her and nodded his head.

"Sorry I was such a basket case when you got here. I had planned to be the one to serve you dinner -- not the other way around. When I saw the mess, I just went to pieces. Thanks for being so understanding."

"It's not a problem; besides, I signed on to this tub as the cook. I don't want the boss messing up my galley. Now, let's eat before I have to warm this up again. Bon appétit!"

"Bon appétit," she replied.

After a few minutes, she put her knife and fork down. She took a swallow of her wine and studied Paul as he applied himself to the food.

"Not bad for ready-to-eat," he said as he finished chewing and reached for his wine, noticing surreptitiously how the moonlight picked out the sheen from her thick, black hair, which was loose tonight, brushing her shoulders.

"Phillip's friend says that a lot of the big charter yachts, the one's with big freezers?"

"Yes, what about them?" he asked.

"Well, they have that store put together a whole list of frozen entrees for their guests," she continued.

"Good thing *Diamantista* doesn't have a freezer, or I'd be out of a job."

"Nah, not really. I'd keep you around; a good-looking first mate's bound to be an asset. Our first charter's a couple of widows."

"Now I feel like a sex object. Or I would, except for being a broken-down old cop."

"That reminds me. I've been meaning to ask you something."

"Will I have to take my shirt off?"

"What?"

"For the widows. What have you promised them? I've got some pride, you know. Gotta draw the line somewhere."

"No, you silly man," she laughed, an easy, musical sound that made Paul wish things were different between them. "I wondered how you decided to become a cop, if it's not too personal."

"Well, compared to being asked to give my all for the team, it's kind of a relief, actually. I inherited it."

"You inherited being a cop?"

"My grandfather was a beat cop in New York. He retired and moved to Florida while my dad was still in school, and my dad became the town cop in this little Podunk place called Two Egg."

"Two Egg?" Connie giggled. "In Florida?"

Paul nodded. "Mm-hmm."

"Where in Florida?"

"You know where Possum Holler is?"

She laughed again, that melodious, full-throated sound that invited him to make her do it over and over.

"Guess not. How about Weewahitchka?"

"At least that sounds like it could be a real place, like an Indian name, maybe."

"Oh, they're all real. Up in the panhandle. That was pretty seriously backwoods when I was growing up. It's not much better now. Once I saw Miami, I was outta there. Finished college, did my time in the Army, and settled in."

"You miss being a cop?"

"No, not a bit. It felt good while I was doing it, but it's behind me now, or almost behind me."

"Almost?"

"Yeah, I need to stick close to Internet and telephone service for a few days. I've got a conference call tomorrow; there's some kind of office services place in Cruz Bay that I can use."

"I know where it is; I passed it going to the Park Service office today."

"Can't be too hard to find; there's not much in Cruz Bay. You never told me what they said."

"The Park Police?"

"Yeah, I guess."

"Well ..." She took a sip of wine, her face turning serious again after the laughter, making Paul sorry he'd asked. "They filled out a report form, but they said petty theft was an occasional problem, particularly from boats that didn't have any close neighbors. They offered to send somebody out with me to make sure it was okay, but I decided to just wait for you."

"You tell them about the other?"

She shook her head, the moonlight on her hair distracting him again. "No. It would have raised way more questions than I wanted to answer, and I didn't think it would do any good in the end."

"Probably not," he agreed, taking a sip of wine.

"Paul?"

"Mm?"

"You think it was related?"

"What do you think?" he countered. "You heard the guy that Phillip and Sharktooth questioned."

"I didn't get much from what he said, but it would be a huge coincidence if it wasn't, wouldn't it?"

He nodded. "You think like a cop," he said.

"Survival instincts."

"That's healthy. You looked for the money?"

"Yes, but we didn't find anything. Besides, the whole Federal government took the boat apart in Beaufort, remember?"

"Yep." Paul stifled a yawn.

"I'm sorry," Connie said. "You must be exhausted."

"Pretty tired," he agreed.

"Why don't you call it a night? I can clean this up. I promise not to mess up your galley, okay?"

He smiled. "Deal." He stood up, stretching his back, his hands on his hips. She saw how flat his stomach looked as the polo shirt stretched across it. She tore her eyes away before he could notice. He took a step toward the companionway and paused, turning to face her again.

She was glad of the dim lighting. As his eyes held hers, she could feel a flush rising from her neck to her face.

"Connie?"

"Yes?" she responded. Her soft, husky voice embarrassed her as she realized how it must have sounded. Her body was betraying her, making a mockery of her resolve to keep their relationship on a professional level; she felt the last of her control melt away as she returned his gaze.

"Try not to worry. We're going to get through this, and those widows will be sending their friends down before you know it." He turned and stepped through the companionway.

"'Night, Paul. I'm glad you're here. Rest well."

"Thanks. You, too."

IT HAD TAKEN Connie less than five minutes to clean up after their dinner, but before she had dried the dishes and put them away, she heard soft snoring sounds coming from the forward cabin. She smiled, finding comfort in Paul's presence, even as she was confused by her own reactions to him.

She had been sure for a moment that he was about to take her in his arms and kiss her good-night as he left the dinner table. She alternated between feeling relief and frustration that he had not. Rationally, she knew it was for the best that he hadn't, but reason seemed to flee when she was alone with him. It would be a long three weeks before those widows arrived.

She wanted a cold shower before she went to bed, but she worried that the noise of the pressure water pump would disturb Paul; it was mounted in a locker in the forward cabin where he was sleeping. She went into the aft head and filled the sink using the hand pump, settling for a cooling sponge bath instead as she tried to make sense of her emotions.

∽

PAUL PASSED from sleep to wakefulness in a flash. He lay still, his eyes closed as he assessed his surroundings. He remembered that he was on *Diamantista* after a second or two. He was trying to figure out what woke him up when he heard a soft, sighing sound and a gurgle from beneath his berth. Water tank, he thought. He had heard the pressure water pump running in one of the lockers as he got ready for bed, but he hadn't heard it just now. Then he realized that Connie must be using a hand pump, worried that she'd disturb him.

That brought a smile to his face. She'd disturbed him, all right, but it didn't have anything to do with running water. The moonlight on that hair, and those big, dark eyes, he remembered. It had been all he could do not to take her in his arms tonight, but he knew that would have ruined everything.

Even though he might be feeling differently about their earlier agreement, this was not the right time to act. She was shaken, vulnerable. She needed a friend and a protector, not some drooling, fawning, middle-aged man with the hormones of a thirteen-year-old boy. He drifted off, dreaming that he was falling into the dark, deep pools of those eyes.

23

"That's the boat, right out there. First one." Tony Ferranti gestured with his head. He and Murano were having breakfast in an outdoor coffee shop overlooking the beach in Caneel Bay. Like everything else about the resort, the coffee shop was overpriced, but it gave them a view of the boat. That was an unexpected bit of luck; they couldn't have planned it better if they'd known what they were doing. Tony was facing away from the water, giving his boss the chair that afforded a view of the beach and the boat.

"First one? Looks like the only one, to me."

"Yeah, well, you can't see the others from here, but there's a string of them mooring balls runs clear down to Cruz Bay."

"How'd you get out to the boat yesterday? Swim?"

"No, man. That's the friggin' ocean out there. There's sharks 'n' shit. I got a dinghy."

"Where?"

"Bought it off a guy. He prob'ly stole it, but ..."

"No. I mean where is it now?"

"Oh. There's a public dinghy dock in Cruz Bay right next to the ferry dock. I locked it up there."

"How long will it take us to get there?"

"To the dinghy? Or to the boat?"

"Both."

"Fifteen-minute drive to town, give or take. Traffic's unfucking believable, man. These damn people stop their cars to talk to one another -- just block the damn road while they shoot the shit. And if you blow the horn, man, they act like you're the asshole, not them."

"And from the dinghy dock?"

"Huh?"

"Once we get to the dinghy, how long to get to the boat?"

"Oh. Ten minutes, maybe. No traffic problem there."

"So the cop's staying on the boat with her?"

"Yeah. I can see 'em real good from my balcony, with binoculars. They went out there late yesterday afternoon. Been there ever since, unless the dinghy's gone."

"No, it's there. How close are the other boats?"

"Too damn close, but they mostly leave by late morning. Guy I bought the dinghy offa told me that, and he was right. The broad went into town a little before lunch yesterday, and by the time I got out there, the boat was all by itself."

"You got any ideas how to handle this?" Murano asked.

"We gotta make the bitch talk, that's all. I'd bet my ass the money's not on the damn boat; I took that sumbitch apart yesterday."

"You're thinking we should snatch her?"

"Yeah, but I don't like the looks of that guy that's out there with her now."

"You afraid of cops?" Murano asked, grinning.

"You said he's retired."

"Yeah. So?"

"So he ain't really a cop. 'Specially down here."

"So what's the problem?"

"You seen him up close?"

"No, why?"

"I was watchin' the broad when she met him at the ferry dock. He's one tough-lookin' hombre. Got them cold blue eyes, always movin' over the crowd, like one of them dudes covers the president."

"I never knew you were a chickenshit, Tony."

"Fuck you, Murano."

"So how are we going to do it?"

"I'd waste him first thing, before he can turn it around on us. That'll shake the broad up, too."

Murano thought about that for a moment. He knew how Giannetti felt about killing cops, but he didn't share that old-fashioned idea. Besides, it would be easy to ditch the body. They could just pick up a weight belt at a dive shop, buckle it on, and drop him in deep water out of sight of land. "All right," he agreed. "We can't really question the woman right out there, though."

"Nah. I figure we go for a sail. Gotta be some places where we could find a little privacy."

Murano nodded. "How long before you figure the boats out there will thin out?"

"Couple or three hours. There's a trail out to the point; we can see from out there. Only take us a couple minutes to walk it."

"What if they leave?"

"Hell, Murano, they just got here."

"Yeah, but ..."

"We still got the tracker. They can run, but they can't hide."

~

CONNIE SAT at the table in the saloon sipping coffee when Paul stepped out of the forward cabin rubbing his eyes. "Morning, sleepyhead."

"Good morning, captain. Got any more of that coffee?"

She nodded, gesturing to the carafe that sat on the table next to an empty cup. He picked up the carafe and filled the cup.

"Have a seat," she invited.

He shook his head. "I'll rustle up some breakfast first. You hungry?"

"I was going to do bacon and eggs for you. It's the one thing I can cook with predictable results. Have a seat."

"I'm the cook; if you've got bacon and eggs in the galley, that's a good start. I need to get in practice at cooking in this galley before those widows show up. Might as well start now."

"I bet if you took your shirt off like you said, they wouldn't care about the food," she said, an impish grin on her face.

"Keep it up and I'll file a complaint with, um ..."

"Yeah? With um? Okay. I'm scared; I apologize."

Paul chuckled.

"You started it," she said.

"What?"

"The thing about taking your shirt off."

"Oh. Well, I'll have to be more careful about what I say." He was rummaging in the top-loading refrigerator, setting things on the countertop beside the stove.

"What time's your conference call?"

"Noon."

"That's an odd time."

"Yeah, but everybody stops to eat, so it doesn't cut into productivity too much. The prosecutor's a real bear about efficiency."

"So you need to leave around 11:30?"

"Maybe a little earlier; I need to get my email. They sent me some reports I need to review. You're coming ashore with me, right?"

Connie was tempted, but she had already decided that she was not going to lean on Paul; she could take care of herself. Besides, she didn't want him to think she was going to cling to him, even though she wanted to. She didn't want to drive him away.

"No, I don't think so. I want to get that lock fixed, where the bastard broke in."

"You got someone coming out?"

"No. I can do it. I've got everything I need to repair it."

"How're you going to do it? Looked like they broke the wood, to me."

"Yes, they did. Nothing a little thickened epoxy won't fix."

"Where'd you learn about stuff like that?"

"Dani. You have to be able to fix things if you want to run a boat; she gave me a crash course on all kinds of minor repairs. Why?"

"Oh, nothing."

"You think that's man's work, don't you?"

"Well, I ..."

"Sexist pig," she teased. "I'm surprised at that, from a man that likes to cook."

Paul chuckled. "Okay, okay. You win, but I don't like the idea of you out here by yourself."

"I can handle myself, Paul."

"I know; I've seen ample proof of that, but it worries me that the people from yesterday might come back. You know they didn't find the money."

"Maybe they did."

"No. It's Cop 101. Basic stuff. Whoever made that search didn't find what they were looking for."

"Because of the way they tore the whole place apart?"

"Yeah, pretty much. You do the job I did for 25 years and you get a sixth sense for things like that."

"I'll be okay, Paul. I'm not going to let these bastards control my day-to-day life; that would mean they won."

"Yeah, but ..."

"Look. I'll put the phone in my pocket; I've got a handheld

VHF radio, and there're tons of people monitoring channel 16. I'll be up in the cockpit, working, so nobody's going to surprise me. Chill!"

"Yes, ma'am." Paul stepped out of the galley with two steaming plates of food. Setting one in front of Connie, he slid into the seat opposite her.

"What's this? I thought you were doing bacon and eggs. This looks like ..."

"Eggs Benedict," he finished her sentence and picked up his fork. "Bon appétit."

"Bon appétit." Connie tasted the eggs. "Yum."

"You like 'em okay?"

"It's wonderful. Thanks."

"Just doing my job, ma'am."

"Paul?"

"Yes?"

"It's not that I don't appreciate your worrying about me. I really do, but I need to ... to ..."

"It's okay. I understand. I'm sort of the same way, I think. You have to be your own person. Sorry if I was bugging you." He saw those eyes, then. The ones he'd been dreaming about; he felt like they were going to swallow his soul as she held him in her grateful gaze. He picked up his knife and busied himself with his food before he said or did something that would embarrass both of them.

～

CONNIE STOOD in the cockpit watching as Paul steered for Cruz Bay in the dinghy. She thought she'd done a good job of maintaining a brave façade until he left, but behind it she was riddled with uncertainty. In spite of what she'd told Paul, she was worried that whoever was looking for Jimmy's money would try again, but that wasn't her only source of anxiety. Between last night and this morning, she had acknowledged to herself that her feelings for Paul went far beyond friendship.

She'd never felt such a sense of comfort, such a willingness to entrust another with her feelings, as she felt with him. She was pretty sure that this must be love; it was a unique experience for her. She was 34 years old and had been on her own for 20 of those years, never daring to put her faith in another person.

Now she wanted to, to ... she shook her head. She couldn't even express to herself what she wanted. She wanted him. Not just physically, although she couldn't deny the warmth that rose in her belly every time he looked at her that way when he thought she wasn't watching. She wanted to be part of him, part of his life, and she wanted him to feel that way about her. She knew that she had no control over his feelings, any more than she had control over her own. She felt a tear roll down her cheek, a tear of frustration.

She could cope with these thugs who thought she had their money; that wasn't a new problem for her. It was frightening, but she knew how to channel the fear constructively. This situation with Paul, though, was beyond her ken. She only knew that she wanted him. She would figure it out; nothing that she ever wanted had eluded her -- not yet, anyway. "But I've never wanted anything this much in my life," she said aloud, surprising herself.

She focused her attention on the splintered wood where the burglar had pried the hardware from the companionway door. After studying it for a moment, she went below to assemble her tools. She couldn't solve the puzzle of what to do about Paul, but she could fix the door, and that would give her some momentary comfort and satisfaction.

∼

PAUL BARELY NOTICED the other boats he passed as he took the dinghy into Cruz Bay. He had registered that several appeared to be getting ready to leave, their engines running as they hoisted their mainsails before dropping their mooring pennants. He had nearly hit one, evoking shouted curses and arm waving on the part of the sunburned tourist at the helm. He tried to focus on the Greco case to get himself geared up for the conference call, but his mind kept drifting back to Connie.

He realized that since he'd met her, all the pain and frustration from his bitter divorce had melted away. At first, he'd attributed that to simple infatuation with a beautiful, vivacious woman willing to spend time with him. Since they passed that night in Beaufort in each other's arms, though, it had become clear to him that there was more to his feeling than that.

He'd had a few tentative relationships since his divorce. They provided enough distraction to mask the pain he carried in his heart, but he always knew it was lurking there, waiting to surprise him when he let his guard down. Now, he could look back on that period of emotional trauma and feel nothing more than a little sadness, a bit of grief, but not the overwhelming sense of anger and hurt that he had borne for years.

Shocked, he found himself holding the dinghy alongside the public dock in Cruz Bay with no recollection of having stopped there. He looked at his watch, alarmed that he been daydreaming and would be late for his call. He was relieved when he saw that only ten minutes had elapsed since he left *Diamantista*. He wrapped the dinghy's security chain around the railing of the floating dock and snapped the padlock through the links. Picking up his vinyl zippered binder, he climbed onto the dock and looked around for a moment to get his bearings. He didn't notice the two men staring at him from the crowd on the plaza in front of the adjacent ferry dock.

~

"SHIT," Murano muttered. They had just found a place to park their rental car. Ferranti had been right; the traffic was 'unfuckin'-believable.'

"That's him, ain't it?" Ferranti asked. "The cop."

"Yeah," Murano said.

They had planned to take their time about picking up the dinghy that Ferranti had left at the dock. Most of the overnight occupants of the moorings around the woman's boat had been leaving, so they had decided to drive to town. They could poke around the harbor in the dinghy, acting like tourists until they saw that all the boats had left. Then they would make their move.

"So what now?" Ferranti asked.

"Let's follow the son of a bitch. See where he goes."

"You think he's got the money?" Ferranti asked.

"Not on him."

"I know that, damn it. I'm the one packed it, remember?"

"Yeah. Take it easy. Let's see what he's up to. He's carrying a briefcase. You catch that?"

"Yeah. Don't look much like a tourist."

"No. Look. He's going in that place that advertises fax and Internet service."

"Yeah, and mailboxes for rent. Maybe the money's in there."

They stood across the street, blending with the crowd for a few minutes.

"Been in there a while," Ferranti said.

"Yeah. I'm going in and check it out. You wait here."

Murano stepped into the air-conditioned store and looked around. There was a woman behind a counter with a couple of people waiting as she searched through a folder. She looked up at Murano and smiled. "Be right with you, sir," she said, in a soft, southern accent. Murano nodded and studied the placards on the wall behind her.

"We're all here because we're not all there," one of them announced.

The other said, "We don't really care how you do it up north."

The two people at the counter left carrying small parcels, and Murano was alone with the woman.

"What can I do for you today?"

"I was wondering, um, do you have, like, private rooms for Internet access, or something?"

She frowned, and he realized what she must be thinking.

"No. Not like that, I mean, like somewhere I could spread out some papers and go on line to do a little work?"

She smiled, blushing. "I thought for a minute ..."

"Yeah. Sorry. My fault. I'm just looking for a place to get away from the wife and kids for a while to get some work done."

She nodded. "We do have a small conference room with a computer that's got high speed Internet access. People use it for video conferences, sometimes."

"That sounds like what I'm looking for. Is it available?"

"Sorry, not right now. It's in use."

"Any idea how long before I could get in?"

She glanced up at the clock on the wall. "Probably a couple of hours, yet. If you have a phone, I could call you when it's free."

He shook his head. "No, thanks. I'll check back with you."

"You're welcome. Have a nice day."

Murano stepped across the street and told Ferranti what he had learned.

"Couple of hours, huh?" Ferranti asked.

"Yeah. What do you think? Should we wait for him, or just go grab the woman?"

"I'm gonna die if I don't get outta the sun, that's what I think."

Murano nodded. "Let's go get a cold drink at that place over there and figure out what to do."

24

Paul did his best to maintain an attentive appearance; that was the thing that he liked least about video conference calls. His active part in the call had long since passed, but he was still on display. He had to look alert and engaged, but they couldn't see his thoughts.

He had spent the last hour working out how to tell Connie what he needed to tell her without spooking her. His worst fear was that she'd think that they had to spend some time apart; he didn't think that she would sever their friendship. She wouldn't reward honesty that way, but she might well be uncomfortable about sharing such a small space with him, knowing how he felt about her. He resolved once again to take that risk. To do otherwise was impossible, but the thought of being separated from her was unbearable.

"Paul?" He heard the voice of the Assistant U.S. Attorney.

He raised his eyes to the screen. "Sorry, ma'am. Just checking my notes."

"I asked if you had anything to add before we adjourn."

"Oh. No, ma'am, I can't think of a thing we haven't covered."

"Good. Thanks for joining us. Get back to your adventures in paradise, but don't forget to check your email every day, please."

"Yes, ma'am. Thanks, and don't hesitate to ask if there's something I can do to keep Greco off the street."

"Will do. 'Bye, everybody."

With a burbling tone, the computer screen went blank. Paul shuffled his papers into his vinyl briefcase, noticing as he did that his notepad was covered in doodles of a black-haired woman with big, dark eyes. He smiled wryly and tore the page off, balling it up and tossing it in the trash can in the corner of the small room. He opened the door and stepped over to the counter.

"All done, Lieutenant?"

"Yes. I'd like to put this on my credit card, please."

"Oh, it's been taken care of; the U.S. Attorney's office has an open account with us."

"Okay, then. Thanks."

"Have a good afternoon," she said, as he eased the street door closed behind him.

He felt like he was wading through quicksand as he made his way through the crowds of tourists to the dinghy dock. He dropped his briefcase into the little boat and climbed down, unlocking it and pushing it away from the crowded dock as he took a seat on the starboard side and pulled the starter cord. He felt a sense of excitement as he twisted the throttle and headed for the harbor entrance; he knew it was because he had made the right decision about telling Connie. His business behind him, he felt free and unburdened, except ... except he knew he had fallen in love with Connie. He had come to grips with that while the other participants in the conference call were droning on about the Greco case.

Despite the fact that she'd spent much of her life as a con artist, she was still a kind, generous person. She radiated a fundamental honesty that spoke of a solid character beneath a wily public persona. Connie had been the one to raise the subject of their mutual attraction back when they had first met. Paul had been surprised at the time, thinking that she was probably just out for a fling. Then she had surprised him when she'd said that she thought they should proceed with caution. She had told him that she wasn't ready to get emotionally involved with a man, even one that she liked as much as she liked him -- especially not one that she liked that much. She had too few friends in her life to risk one by getting into the complexities of a sexual relationship, as attractive as she might find it.

As they had talked, he had seen the wisdom in her viewpoint. He had taken stock of his own feelings and confessed that he agreed with her. The comfort that they provided one another was too rare to risk losing for a roll in the hay, as he had put it in his down-home way.

He still felt that way; it was just that there was something new in the mix. He couldn't look at her without wanting to take her in his arms, to hold her and comfort her and protect her. And while those were the limits of his conscious desires, he wasn't naïve enough to believe that he could stop there.

He was ready to move their relationship beyond friendship, but until she felt the same way, he knew he owed her the kind of honesty that she had shown him. As difficult as it would be, he'd have to tell her how he was feeling about her, and sooner rather than later. As risky as such a confession might be, it was the only right path for him to follow.

As he rounded the point, the mooring field that stretched from there up to Caneel Bay came into view. He was a little surprised at how many of the moorings were occupied now; they had been empty except for *Diamantista* and a few other boats when he had come in just two and a half hours ago. Now, there were few unoccupied mooring balls; the population of boats was so dense that he couldn't even pick out *Diamantista* on the farthest mooring.

He was about a hundred yards back when he realized that the

boat on the far mooring was not *Diamantista*. Perplexed, he thought Connie must have moved for some reason. Maybe she wanted to be closer to town, but he was surprised that she would do that by herself. A 56-foot boat was a handful for one person when it came to picking up a mooring. She had worked hard at becoming an expert boat-handler. He didn't doubt that she could have done it, but he couldn't imagine why she would have.

He throttled back and stood up in the dinghy, looking around, but he didn't see *Diamantista*. "Must have passed her," he muttered, turning the dinghy around and weaving through the boats at full throttle as he headed back to town. Having failed to spot her, he went back to the boat on the mooring *Diamantista* had occupied when he left a few hours ago.

There were several people in the cockpit when he pulled alongside. He willed his heart to slow down, sure that his blood pressure must be setting a record.

"Excuse me," he said, "but I'm looking for a boat called *Diamantista*. She was on this mooring about three hours ago."

One of the men shrugged and shook his head. "It was empty when we got here."

"Could you please tell me how long ago that was?"

"I made a note in our logbook. When I shut the engine down, it was 2:15. Couldn't have been too long ago; we're still on the first round of beers." He chuckled.

Paul glanced at his watch; it was 3:00. He released his grip on the side of the boat and sat down. "Thanks," he said, as he turned to start the outboard.

"No problem," the man said.

"Hey!" one of the women yelled as Paul started to accelerate.

He throttled back and returned.

"Yes, ma'am?"

"Check the third boat from the front. It was here when we got here; the rest of them came after we did."

"Thank you very much," he said, and roared away. He throttled back as he approached the third boat, finding a couple relaxing with books in the shade of the cockpit awning. They looked up from their books as he came alongside.

"Sorry to disturb you," he said, and explained his quest.

"Well," the woman said, "I don't know about the name because we didn't get that close, but there was a boat on that mooring when we got here. There were only a couple of others back toward town, us, and that one on the first mooring."

"Do you know about what time that was?"

The woman and her companion exchanged glances.

"Not exactly. We're on vacation, so we're deliberately not looking at the time," the man said.

"But it was lunch time," the woman added. "While we were eating, the two men came back to that boat and left in a big hurry."

"Two men?"

"Yes, in a really trashy-looking dinghy. I was surprised, because the boat was so well kept."

"Any chance you could describe them?" Paul asked.

"I didn't get that good a look; they were going pretty fast, but I guess they were average looking. Shorts, T-shirts. Nothing that caught my eye but the dinghy."

"Were they white or black? Fat? Skinny?"

"White, I think. The dinghy was kind of a dark gray with paint splotches on it, and the outboard was painted day-glow orange," the woman said. Her husband nodded.

"Thanks," Paul said, his heart in his throat.

∽

CONNIE COULD HEAR voices as she recovered consciousness, but she could not make out what they were saying. She lay still, feigning sleep as she assessed her surroundings. The rumble of the diesel from below sounded familiar, like *Diamantista's,* but that wasn't right. Could Paul be moving the boat, or charging the batteries, or something? That didn't add up either. She remembered that he had gone into Cruz Bay for some reason.

Cruz Bay. That's right. They were on a mooring in St. John. God, her head was splitting. She kept her eyes nearly closed and cast a furtive glance at her immediate surroundings. She was on the starboard settee in *Diamantista's main* cabin, and she could tell now that the boat was underway. Alarmed, she rolled to a sitting position, her vision spinning as she opened her eyes.

"Well, well. Sleeping Beauty awakens. I was beginning to think I'd hit you too hard."

She focused on the grinning man with difficulty, taking in the carefully groomed hair and the closely clipped beard that covered his face. At first, she thought he needed a shave, but then she realized that the whiskers were a fashion statement of sorts, like the piercing through the bridge of his nose.

"Like what you see?" he asked, still grinning.

"Who are you?" she asked, still befuddled.

"Just call me Tony, sweet thing. And I'm betting you go by Connie, right? Not Constanza?"

So he's looked through the papers, she thought.

"Well? Which is it?" he asked in a pleasant enough tone of voice.

"Connie."

"Good. I like Connie. It suits you. Constanza sounds like some old bat from a vampire movie."

"What do you want?" she asked.

"Now that's my kind of girl," he said softly, smiling. "Friendly and accommodating."

They looked at one another in silence for a moment, and then he got to his feet and stepped across the cabin, invading her space as he bent down and put a hand on the cushion on either side of her, bracing himself against the motion of the boat.

He screamed suddenly, "I want you naked, right now, bitch!"

She felt the spray of his spittle on her face as she recoiled from his reeking breath. She saw a flash of blinding light and felt an excruciating pain on the right side of her head, realizing as she fought to hold onto consciousness that he had hit her. She tasted blood in her mouth; the inside of her cheek must have been cut by her teeth.

He stepped back, jerking her to her feet. "Right now, bitch. Strip!"

"No, please," she said, feeling a surge of panic. She thought of kneeing him in the groin, or kicking his knee out; that had worked well with Jimmy, but she was so shaky she didn't know if she could do it.

As if reading her mind, he stepped back again. A straight razor appeared magically in his right hand.

"Naked. Now!" he screamed, his eyes bugging as he brandished the razor.

"Look, Connie," he said, his tone now conversational. "You're going to be naked in the next thirty seconds. You can strip, or I can cut away your clothes. Now, I've done it before, but I'm a little out of practice, so I might cut you. I'd recommend that you strip." He smiled pleasantly.

"Now!" he screamed, lifting the razor over his head and starting to bring it down toward her chest.

"Okay!" she said, thinking that maybe she could distract him and tangle the razor in her clothing as she removed it. She began unbuttoning her shirt as he smiled sweetly and nodded his encouragement.

"Good," he said, in a soft tone.

"Tony!" a man's voice bellowed from above deck.

"Busy," he yelled in reply, winking at Connie.

She'd been wondering about whether he was alone. Now she knew there was at least one other person aboard.

"Quit screwing with her and come here for a second," the man on deck called.

"We're not screwing ... yet," Tony yelled in reply, grinning at Connie as she took her shirt off. "I'll be up in a bit. Just head north and don't hit anything for now. I gotta finish what I started down here."

He licked his lips theatrically as Connie unbuttoned the waistband of her shorts and let them drop to the floor. She pushed them aside with her foot and stood, hands at her sides.

"Naked!" he screamed again, lifting the razor and stepping toward her. "You're not naked yet," he murmured. "You have to be naked for what happens next."

She measured the distance to his near knee, keeping the razor in her peripheral vision. She knew it was intended to terrify rather than to inflict a mortal wound. She decided she'd risk a few razor cuts before she'd let him rape her. These bastards wanted the money, she was sure, so they wouldn't kill her. The longer she could drag this out, the more likely Paul would come looking for her. She realized that the adrenalin had cleared her head. She reached back and undid the hooks on her bra, sliding it from her shoulders as she watched his eyes. It worried her that they never once flickered toward her exposed breasts. The clock on the bulkhead chimed six times; it was three in the afternoon. Paul should be discovering that the boat was gone about now. She slipped her panties down over her hips and stepped out of them, dangling them on her right index finger as she locked eyes with Tony.

"Happy?" she asked.

"Not yet, but soon," he grinned.

He tossed the razor from his right hand to his left, watching her eyes follow it. As he caught it, he brought his right fist up in a vicious punch that landed just below her left ear.

~

CONNIE HEARD the clock chime as she felt her head throbbing

again. She recovered consciousness much more quickly this time, aided by the pain that seemed to radiate through her body. She was face down on the saloon table. Her shoulders and hips ached, and she couldn't feel her fingers and toes.

She tried to change her position, but her arms were extended over her head. She tugged on them a little bit and felt something cut into her wrists. She lifted her head enough to see her hands; there were cable ties around her wrists and a short length of quarter-inch nylon line secured them to the part of the mast that came down through the cabin.

She couldn't see her feet, but she didn't need eyes to know that her ankles were cable-tied and probably roped to one of the fittings on the waist-high bulkhead that divided the galley from the saloon. Her bare skin stuck to the varnished surface of the table, so that any movement, even taking a deep breath, brought tiny needles of pain from her breasts as her skin stretched, the parts touching the varnish held firmly in place by her dried perspiration.

The engine was silent. She held still for a moment, concentrating, and decided from the boat's motion that they were at anchor in reasonably calm water. She could hear the murmur of voices from the cockpit. She only identified two different ones, both male. She closed her eyes and concentrated on breathing evenly, feigning unconsciousness.

She knew they would rouse her when it suited them, whether they thought she was conscious or not. In the interim, she might hear something useful if they thought she was out cold. One of them came below and lifted the top on the refrigerator

"We should have grabbed the cop, too," the one below deck said.

His was the other voice. She dubbed him 'Not Tony.' They knew about Paul, so they must have been watching them for some length of time. She searched her memory, but she couldn't recall having seen Tony before, nor could she remember seeing anyone suspicious since Paul arrived. "Not that I would have noticed," she thought, ruefully.

"Yeah. We coulda worked on her and let him watch. He woulda talked for sure then."

"You'll get it out of her. Shit, you scared the hell out of me with that lunatic screaming fit, and we're on the same side."

"You like my evil twin, huh?"

"I wouldn't go that far, but it's effective."

"Trick I learned back when I was running women. Not much scares crack whores, but crazy is somethin' that seems to rattle 'em. 'Specially if you threaten to cut 'em up a little. Somethin' about a straight razor and a lunatic, I guess."

"You teach that to Willie?"

"Nah. He got his own shtick. He likes needle nose pliers."

Connie heard the sound of a pop top opening from the galley. She wondered if Willie was Jimmy's friend, the pimp that he used to threaten Kirsten. Probably, she reasoned. She shuddered at the memory of the girl stabbing Jimmy in the back, remembering the look on her face. Connie knew she could kill; she'd been forced to, but it still bothered her. The look of pure insanity on that girl's face as she had ripped the knife through his kidneys was a stark contrast to the look on Tony's face when he was waving the razor around. Not that he was not scary, but he didn't project insanity -- not if you had first-hand experience with the real thing.

"You want a beer while I'm down here?" Not Tony asked.

"Yeah, sure. Might as well relax. Time's on our side, now."

"How do you figure that?"

She could tell he was going back up the companionway ladder from his voice.

"The longer we leave her stretched out like that, the worse she's gonna hurt when we start messin' with her."

"We don't have a lot of time. Giannetti wants his damn money."

"We'll get it for him."

"Did you put it to her yet?"

"Nah. But she's expecting it. Anticipation, man. It's worse waitin' for it than it is havin' it happen. Once you do it, whatever it is you're threatenin', some of the scare goes out of it. It's the not knowin' when it's gonna happen that scares 'em shitless."

"I don't know about that. Remember, this woman's not one of your crack whores. She's got her shit together."

"Had," Tony said.

"What?"

"She had her shit together, but not now, man. She's ours, now. You can mess with her all you want once she talks. I seen the way you look at her."

"Well, she's an eyeful, Tony."

"They're all the same after a while, Murano. All the same."

Connie had a name for 'Not Tony," now. Murano. She heard the clock strike two bells. 5 p.m., she thought. They had come aboard not long after Paul left, and they had run the engine until sometime between three and four o'clock. They could have covered twenty or thirty miles in that time. She wondered where they were, and how Paul would find her. Surprised, she realized that she had no doubt he was coming for her, or that he would know how to find her. She didn't know why she was so sure, but it didn't matter. The important thing was to hang on as long as she could.

25

She could hear them talking in the cockpit as they drank their beer.

"You think that quarter mil is on this tub somewhere?" Murano asked.

"Nah. It filled a good-sized duffle bag; we woulda found it," Tony said.

"How come the cops didn't find it in North Carolina, then?"

"Good question. Maybe they did."

"But you said your guy didn't know anything about it," Murano protested.

"Yeah, but you know cops. Maybe they're runnin' some kinda game here. Leave the money on the boat, keep an eye on it, like."

"That's paranoid, Tony. Why would they do that?"

"Cops forever do shit that don't make sense. It's almost dark. You want another beer before we go to work on her?"

"I guess. Why're you waiting until dark?"

"Psychology, man. Dark is scary and hopeless. I'll get us this round."

∽

CONNIE'S MIND WAS RACING. She figured Paul had to be on his way; maybe the conference call had run late. She needed to buy some time, but how? She rehashed everything she had learned from Jimmy and Kirsten, matching it against what Paul had told her about them. She did her best to mesh those facts with what she had picked up from listening to her captors. She also thought about what she had learned about the economics and logistics of the drug business from her encounters with Sam Alfano. She'd just have to wing it and hope she could fake these guys out long enough for help to arrive.

Lost in thought, she jumped and squealed when she felt an icy touch on the side of her right breast, just beneath her armpit.

"It's okay, babe," Tony said. "It's not the sharp edge of the razor; not just yet. I just wanted to kinda measure it out before I cut. I don't want to mar that beautiful skin, see. My friend, he's gonna make me something really nice from it after this is over."

She steeled herself, but she still flinched and trembled as he drew the blunt corner of the straight razor down along her ribcage and up over her hips. She felt it stop and reverse direction at the cleft between her buttocks as he traced a line over her left hip and up her left side, pausing at the swell of her left breast and then dragging it across her shoulder blades to stop under her right armpit again.

"Too bad about the tan lines," he said, "but maybe he can work around those. Like, put them in a seam, or something."

He withdrew the razor and laid his hand on her hip, stroking gently. "They tell me that it don't really even hurt. One girl, she said it felt the same when I made the cuts as it did when I was tracing it out, like I did just now. She didn't even start screaming until I was through with the cuts. It was when I started to ..."

"Shut the fuck up for a minute, you monkey-brained bastard," she hissed.

"What did you call me?"

"You're wasting time we don't have," she said.

"Huh? We got ..."

"You got shit, moron. Get Murano in here. I've got something to tell him."

"Smart. You give up the money, things could go better for you."

"You've got somewhere between a few minutes and a few hours to live if I don't save your sorry ass. Get me Murano, you miserable piece of shit."

"Hey, Mark! She's askin' for you. Got something to tell you."

"What is it?" Murano asked. "You want to tell me where the money is?"

"That's not your biggest problem. Neither is Giannetti and whatever he threatened to do to you for being a dumb ass."

"How do you know about Giannetti?"

"Uh-uh," she said. "I think I may still be able to work something out to save you two shit-heads, but I'm not talking any more until you cut me loose. Or are you scared I'll hurt you?"

"Why would I cut you loose?"

She grinned at him and shook her head, watching as he chewed nervously on his lower lip. His eyes oscillated between her and Tony. After a couple of seconds, he nodded at Tony. "Cut her loose."

"But ..."

"Don't make me tell you a second time."

Her hands stung from the sudden rush of blood when he snipped the cable ties. She massaged her wrists and said, "Ankles, too."

Tony clipped the cable ties around her ankles and stepped back.

"Hand me my clothes, please," she ordered Murano as she tentatively put her feet on the floor and tested them with her weight.

"What are you ..." Murano started to say.

"The clothes. You're wasting time you don't have."

"But ..." he said as he handed them to her in a wad.

"But I'm going to the head and get dressed. You and your yard ape figure out whether you want to live to see morning while I freshen up."

She took the clothes and walked gracefully into the aft cabin, smiling at their stunned looks as she closed the door. She filled the sink and splashed water on her face as she listened to their whispered argument. She couldn't tell what they were saying, but she knew Murano had taken the bait. Now she had to set the hook and play him until help arrived. She put on her clothes and ran a brush through her hair, grinning at her reflection in the mirror to get herself in the right frame of mind. When she put her hairbrush back in the drawer, she saw an old-fashioned steel nail file. She slipped it in her pocket before she opened the door, thinking she might use it as a weapon.

"Okay," Murano said. "So start talking. Tony said you threatened us."

She smiled. "Like I told your yard ape, you boys are in trouble. I might be able to save you, but no guarantees."

"I don't ..."

"I know you don't get it, but you will if you pay attention."

"I say we just waste her. I'll make her tell us where the money is, and we'll ..."

"Can you shut him up?"

Murano backhanded Tony across the mouth, knocking him off his feet. He landed on the settee and fixed Connie with a malevolent glare.

"Thank you. Just so it doesn't distract you any more, I'll tell you about the money; it's safely in a numbered account in the Cayman Islands. There's no way you're going to get your hands on it, no matter what you do to me."

"How did ..."

"Time is precious. You'd better pay attention."

"Okay, but ..."

"Why is time critical?" she finished his question, raising her eyebrows.

"Yeah."

"The short version is you and dumb-ass over there walked into a trap."

"A trap?"

"Yes. I'm the bait; the helpless female, all alone on a big boat, and you two stupid shits stepped right into it. Giannetti must like to hire the handicapped. You boys wouldn't last 30 seconds working for me."

"Working for you?" Murano's mind was racing, remembering what Alfano had said.

"Here's the rest. Giannetti has seriously pissed me and my associates off; he's shown a total lack of respect."

"I'm lost."

"I know, sweetie. Listen to Mama, now, okay?"

He nodded and she continued.

"He thought he could move product through our turf without paying the tariff."

"Your turf?"

"Mine and my partners, yes. We control the Caribbean basin. Like I said, he stepped out of bounds."

"So what happens now?"

"Depends on whether we can come to an agreement before my partners show up."

"What happens when they get here?"

"Well, you know about Omaha Steaks?"

Murano looked puzzled. "Yeah," he said in a tentative tone. "The frozen beef people?"

"Right. My partner's planning to send Giannetti a delivery from Omaha Steaks."

"I don't get it."

"No, Giannetti gets it. *You*, handsome *are* it. Picture Giannetti opening that white styrofoam box with the dry ice fog coming out and looking down in there. Guess what he'll see?"

"I don't know."

"No imagination. Your handsome face looking back at him, with two sets of male genitals in your mouth."

Murano blanched. "Two sets?" he squeaked.

"Just so Giannetti knows that you both tried to earn your pay, you and dipshit over there."

"But how ..."

"They'll be here any time. If we don't have a deal when they get here, you're done."

"Wait!" Tony interrupted. "This don't make sense. Why would you do a deal instead of just lettin' them kill us?"

"He's smarter than I thought," Connie said, smiling at Murano.

"Yeah. Well, it's a good question. You got an answer?"

"Testosterone." She used the grin that she'd practiced in the mirror a few minutes ago, imagining that she was a shark about to sink her teeth into her prey.

"Tes ... testosterone?" Murano asked.

"Yes. I'm not hampered by it like you ball-bearing thugs are. This is business. I'm in it for the money; I don't need to show Giannetti that my dick's bigger than his."

Murano swallowed hard, thinking. "You said something about a deal."

"I can hold them off, unless you do something stupid when they get here."

"And what do you want in exchange?"

"I like round numbers. Let's say one."

"One?"

"Million."

"One million dollars?"

"See. That wasn't so hard, was it?"

"Wait. You already took a quarter mil."

"Oh, think of that as a fine; like a penalty for not paying taxes."

"What do we get for the million?" Murano asked, stalling for time. He knew what Giannetti would say to her proposal.

"You and your buddy here might get to go home. But I'm not sure about him. I don't like guys that pick on women. Maybe we'll neuter him before we let him go. One of the guys coming is pretty handy with a filet knife. Other than that, the million would get Giannetti a chance to start clean with us."

"What does that mean?"

"It means we'd guarantee his shipments through the islands. For 50 percent."

"Fifty percent!"

"Of street value."

"That's outrageous!"

"We could work on a sliding scale, maybe, if the volume's high enough."

"I'd have to talk to Giannetti."

"Be my guest, but I'd be quick."

"I don't have any way to reach him; our cell phones don't work. Already tried."

"Mm." Connie smiled and shook her head.

Murano blinked several times. He chewed at a hang-nail on his right index finger, and scratched behind his ear as Connie studied him with an amused expression on her face.

"Look," he said, "I can't guarantee what Ralph will say, but I'm pretty sure I can make it happen."

Connie held his eyes until he looked away.

"About the million," he said, "I can do that on my own account."

She continued to stare at him, her predatory grin unchanged. She nodded slightly.

"That's yours, no matter what Giannetti says, if you let me go."

"Me, too, damn it," Tony protested.

Murano raised his eyebrows. Connie shook her head.

"How much for me?" Tony asked.

Connie studied him for a minute. "Fifty thousand."

"Okay, I'll do it," Tony said.

"Plus another nine hundred fifty if you don't want the free surgery, but I hope you'll let us help you. It would make you a better person." She smiled as she watched the sweat break out on his forehead.

"Think about it, Tony. I'm still pretty upset with you; it would be better for you to wait and talk with my partner man-to-man. You'll still be a man after he gets here, at least for a little while. I think I'm going to just stick with my deal with Murano, here. You can work something out with my partners, or not."

She turned back to Murano. "Now, about that million dollars."

"What about it?"

"You need to make that happen."

"Tomorrow morning. First thing. Swear to God; the money's in the bank. I'll wire it wherever you say. Nine o'clock, Eastern time," he stammered.

"I think you will. Let's have a drink to seal the deal."

"Um, I er ..."

"Don't trust me not to drug you, Murano?"

"Well, uh ..."

"I don't blame you. There's some nice red wine in the locker right behind your pet monkey. Pick out a bottle, and I'll get the glasses and a corkscrew." She rose from the table and stepped into the galley.

As she opened the galley drawer, she heard Murano shifting the wine bottles.

"Hey, Connie?" he called.

"What?"

"Okay if I call you Connie?"

"Sure, Murano."

"You can call me Mark."

"I like Murano better. You were going to ask me something?"

"Yeah. What about the cop?"

"Paul Russo?"

"Yeah. He crooked?"

She thought hard about how to answer that, finally deciding that Paul was well-known to the criminals in south Florida. "No way. Not him. Why?"

"What are you doing hanging out with him, then," Murano asked, suspicion creeping into his voice.

"You know who Joe Greco is?" she asked, winging it.

"Yeah?"

"Russo's on the task force that's prosecuting him. In fact, he put the cuffs on Joe."

"I heard. So what?"

"So Paul's my inside track on the Greco thing; we've got a big stake in Greco keeping his mouth shut."

"But Greco works for Giannetti."

Connie's heart was in her throat. She raked through her memories of Paul's comments about Joe Greco, one of the deadliest killers to come out of the drug culture in years.

"You're not that naïve, Murano." She took three wineglasses from the locker beside the stove and polished them as she thought. "A guy like Greco, he worked for a lot of people. If Giannetti thought he owned Greco, he must have caught a case of the stupids from your pal Tony."

"Ah," Murano muttered. "So Russo won't be coming tonight?"

"I hope not. If he shows up, play it cool. I'll handle him."

She was wondering where Paul was when she felt a subtle shift in the boat's motion. The rhythmical movement imparted by the waves had become part of the background. This was something else. She saw a flicker of movement in the dark outside the companionway and turned to see Paul peering cautiously below, a finger to his lips. His face was smeared with black camouflage paint, and he wore a dark-colored wetsuit. Raising his eyebrows, he extended one finger, then a second, then a third. He wiggled his eyebrows as he folded his hand closed. Connie held up two fingers. He nodded and turned away, rising from his crouch.

"Connie?" Murano called.

"Coming." She put the wine glasses and a bowl of salted nuts on a small tray and went back to the saloon.

~

CONNIE PUT the tray on the table and slipped into the seat between the table and the port side of the saloon. She set a glass in front of herself and another across the table, indicating with a nod that Murano should sit there. He complied and she handed him the corkscrew. She looked over at Tony, still sitting where he had fallen when Murano hit him. Catching his eye, she raised a third empty glass. He shook his head. She smiled.

"Smart. You're going to need your wits about you to get through this in one piece," she said, laughing out loud when his face went pale.

As Murano filled the glasses, she saw Phillip and Sharktooth slip into position, one on either side of the door leading from the forward cabin. They must have dropped through the forward hatch into Paul's cabin. Phillip was wearing a dripping black wetsuit and camouflage face paint, just like Paul. They smiled at her and nodded.

Murano raised his glass. "To a profitable partnership with a lovely lady," he said. Before Connie could respond, Paul and Freddy Johnson, Phillip's fishing buddy, stepped from the galley holding pistols with silencers attached.

"Nobody moves; nobody gets shot," Paul said, as Phillip and Sharktooth entered from the other direction. The four men spread out to give themselves clear lines of fire.

"I'll be damned," Paul said. "Mark Murano."

"Up yours, Russo."

"You know this guy?" Phillip asked.

"Yeah. He's a spineless piece of shit that works for a hood named Ralph Giannetti. Who's the other one?" Paul looked at Connie.

"Tony, but I didn't catch his last name."

"How about it, asshole? Who are you?" Paul asked.

Murano's mind was racing. Could it be that Ralph was right all along? Was Connie some kind of undercover cop? He looked at her, wondering.

"The mon, he ask you a question," Sharktooth said, stepping within arm's reach of Tony.

"I want a lawyer," Tony said.

Everyone except Paul laughed, including Murano.

"No lawyers here, I'm afraid," Phillip said. "You're on your own."

"Bullshit. You guys are cops. I'm not sayin' nothin' until I got a lawyer."

Freddy raised his pistol, pointing it at Tony. "Anybody think he knows anything worth hearing? Or should I just do it now?"

"Wait," Paul said. "We can take them back to the U.S.V.I."

"No, man," Freddy said. "Too much trouble, and the fish are biting. These two already caused us enough grief. Let's just waste 'em. We'll chop 'em up and put them through the chum grinder. Maybe they'll attract enough big fish to make up for the time we lost."

"I want his name, first, at least," Paul said.

"Fair enough," Phillip said. "Sharktooth?"

Sharktooth grinned from ear to ear as a twelve-inch filet knife materialized in his hand. "Stan' up," he ordered Tony.

Tony shook his head. "I want a ..."

Sharktooth's big left hand closed over the top of Tony's head. Tony screamed in pain as Sharktooth lifted him to his feet. "Pants off," Sharktooth ordered.

"Look out," Connie cried, as the razor flashed in Tony's right hand.

Sharktooth was the faster of the two. He released Tony's head and caught his right wrist, stopping him in mid-slash. He put the tip of his filet knife just below Tony's left eye. "Now doan move," he cautioned as he squeezed his left fist, crushing the two bones in Tony's forearm with a grinding sound, followed by a crack. Tony screamed again. The razor dropped from his fingers, but Sharktooth held fast to his broken arm. "Now, the pants. Underpants, too. I know it's not much but it's all you got, so doan be shy. You gonna have to show us what you got befo' you lose it."

"T-T-Tony F-F-Ferranti. Don't cut me, please. I'll tell you anything."

"He doesn't know anything," Connie said.

Murano had relaxed, realizing that these guys weren't cops after all. He could tell by the look on Russo's face that he wanted no part of what the big Rasta was doing. His blood ran cold when Connie said, "Murano's the brains, if there are any between the two of them."

Sharktooth put his knife down on the settee and slapped Tony on the side of his head with his baseball-glove-sized right hand, knocking him unconscious and lowering him to the settee. He picked up his knife and turned to Murano, grinning again, a trickle of saliva running from the corner of his mouth.

"Tell them," Murano squeaked, looking plaintively at Connie.

"Tell them what?" she asked, smiling.

"About our deal."

"You haven't paid me. We don't have a deal. Sorry."

"B-But, f-first thing in the morning. When the b-bank opens. A million dollars. You agreed."

"I changed my mind. Woman's prerogative."

"The fish are waiting," Freddy said.

"Paul?" Phillip asked. "Your call."

"I don't like it, but I can live with it."

Freddy raised his pistol again, flicking the safety off with his thumb.

"No! Wait!" Murano pleaded. "Russo, I can make it worth your while."

"Good-bye, Murano. There's nothing you can do to make it worth my while."

"Greco's boss! I can give you Greco's boss."

"Greco is the boss. You're bullshitting me. Shoot him, Freddy. I'm retired. Besides, this is outside my jurisdiction."

"No. Give me one phone call, and I'll call Giannetti. You can listen, and I'll prove to you that Greco was working for him all along."

"Hold on, Freddy," Paul said.

Freddy lowered the pistol again.

"You still willing to hold them for a while?" Paul asked Phillip.

"Freddy?" Phillip asked.

"Sure. Get 'em aboard *Fin Dancer* and we'll hog tie 'em and gag 'em while we get back to the fish. Send us out a cooler of beer and we'll keep 'em long as the fish keep biting. Like I said, they'll always make good bait if we grind 'em coarsely."

26

Ten minutes later, Connie and Paul were alone on *Diamantista*.

"What took ..." Connie started to say, as Paul spoke simultaneously.

"Thank God," he said, the quaver in his voice betraying his emotion.

They both smiled weakly and hugged one another.

"You first," Paul said, patting her shoulder as she buried her cheek against the clammy neoprene of his wetsuit.

"Yuck," she said, stepping back. "You smell like dead fish."

"Sorry. It came from Freddy's boat. Everything there smells like dead fish. I need a shower; this camouflage face paint is bugging me every time I try to scratch my cheek."

"I was sure you were coming any minute, and I, I ..." she sobbed. "Sorry. I'm so glad ..."

"I knew something was wrong when I got back to the mooring about three o'clock. Took me about five minutes to piece together what happened from a couple on a nearby boat. They saw two men in a dinghy board *Diamantista* and leave in a hurry."

"I was hoping you'd go online and check the satellite tracker. I forgot to turn it off when we got here."

"I was hoping you'd forgotten it. That's the first thing I thought of, and then I called Phillip. I went ashore and got online while they were coming to get me."

"Were they far away or something?"

"No. By the time I got through at the Internet café, they were idling in the harbor at Cruz Bay, waiting for me."

"Then what took you so long? I've never been so scared, Paul." She sobbed again.

He put his arm around her and pulled her into another hug. "The damned server was down."

"What?"

"The web server for the company that sells that tracking service was offline."

"Oh. So how'd you find me?"

"Freddy. He's plugged in to this whole subculture that makes a living off tourists -- charter boats, fishing boats, dive boats. He got on the radio and finally found somebody that had seen *Diamantista* at anchor; they were on their way into the marina."

"What marina? I haven't a clue as to where we are."

"We're anchored in the lee of Buck Island, off the southeast end of Tortola. There's a big bareboat charter operation in the marina about a half a mile west of here."

"Is that were Freddy's boat is?"

"No. We anchored in Fat Hog's Bay. It's about a quarter of a mile north of here, and there's a shallow sand bar that cuts it off from this bay. We took the dinghy to the sand bar and swam up."

"You guys really dressed like commandos, or something. If I hadn't recognized you, I'd have been more scared of you than the assholes that kidnapped me. Freddy had all this stuff on the boat? I mean guns with silencers and everything?"

"Yeah. Phillip and Freddy were in some kind of super-secret military unit years ago. I think Freddy may freelance a bit, or maybe he just likes the paraphernalia. They don't encourage idle questions, those two. You know, the old 'ask me no questions and I tell you no lies' cliché. Anyway, all three of them have done this kind of thing before -- more than once, and together, I think."

"I don't think I want to know more, but I'm glad they were around to help you."

"Me, too. You can't imagine what was going through my mind; I was crazed. It's a good thing they're such cool heads."

"I thought you'd call the police or the Coast Guard."

"Too cumbersome; you'd only been missing for a few minutes. I would have spent hours convincing them we didn't have some quarrel that caused you to ditch me."

"I can see that. God, Paul, I was so scared."

"Well, I confess I wasn't expecting to find you calmly drinking wine with a Miami mobster; I was worried that I was going to be too late."

"You nearly were, but before I tell you my part of the story, can we clean up a bit? I'm in serious need of a long shower, no matter how much of our precious water I use, and you're stinking up the whole boat with that skanky wetsuit."

"Sounds good to me."

~

"After I watched you head into Cruz Bay, I came below to gather up the things I needed to fix the lock on the companionway door. It didn't take too long to repair it, and then I went below again to put my tools away. I guess that's when they came aboard. I don't have any recollection of that; the first thing I remember is coming to on the settee with a splitting headache. The engine was running, and I thought maybe you were charging the batteries or something. I'm sure I have a concussion; I've got a huge knot on the back of my head."

"That's why you can't remember getting whacked, probably.

Concussions will mess up your memory; usually it comes back after a while."

"You sound like an expert."

"I don't claim to be an expert, but I've been hit over the head a few times. What happened after you came to?"

"Well, it's kind of fuzzy, still, but Tony was below with me, watching for me to come around, I guess. How long would I have been out from a blow like that?"

Paul shrugged. "No clue. I think that's one of the great medical mysteries. It varies from seconds to hours, for no reason anybody ever managed to explain to me. So Ferranti was there?"

"Right. He was grinning at me, and he made some kind of 'Sleeping Beauty' remark and said something about maybe he hit me too hard. I can't remember exactly, but then he jerked me to my feet and threatened me with that straight razor. He made me undress, acting like he was going to rape me. I was scared, but I decided to go down fighting. I surprised myself, there.

"I was measuring the angles, trying to figure out whether to go for his kneecap or his groin, but he flipped the razor from one hand to the other, and I watched it instead of him. He blind-sided me with a punch to my jaw that literally made me see stars. I always thought that was an exaggeration, but ... anyway, the next time I came to, I was stretched out face down on this table, with my wrists tied to the mast and my feet tied to that handrail on the bulkhead. I was stark naked, and every joint in my body ached, but my head was much clearer. The engine had stopped, and I could hear them talking up in the cockpit.

"They were drinking beer, and Tony kept saying that the longer they left me, the easier it would be to make me talk, because my fear would build. Finally, just after dark, he came below and started dragging the blunt edge of the razor over my sides and back, telling me he was measuring the hide, or something. He spun this tale about how some friend of his would make something nice out of 'that beautiful skin,' or something like that."

"You must have been ..."

"What I was by then was furious. I'd been listening to the clock strike, and I figured that something must have gone wrong -- that your call had run overtime or something. I still figured you were coming, but I was running out of time. I decided I had nothing to lose by trying to run a con on them."

"A con? What kind of con?"

"Well, I'd been listening to them, plus I'd talked to Kirsten, and you'd given me some information, so I decided to sell them a ticket on the plane to heaven. I figured I could drag it ..."

"Wait, wait. A ticket on the plane to heaven?"

"It's just shorthand for a kind of scam. You figure out what the mark wants, and then you convince him that you, and you better than anybody else, can get it for him. You have to establish some credibility, and you have to demand some exorbitant fee for your service. Once he forks over the money, you give him something that's worthless, but you're long gone by the time he figures out what happened. The name comes from a scam where this preacher sells people reserved seat tickets on a plane that's supposed to take them to heaven."

Paul grinned and shook his head. "Now you sound like an expert. I'm not sure I want to know how you ..."

"You know about the diet clinic; that's exactly what I'm talking about. Instead of trying to lose weight, these two wanted ..."

"Their quarter of a million dollars back, but you couldn't give that to them because we can't find it."

"Well, that was only part of it, see. What they thought they wanted was to set up a smuggling operation that used the eastern Caribbean islands as transshipment points and to move the drugs on private yachts under the command of innocent people."

"Right. I see how you pieced that together, but what could you offer them that ..."

"Wait. That's what they thought they wanted. What they really wanted was to stay alive; immortality is the ultimate ticket on the plane to heaven."

"Okay, but how did you ..."

"I convinced them that my partners and I controlled drug transshipment in the islands, and that Giannetti and Murano had thoroughly pissed us off by not respecting our turf."

Paul chuckled. "Wait a second. How'd Giannetti get into this?"

"I heard them talking about him; it was clear from the conversation that he was Murano's boss."

"I see. What next? How did you get them to untie you?"

"I told that creep Ferranti that they had between 30 minutes and a few hours to live if he didn't get Murano below to talk to me. When Murano came down, I taunted him into releasing me before I told him where the money was."

"So what did you tell him?"

"That it was safe in my numbered account in the Cayman Islands, and that they'd never see it again; that it was a fine for their disrespect."

Paul laughed. "And he bought that?"

"Why not? The money wasn't his biggest problem."

"What was?"

"My partners and I set this up as a trap with me as the bait so that we could send Murano's head to Giannetti in an Omaha Steaks box."

"How did you get from there to drinking the wine? What was the deal that Murano mentioned?"

"I told him that I might be able to save his ass for a million dollars and fifty percent of their action; that we'd go into a partnership with them, but that the deal didn't include Ferranti. He just really pissed me off, and it was fun to make him beg after I got Murano on my side."

"But Murano knows I'm a cop."

"Yes, and they know you're a straight cop, too. Your Involvement was a problem for me. I had to waste you, just a little bit."

"How'd you do that?"

"I led Murano to believe that I'd seduced you to get information about the Greco task force."

"What? How'd Greco figure in it?"

"He didn't, until I brought him in out of desperation to explain why you were hanging around with me. I guessed that he'd heard of the Greco task force."

"But Murano ..."

"Yes. He asked me why I cared about Greco. 'Greco works for Giannetti,' he said, when I told him that."

"Holy shit! I need to make some calls, fast." Paul got up and scrambled to the chart table to retrieve the satellite phone. When he turned back around, Connie's arms were crossed on the table, her head resting on them. The adrenalin had worked its way through her system and she had fallen asleep.

He set the phone down for a moment and picked her up, one arm under her knees, the other around her shoulders, her head falling against his chest. As he carried her to the aft cabin, she roused enough to wrap her arms around him and murmur something unintelligible. He eased her onto her berth, arranging a pillow under her head. He stood there for a moment, waiting to be sure he had not awakened her, and then he went back to the main cabin and picked up the satellite phone.

~

PAUL SAT at the table in the saloon for a few minutes collecting his thoughts. The task force had been operating under the assumption that Greco ran his own operation, subservient to no one, but Murano wanted to cut a deal and give up Greco's boss. That in itself was enough to get Paul's attention, but Murano's statement to Connie that Greco worked for Giannetti would change the whole prosecution strategy. Everyone in law enforcement in south Florida knew Giannetti was dirty, but no one had ever managed to pin anything on him.

He decided this information was worth waking up Mandy Cantrell, especially this close to Greco's trial date. The hard-driving prosecutor would be angry if he didn't call her. He looked up her home number in his cell phone, noticing as he did that there was no service. Thankful for the satellite phone, he entered her number and waited, listening to the ringing for what seemed like a full minute. He was beginning to wonder if she'd slept in her office and was about to disconnect and call her there when she answered.

"Mandy Cantrell." Paul had been expecting a groggy answer, but she sounded wide awake and ready for business.

"It's Paul Russo, Mandy. Sorry to disturb you so late, but I've stumbled across something that could change the whole game plan for the Greco trial."

"Damn, Paul! I'm glad you called. I was just rehearsing my opening statement. The judge finished the case she was hearing a day early; the trial's been moved up. We start day after tomorrow. What do you have?"

He gave her a concise summary of what had happened from the time Connie took on her pick-up crew in Annapolis up through this evening's excitement. "Murano and the other guy, this Ferranti, are being held by a friend of mine on a boat that's in international waters until I can hand him over; I'm still a Deputy U.S. Marshall, remember, and I caught the two of them red-handed kidnapping a U.S. citizen on a U.S. flagged vessel. They've only been in custody a couple of hours. I think it's a decent bust, especially if we act quickly. I'm guessing we want to cut some kind of deal, right?"

"Oh, yeah! I see serious problems here, though. Murano's not got access to counsel, and it sounds like he could argue that you coerced him to talk."

"Well, we were headed that way," Paul said, "but he pre-empted us and offered to give up Greco's boss. I put the brakes on at that point, and asked my friends to keep the two of them until I had time to talk with you."

"And he gave up Giannetti already? He's a Harvard MBA -- new mob-type -- I figured he was smarter than that. Sure you guys didn't beat it out of him?"

"No, Mandy. Nobody touched him, although one of the guys who helped me rescue Connie was about to shoot him."

"Shit, Paul! A good defense attorney will cut us to pieces if I put Murano on the stand."

"I've got an idea, Mandy. Have I given you enough to get a wiretap order for Giannetti?"

"Yeah, I think so. Where are you going with this?"

"Murano suggested that I listen in while he talks to Giannetti on the phone. He says he'll get Giannetti to incriminate himself. If you get that on tape, can you make it work?"

"Maybe so. I'm liking that. You guys have any video recording capability out there?"

"Several of us have smart phones. Why?"

"Okay, here's the plan. I'll call you back when we've got Giannetti tapped. Meanwhile, tell Murano we're gonna deal, but I want video of you reading him his rights. On that same video, I want him to make the offer again, and I want him to waive his right to counsel. Think you can make that happen?"

"Shouldn't be a problem."

"Good. I've got a lot of work to do; I'll call you back in the morning. This number in my caller i.d., is it a good one?"

"Yes. It's a satellite phone, and it's in my possession. Hey! Just occurred to me -- we'll place the call to Giannetti from this number, so you can monitor it when the time comes. That way, if Giannetti's got some unknown number for Murano to use, it won't matter."

"Perfect. Now, I want to get this done as early tomorrow as

possible. If it works, I'll be asking for a continuance on the Greco case while we sort this out. Figure on placing the call to Giannetti around lunch time."

"Got it. I'll be in position with Murano and get the videos done by around ten tomorrow."

"Okay, great. Paul?"

"Yeah?"

"Sounds like you've got yourself one brave lady."

"I wish. She's just a good friend, though."

"Bullshit. If she doesn't snag you she's nuts. I'd have been after you myself if I didn't play on the other team."

"Thanks, Mandy. Talk to you later."

"G'bye, handsome."

27

Diamantista and *Fin Dancer* occupied adjacent moorings in Francis Bay on the north coast of St. John. Paul had called Phillip early that morning and arranged the rendezvous. The set up with Murano had gone off flawlessly; Giannetti had jumped into the trap with both feet. The rest of the day had been filled with conference calls until about an hour ago, when a U.S. Coast Guard boat had arrived carrying two U.S. Deputy Marshals. Paul had done the paperwork to transfer Murano and Ferranti to their custody. Mandy Cantrell had sent them an arrest warrant for both men, and the prisoners would be flown to Miami on a DEA jet this evening. Paul had just disconnected from a last minute phone call with Mandy and was preparing to join the others on deck for a round of drinks.

"Sorry about the delay," he said, emerging from the companionway with a tray that held six ice-cold beers in moisture-beaded glasses.

Phillip and Sharktooth helped themselves after Paul handed a glass to Connie. Sitting down across from Freddy, Paul passed him one of the two remaining beers. They were seated around the fold-out table in *Diamantista's* cockpit, large bowls of chips and mango salsa in the center.

"Freddy, I'm sorry we spoiled yet another day of fishing," Paul offered.

"No problem, Paul. It's for a good cause, and there's always tomorrow. The fish'll still be there. Besides, I haven't had so much fun since Phillip and I were down in Central America a few years ago."

"What's the latest from Mandy?" Connie asked.

"They picked up Giannetti this afternoon."

"So, this whole mess is really over, you think?"

"Probably, but who knows? There's still the question of the missing quarter of a million dollars."

"I'll bet those kids had some deal going to take off with it; maybe they gave it to somebody else," Phillip said.

"Anything's possible in the drug business," Paul agreed, "but if they were going to run off with the money, why bother with sailing to the islands?"

"Kirsten said that Jimmy wanted to set himself up as a pimp in St. Thomas; could be that he had some connections there," Connie said.

"Speaking of Kirsten, they arrested the matron in Carteret County who gave her the coke. She said that Tony paid her to do it and provided the coke. She didn't know it was uncut until Kirsten died and she heard about the coroner's findings. She thought she was just helping out a junkie who was hurting for a fix, or so she says."

"We 'bout to get one fine sunset," Sharktooth said, watching the light reflecting from the trade wind cumulus clouds. "Too bad we in this cove an' can't see the horizon. Bet we gonna miss the green flash."

"It's a beauty, all right." Paul drained his beer as he gazed at the deepening colors. "Anybody hungry? Or should I set up another round?"

"I'm starved," Connie said. "You get dinner going; I'll come down with you and get everybody another beer."

As they stood, Sharktooth asked, "What's for dinner?"

"Fresh tuna steaks, thanks to you guys. Seared and drizzled with wasabi-balsamic vinaigrette. But don't worry if that sounds too healthy, Sharktooth. Connie warned me that you're trying to recover your strength. There'll be a side of risotto with pancetta and radicchio, just for you."

~

TWO HOURS LATER, Paul and Connie were alone on *Diamantista*. *Fin Dancer* would be departing at first light to go fishing, so their three guests had made an early evening of it. After Paul had refused to let Connie help with the after-dinner cleanup, she had taken the satellite phone up into the cockpit. She wanted to call Dani and Liz and let them know that she and Paul were finally in the islands and would like to meet up with them somewhere. They still had a little more than two weeks before their first guests would arrive in Antigua, and Connie was hoping that their friends might have a break between charters so that they could meet somewhere between Antigua and Martinique.

Paul knew that she wanted to show them *Diamantista*; she had consulted with them by phone numerous times during her search for a suitable vessel. She made no secret of the fact that she had really wanted to buy a Herreshoff 59 like *Vengeance*, and he had been surprised when she called to tell him she'd signed a purchase contract for this boat.

He was struggling with the need to have his long-delayed conversation with her. Tonight didn't seem like the right time, but he wondered if he was looking for reasons to put it off. Drying the last of the dinner dishes, he put them away and decided to join her on deck and see where the conversation went.

He dried his hands and mounted the companionway ladder,

stopping when he saw that she was stretched full length on the starboard cockpit seat, the phone on the cushion beside her with her right hand on top of it. He climbed into the cockpit, moving quietly. As he suspected, she was sound asleep, her beautiful face completely relaxed for the first time in days.

He thought for a moment about covering her with a light cotton throw and letting her sleep in the cockpit, but rain showers often blew through in the early morning. With regret, he roused her enough to help her get below and settled her in her bed in the aft stateroom. Spared from his dreaded conversation about their relationship, he mixed himself a stiff drink and retired to the forward stateroom, vowing that tomorrow, he would tell her how he felt, no matter what.

28

Paul woke up to the smell of strong, freshly brewed espresso. He opened his eyes and rolled onto his side, freezing when he saw Connie standing beside his berth, a cup of steaming espresso in her hand. She was wearing something almost big enough to qualify as a bikini; he saw her smile at the surprise in his eyes. He was glad it had been cool enough for him to sleep under a sheet, given his body's immediate response to her.

"Good morning, sleepyhead."

"Morning. Did I oversleep?" He reached for the coffee.

"We're not really on a schedule. I figured you needed the rest."

"Thanks. I guess I did. You been up long?"

"Couple of hours, but remember, I crashed pretty early last night."

"Yeah." He sat up on the edge of the berth, letting the sheet fall from his chest into his lap, surreptitiously checking to be sure he had slept in his boxer shorts. He didn't remember going to bed, but he usually slept in his underwear. His relief at finding that he was wearing them was short-lived, though. He was in no condition to get out of bed with her standing there like that. He inhaled the fragrant scent of the espresso and took a sip, studying her face to keep his mind off the rest of her. The bruising on her jaw was still noticeable, but the swelling had gone down.

"You sleep okay? The jaw looks better."

She touched it with her fingertips. "It's still tender, but it's not bothering me unless I touch it. I rolled over on it a time or two and it woke me up, but I was so beat that I went right back to sleep."

"What time is it?"

"Eleven."

"Eleven? Wow! I did sleep in. We still going back to Caneel Bay?"

"Well, I was thinking that unless you need to do a video conference or something, maybe we could stay here for a while and go back later."

"Fine with me. You had breakfast?"

"Some toast. I wasn't very hungry after that dinner you cooked. Even Sharktooth got enough, I think." She smiled.

"Me, too. My grandmother's risotto's pretty filling. So what's on your agenda today?"

"We're the only boat in the cove; everybody else left, and Freddy said that little reef just along the north shore is really pretty. Want to play tourist and go snorkeling?"

"Sounds great." He slugged down the rest of his espresso. "Give me a few minutes to shave and get my trunks on?"

"Sure. No problem. I'll go get our stuff out of the cockpit locker while you get ready."

Paul waited until he heard her open the cockpit locker, not wanting her to come back for some reason and see him in, or mostly in, his boxer shorts. He grabbed his baggiest swim trunks and stepped into the forward head. He shaved, careful not to make it too close. He didn't want any nicks that would burn in the salty water. He brushed his teeth and took off his underwear and the T-shirt he'd worn to bed. He caught a glimpse of himself in the mirror, noticing how pale his shoulders looked. He put the T-shirt back on, remembering how easy it was to get a painful sunburn while paddling around face down in the 82-degree water. The coolness of the water hid the damage until later. He snugged up the drawstring in his trunks and opened the door.

He did his best to forget how Connie had looked in that bikini when he first opened his eyes. He had thought at first that he was dreaming, but then she handed him the coffee and he had burned his tongue. That was when he was sure he was awake. He knew he'd probably gawked like a teenager; he'd seen her embarrassed smile as she watched his face. There was nothing he could do about that now, but he definitely needed to find time to have that conversation with her today. Maybe after their swim; if not then, maybe he could work it in while they were sailing around to Caneel Bay.

~

WHILE CONNIE SORTED through the locker picking out snorkeling gear, she thought about Paul's reaction when she had awakened him a few minutes ago. She had seen the look on his face before his guard came up. She was a little ashamed at how pleased she had been to see the undisguised lust in his eyes. She hadn't even thought about the bathing suit until then, but it was pretty revealing. She'd picked it up in a wild moment when she was hanging out in South Beach a few years ago and hadn't worn it since the day the Miami Beach police car ran over her foot.

She hadn't meant to tease him, but at the same time, she was happy that he found her attractive, even if he was too much of a gentleman to make a move. She didn't know how Paul felt about their agreement to keep their relationship platonic, but she was ready to move beyond that. What she had seen in his eyes and his overall reaction led her to believe that he had the same need, whether he'd realized it or not. She had to find a way to talk this over with him, if not immediately, then certainly before their guests arrived in two weeks. She didn't want to rush Paul; she might scare him away. On the other hand, she sensed that if she didn't take the risk, she might end up as a frustrated old-maid skipper with a good-looking, celibate cook.

Remembering the bikini, she reached into the locker for her shorty wetsuit. Besides providing for modesty, it would keep the sun off her shoulders and back while they explored the reefs in the cove. She managed to contort herself enough to get into the suit in spite of some residual stiffness from yesterday's experience. She had just reached over her shoulder and zipped the wetsuit when Paul came up into the cockpit. She saw the relief on his face as he saw that she was covered.

"Hey," she said. "It was thoughtless of me to rush you out here. Do you want something to eat first?"

He smiled and shook his head. "I'm okay. I'll do us up a brunch after we swim."

"You sure? I don't mind waiting."

"I'm fine, really. You got a wetsuit that'll fit me, by any chance?"

"Yes. I bought two of each size from medium through extra-large. What do you think?"

"Probably an extra-large."

She handed him the suit and watched from the corner of her eye as he peeled off his T-shirt. He was nicely muscled -- fit looking without the overdeveloped muscles of a gym-rat. She wondered about the long, ragged scar up the left side of his ribcage.

Apparently her examination wasn't as subtle as she thought, because he volunteered, "Knife."

Flustered, she felt the color rise in her cheeks. "Sorry to stare," she stammered.

He smiled. "It was when I was a rookie patrolman. Domestic disturbance, both of 'em high as kites."

"He cut you?"

"She. It's the women who do unpredictable things. She'd

called because he was beating her. He had a gun, and my partner got the drop on him -- made him drop the gun and stand facing the wall. When I put the cuffs on him, she cut me."

"Wow! Then what?"

"My partner shot her; it didn't do much damage, but I got the knife away from her." He pulled up the zipper on his wetsuit. "Want to take the dinghy over to the reef? Or swim from here?"

"Let's swim," she said. "It'll help work the kinks out of my shoulders."

∽

CONNIE WAS ENTRANCED by the schools of tiny, colorful fish that flitted around the reef. They were ignored by a three-foot-long barracuda that hovered just off her shoulder. The barracuda darted out of sight just moments before she felt a tap on her leg. Frightened, thinking the barracuda was attacking her, she whirled to see Paul charging away in pursuit of a large hawksbill turtle.

They had noticed the turtles surfacing while they were sitting in the cockpit, but this was their first encounter with one in the water. Her fear forgotten, she took off in Paul's wake. The turtle seemed oblivious to their presence, although it was swimming fast enough that they could barely keep up with it. As they approached the middle of the cove, the turtle plummeted to the bottom, where it began foraging on the grass. They watched the turtle until Connie reached out and squeezed Paul's hand. They both popped their heads out of the water.

Taking her mouthpiece out, Connie said, "I'm kind of chilly. Think I've had enough for now."

"Let's go back to the boat. I've worked up an appetite," Paul agreed.

29

After their swim and brunch, Connie and Paul had both confessed to being tired, so they slung hammocks in the shade of the cockpit awning and napped away the better part of the afternoon. When Paul woke up, he saw that Connie's hammock was empty. Rolling to his feet, he stepped to the companionway and found her below, studying a chart spread out on the chart table.

"Going somewhere?" he asked.

"Thinking about it. I've had a lot of fun being a tourist with you."

"Me, too. What're you thinking?"

"We've got two weeks before we have to be in Antigua. It's five miles to Great Bay on Jost van Dyke. Looks like we could get in there and anchor in the dark okay."

"If we leave now, we'll make it before dark."

"Well, I was remembering Sharktooth's comment about the sunset last night."

"Yeah?"

"I was thinking we could leave now and sail about halfway

and heave to. We could have sundowners with a clear view of the horizon, and then sail on in."

"You're the captain."

"We need to learn to think of stuff like this. It's the kind of thing that we should do to surprise our guests."

"Sounds good to me. There's mango salsa left from last night, and I can open a fresh bag of chips."

An hour later, they were sitting in the cockpit, sipping rum punch; *Diamantista* was hove to about two miles northwest of Francis Bay. They enjoyed a comfortable silence as they munched on chips and watched the sun drop toward the horizon. Paul, thinking there would never be a better time, cleared his throat. "Connie?"

"Mm-hmm?"

"I've been struggling with this for a while. We need to have a serious talk about where we're going with our relationship."

"You're right, we do. But there's something that I have to do first. Indulge me, okay?"

Paul nodded grudgingly, his frustration clear in the frown on his brow. Connie rose slightly and shifted to her left, settling herself squarely in his lap. Before he could react, she put her arms around his neck, closed her eyes, and kissed him. His response was immediate, and more ardent than she could have imagined. Within seconds, both were lost, oblivious to the sunset, the green flash, and everything except each other. Connie did notice at some point that there were fragments of chips in Paul's hair, and he was vaguely aware that one of her nipples tasted like mango salsa.

"We'd better get dressed before we have that talk," Connie said later, after her pulse had settled into a normal rhythm. "Even though it's getting dark, there are other boats around, and we aren't showing any lights."

Paul stepped below and turned on the running lights. When he returned to the cockpit, Connie handed him his clothes.

"Now," she asked, "what about this talk?"

"Um, I think maybe we just had it."

"Man of few words. I like that about you."

"Mm," he said. "You okay with this?"

"Well, no. I mean yes, but some things need to change."

"Uh-oh. Like what?"

"We need to move my stuff into the forward cabin."

"But my stuff's already in there."

"Right. No point in us settling into the aft cabin. Those widows are going to be here before we're ready."

She snuggled up to him, and he put his arm around her shoulders.

"That feels right," she said.

"It does, but I guess we'd better get under way."

"In a hurry to get to the anchorage?" she teased.

"Yes."

"Are you worn out, old man?"

"No."

"Good. Let's hurry up and get there," she said, with a throaty chuckle.

"You take the helm; I'll get the headsails," Paul said, his blood racing from that laugh of hers.

"It's easiest if we jibe. Ease the main and we'll let the bow fall off. Once we get some way on, I'll swing the stern through the wind and you can sheet it in."

"Aye-aye. You're the boss."

"Remember that later, okay?"

"Uh-oh," Paul said a moment later. "The staysail sheet's fouled on something. I'll go free it."

"All right. Careful, please."

Paul went forward, and a few seconds later, the sail was drawing. He came back to the cockpit as Connie was trimming the sails.

"What've you got?" she asked.

"A duffle bag. The sheet was fouled on the life raft canister; it ripped the top open when it came free. This was inside." He unzipped the bag and they peered into it in the rapidly waning light.

"So that's where they hid it. Nobody looked; the canister was sealed."

"It was just sealed with some kind of tape. I'll bet he brought some with him to replace what he tore off."

"He threw away my brand new life raft."

"We'll get another one. There's bound to be a dealer in St. Thomas."

Paul settled in beside her behind the helm and she reached over and took his hand. She looked over at him. "How about you?"

"What about me?"

"You asked if I was okay with this. I most definitely am, but I want it all to be right. If you're not ready, I'll wait."

"I'm so ready. That's exactly what I wanted to say to you."

"You said it. I just wanted to hear it vocalized as well as acted out."

They sailed for several minutes, enjoying the sounds of the boat as she sliced through the nearly calm sea, driven by the steady evening breeze.

"Connie?"

"What?"

"What about the money?"

"You found it; I guess it's yours."

"Then I'd like to put it into *Diamantista*; buy a share in the business."

"I've got a different idea, if you're serious."

"I'm serious."

"We'll sell *Diamantista* and go in together on another boat. There's a Herreshoff 59 for sale in Maine. I almost bought it."

"Like *Vengeance*?"

"Right."

"Why didn't you?"

"It's only got two double staterooms."

"So?"

"I needed more sleeping accommodations."

"Then why ..."

"I wasn't sleeping with my crew when I bought *Diamantista*."

"Would we call her *Diamantista II*?"

"No. I've got some bad associations now with *Diamantista*. I've got another name in mind, if it's all right with you, partner."

"What's that?"

She pointed at the red glow on the western horizon and prompted, "Red sky at night ..."

"*Sailor's Delight?*" Paul asked. "Done."

THE END

MAILING LIST

Join my mailing list at http://eepurl.com/bKujyv for notice of new releases and special sales or giveaways. I'll email a link to you for a free download of my short story, **The Lost Tourist Franchise**, when you sign up. I promise not to use the list for anything else; I dislike spam as much as you do.

A NOTE TO THE READER

Thank you for reading *Love for Sail*, the first book in the *Connie Barrera Thriller* series. I hope you enjoyed it. If so, please leave a brief review on Amazon. Reviews are of great benefit to independent authors like me; they help me more than you can imagine. They are a primary means to help new readers find my work. A few words from you can help others find the pleasure that I hope you found in this book, as well as keeping my spirits up as I work on the next one. If you would like to be notified by email when I release a new book or have a sale or giveaway, please visit http://eepurl.com/bKujyv to subscribe to my email list. I promise not to use the list for anything else; I dislike spam as much as you do.

If you haven't read the other **Connie Barrera Thrillers**, please take a look at them. If you enjoyed this book, you'll enjoy them as well. I also write another series of sailing thrillers set in the Caribbean. The **Bluewater Thrillers** feature two young women, Dani Berger and Liz Chirac. They sail a luxury charter yacht of their own. They are friends of Connie's; they met her when she chartered with them in *Bluewater Ice*.

Connie had a key role in *Deception in Savannah*, my first

book. I enjoyed writing about her so much that I wrote her into the **Bluewater Thrillers**. She plays prominent parts in both *Bluewater Ice* and *Bluewater Betrayal*. The **Connie Barrera Thrillers** are a spin-off from the **Bluewater Thrillers**, and feature some of the same characters. Dani and Liz taught Connie to sail, and they introduced her to Paul Russo, her first mate and husband.

Bluewater Enigma, the thirteenth book in the series, was published in June 2017. Now, I'll turn my attention back to Connie and Paul in their eighth adventure. You'll find progress reports and more information on my www.clrdougherty.com. Be sure to click on the link to my blog posts; it's in the column on the right side of the web page. Dani Berger has begun to blog about what's on her mind, and Liz and Connie are demanding equal time, so you can see what they're up to while I'm writing.

A list of my other books is on the last page; just click on a title or go to my website for more information. If you'd like to know when my next book is released, visit my author's page on Amazon at www.amazon.com/author/clrdougherty and click the "Follow" link near the upper left-hand corner, or sign up for my email list at the link in the opening paragraph above.

I welcome email correspondence about books, boats and sailing. My address is clrd@clrdougherty.com. If you'd like personal updates, drop me a line at that address and let me know. Thanks again for your support.

ABOUT THE AUTHOR

Welcome aboard!

Charles Dougherty is a lifelong sailor; he's lived what he writes. He and his wife have spent over 30 years sailing together. For 15 years, they lived aboard their boat full-time, cruising the East Coast and the islands. They spent most of that time exploring the Eastern Caribbean. Dougherty is well acquainted with the islands and their people. The characters and locations in his novels reflect his experience.

A storyteller before all else, Dougherty lets his characters speak for themselves. Pick up one of his thrillers and listen to the sound of adventure as you smell the salt air. Enjoy the views of distant horizons and meet some people you won't forget.

Dougherty has written over 25 books. His **Bluewater Thrillers** are set in the yachting world of the Caribbean and chronicle the adventures of two young women running a luxury charter yacht in a rough-and-tumble environment. The **Connie Barrera Thrillers** are also set in the Caribbean and feature some of the same characters from a slightly more romantic perspective. Besides the **Bluewater Thrillers** and the **Connie Barrera Thrillers**, he wrote *The Redemption of Becky Jones*, a psycho-thriller, and *The Lost Tourist Franchise*, a short story about one of the characters from *Deception in Savannah*.

He has also written two non-fiction books. *Life's a Ditch* is the story of how he and his wife moved aboard their sailboat, *Play Actor*, and their adventures along the east coast of the U.S. ***Dungda de Islan'*** relates their experiences while cruising the Caribbean.

For more information, visit my website or send me an email
www.clrdougherty.com
clrd@clrdougherty.com

Other Books by C.L.R. Dougherty

Bluewater Thrillers

Bluewater Killer
Bluewater Vengeance
Bluewater Voodoo
Bluewater Ice
Bluewater Betrayal
Bluewater Stalker
Bluewater Bullion
Bluewater Rendezvous
Bluewater Ganja
Bluewater Jailbird
Bluewater Drone
Bluewater Revolution
Bluewater Enigma
Bluewater Thrillers Boxed Set: Books 1-3

Connie Barrera Thrillers

From Deception to Betrayal - An Introduction to Connie Barrera

Love for Sail - A Connie Barrera Thriller
Sailor's Delight - A Connie Barrera Thriller
A Blast to Sail - A Connie Barrera Thriller
Storm Sail - A Connie Barrera Thriller
Running Under Sail - A Connie Barrera Thriller
Sails Job - A Connie Barrera Thriller
Under Full Sail - A Connie Barrera Thriller

Other Fiction

Deception in Savannah
The Redemption of Becky Jones
The Lost Tourist Franchise

Books for Sailors and Dreamers

Life's a Ditch
Dungda de Islan'

For more information please visit www.clrdougherty.com
Or visit www.amazon.com/author/clrdougherty

READ AN EXCERPT FROM SAILOR'S DELIGHT – A CONNIE BARRERA THRILLER (BOOK 2)

CHAPTER 1
SAILOR'S DELIGHT

Connie had a smile on her face as she pushed the cart down the dock to *Diamantista*. Before she lifted the first bundle of laundry from the cart, she glanced at her wristwatch. She had hours before Paul's flight arrived — plenty of time to stow the laundry and make up the berths for their guests who would arrive tomorrow. She set both bundles in the cockpit and opened them, separating the sheets and towels from the clothing. She put her things in one pile and Paul's in another, feeling quite wife-like as she took their clothes below and started putting them away in the stateroom that she and Paul shared. She was excited that he'd be back tonight; this was the first time they had been apart since they became a couple, and the three days since he left had seemed to drag on forever. As she stowed a stack of Paul's folded boxer shorts, she felt a small wad of cloth in the back of his top drawer. Curious, she extracted it and shook it out to see what it was. Her heart sank as she recognized the orange thong bathing suit bottom that was the principal garment Karen Gilbert had worn during their last charter.

Besides the crushing pain in her chest, she felt a flush of

anger as she recalled her sappy conversation with the woman in the marina office a few minutes ago.

"Where's Paul? He not been aroun' for a while. You send him Packin'?" The receptionist had teased Connie as she had entered the office.

Connie had laughed. "He'll be back tonight, Helen. He's been in Miami for the last few days. He had to take care of a bunch of stuff; his condo sold last week."

"Wow! Look like you really got him for good, huh?" Helen had smiled. "Guess there's no hope for the res' of us, now."

"Well, we're committed at this point. Once I sell *Diamantista*, we'll make it official."

"How come you wait for that?" The woman had frowned, puzzled. "Better you hook him solid befo' somebody else decide to." She grinned, pretending to primp for an imaginary man.

"He's hooked solid. Don't you worry. We're buying another boat together; we'll have the wedding aboard, once we take delivery."

"I see. When you gon' get the new boat?" Helen had hefted the two big bundles of freshly laundered linens onto the counter.

"We've already bought her; we're having a refit done up in Maine. It'll be a few months, yet."

"You gon' name her *Diamantista II*?"

"*Sailor's Delight*," Connie said. "From when we made the decision."

"You mean like, 'red sky at night, sailor's delight' — that ol' sayin'?"

"Right. Or maybe *Red Sky*. I like that one better, but Paul likes *Sailor's Delight*. We were sitting in the cockpit watching a gorgeous sunset when we decided to go for it."

"Tha's a nice story, Connie. You are two lucky people; I'm happy fo' you."

"Thanks, Helen. Guess I'd better go get this stuff put away. Our next guests arrive tomorrow."

"Don' work too hard, Connie. I jus' put this washin' on the bill, all right?"

"Sure. That'll be great. Thanks, Helen." Connie had shifted the bundled laundry from the counter to the dock cart and walked out of the office with a spring in her step.

That was then. This thong was now. Blinking back tears, she crushed the thong into a ball and shoved it into the back of the drawer where she'd found it. She was in a daze as she put the rest of the laundry away, remembering every minute of the charter with Karen and the other young widow, searching for some explanation. Finished with her chore, she collapsed on the bed and gave in to the urge to cry — something she hadn't done since childhood.

~

PAUL RUSSO WAS SAVORING a colada with his old friend, Mario Espinosa, in Mario's favorite Cuban restaurant on Calle Ocho in Miami's Little Havana. He sipped at the thimble-sized cup of thick, sweet Cuban coffee, thinking it was the perfect finish for their late lunch of roast pork with black beans and rice.

"So, you're really giving up the bachelor life?" Mario asked.

Paul grinned. "It's not a tough choice, Mario."

"Well, I've been married all my life, but I had you figured for a confirmed bachelor. That Connie must be some gal."

"I've never been struck by lightning before, but it's gotta be something like what happened to me the first time I kissed her. Damnedest experience I've ever had — blinding flash of light, ears ringing ... "

Mario chuckled, shaking his head. "The two of you gonna keep running charters? You said you were getting another boat."

"Yeah. We've bought one together; it'll be a few months yet before it's ready. Connie wants to make a go of the business; it's a challenge for her."

"Sounds like a good life," Mario said.

"I don't know. Based on the first charter, I'm not so sure."

"Bad experience?"

"That's putting it mildly. These two widows booked us for a month. We had visions of little old blue-haired ladies, but they were both in their twenties. Knockouts, too," Paul mused, shaking his head and scratching behind his right ear with his index finger.

"That doesn't sound bad — you had a month in the sun with three beautiful young girls. Tough job, amigo."

"*One* beautiful young girl, Mario. Those widows were like poison. Well ... I guess the one was okay ... or would have been, by herself. The other one, though ... she treated Connie like dirt. And she kept trying to grope me, every time she thought she could get away with it."

"Sounds like a young man's fantasy, Paul. You gettin' old?"

"It was disgusting, Mario. She was looped on rum most of the time. Besides, I'm a one-woman man. I never went for the loose, trashy type."

"I know that. Just teasing you, 'migo. I hope Connie knows what a lucky woman she is."

"I don't know about that, but I'm one lucky guy. Not sure about the charter thing, though."

"You got any more guests lined up?"

"Yeah. There's a couple with a teenaged daughter joining us tomorrow."

"A family, huh? That ought to be better," Mario said.

"I sure hope so. Speaking of that, I'd better get to the airport."

"Glad we got to have lunch. Too bad the rest of the guys couldn't make it; they all send their best."

"Thanks, Mario. It's good to see you; tell the others I'm counting on them to come to the wedding."

"We wouldn't miss it. Everybody wants to meet the bride."

CONNIE STOOD in the waiting area outside Customs and Immigration at Maurice Bishop International Airport in Grenada. It was early evening, and the air was refreshingly cool, but she didn't notice. She was determined to suppress her instinct to confront Paul. There was only this evening; their guests would arrive early tomorrow. She didn't want to start something that they couldn't finish. An ongoing quarrel between the two of them was certain to spoil the carefree atmosphere that people had a right to expect when they were on holiday.

She had a lifetime of experience at hiding her emotions, but she couldn't recall ever feeling this distraught. She'd never risked letting herself fall so selflessly in love with a man before Paul came along. Until the last couple of years, she'd been focused on achieving and maintaining financial stability. Falling in love had been a luxury that she could never afford, so this kind of heartbreak was a new experience for her.

She still couldn't believe that Paul would have dallied with that vixen; it seemed out of character for the man she had trusted so implicitly. But, she reminded herself, she really hadn't known Paul for very long. While their romance hadn't been love at first sight, it still fell into the whirlwind category. Both of them had plunged headlong into this relationship while protesting that neither wanted to rush things. Reflecting on the joy of their first unguarded encounter, she momentarily forgot the pain and anger that she had felt earlier this afternoon. She felt a smile forming on her still tear-swollen face, and then a wave of grief washed over her as she remembered the thong. How could he have done that to her? How could he have fallen for such an obvious piece of trash as Karen Gilbert?

She remembered the inebriated woman flaunting her gym-toned body as she flitted around *Diamantista* in her orange thong, her augmented breasts well-oiled and displayed to their greatest advantage. Since the age of puberty, Connie had known that she was blessed with the kind of natural beauty that set her apart from the crowd, but she felt frumpy around Karen Gilbert. Thinking back, she remembered how Paul had averted his eyes from the spectacle of the woman doing yoga on the foredeck, practically naked. At the time, she had been embarrassed for him because of the woman's aggression.

They had several whispered conversations about Karen's increasingly overt play for Paul, and Connie had discouraged him from a frank confrontation with the woman. She was, after all, a paying guest. Connie and Paul had joked at the time about his 'taking one for the team,' but he had seemed genuinely put off by Karen's behavior. Connie wondered again how she could have misread the situation so badly.

~

CONNIE WAS LOST in thought as Paul came through the door from the baggage claim and customs area. When he dropped his duffle bag and wrapped his arms around her, she stiffened, caught off guard. Surprised by her reaction, he released her and stepped back, frowning.

"What's wrong?" he asked, the frown melting into a worried look as he took in her puffy eyes and tense manner.

"Sorry," she said. "I was miles away; you just startled me. How was Miami?"

Paul studied her for a moment, assessing the expression on her face. "Okay," he said. "The closing's done, and my stuff's all in storage. You okay?"

She forced a smile. "Fine. Just tired, I guess. The Regan's will be here tomorrow morning."

He picked up his duffle bag. "You take a taxi from the marina?"

"A bus," she replied.

"Let's take a taxi back, then."

She nodded her assent as they walked toward the taxi stand.

"Hungry?" he asked. "We could stop somewhere."

She shook her head. "I had a sandwich."

"Peanut butter and jelly?" he asked.

She nodded. "I like it."

"You eat anything else while I was gone, or is that it?"

That got a little smile from her. "I ate lunch in the marina restaurant every day. I only ate PB&Js for supper."

He chuckled as he put his bag into the back of the van at the front of the taxi queue. She ignored the hand he offered, climbing into the center seat without his assistance.

"We can stop somewhere if you're hungry," she said, as he settled into the seat beside her.

"I'm okay. Had a big lunch with Mario, kind of late in the day."

"Let's make it an early night then," she said. "I'm beat, and we still have to go shopping for provisions in the morning before they show up."

"Okay," he agreed, turning in his seat to look at her, noticing that she wouldn't return his gaze but stared out the windshield instead.

"I'll take care of that; you can sleep in if you want."

"Good," she said, still not looking at him.

He sighed with resignation, puzzled by her cool reception.

CHAPTER 2

SAILOR'S DELIGHT

Mary Nolan sat alone at the table for two in the Grande Anse Resort's beach bar, checking out the men. She took a careful sip of her rum punch, remembering what she had learned from her experience last night. The drinks were deadly; rum was less expensive in the islands than fruit juice, and while the taste was luscious, the aftereffects were hideous. She'd gotten smashed last night and stumbled back to her room alone — not exactly what she had in mind. She was here to celebrate her escape from a bad marriage that had ended in a worse divorce. She'd been celibate for months, not by choice, but to avoid giving her ex any ammunition in their protracted court battle. It had been tough, but the money at stake made it worth her while. Now she was free, and she wanted a man, but not just any man.

There were some stunningly handsome locals. She'd already been approached by a few in her two days here, but she'd made them for the hustlers that they were and sent them on their way. She wasn't looking for a rented boy-toy, nor was she looking for true love. A little honest sex with somebody whose company she could enjoy for a few days was what she had in mind. She'd been watching the two men seated a couple of tables away. They were checking out the women in the bar, and not in a subtle way, either. She'd felt their gaze lingering on her several times already; she told herself it was just a matter of time before one of them made a move. She knew she looked good, and she was dressed for the hunt. She hoped it would be the younger of the two; he was cute, and he looked to be in his late teens – a little young for her, but he was gorgeous. His companion wasn't bad looking, but he was older. He'd do, if that's what fate ordained, but a girl could dream in the meantime.

She had noticed the two of them on the beach earlier. The older one had once been fit, but he was running to fat; he appeared to be in his late thirties. Of average height with dark hair that was thinning on top, he wasn't unattractive, but his younger friend was more what she had in mind. He was tall, slender, and athletic; she'd watched him swim out to the buoys that marked the edge of the boat-free zone off the beach. He moved through the water with the grace of a dolphin, and when he came back to shore and stood up in the knee-deep water, she felt the warmth spread from the root of her being. He was slim, but his smooth, golden skin rippled as the hard ridges of muscle played beneath it, making her squirm with want. He stood for a moment, dripping seawater, and then brushed the droplets from his medium-length blond hair, smiling at her when he caught her watching.

She'd thought for a moment that he'd approach her then, but the older man had said something to him, and he had turned away from her and taken the towel proffered by his friend. He had settled on a lounge chair and warmed himself in the sun for a few minutes, and then the two men had gotten to their feet and walked up the beach to the little pier where several small boats bobbed in the gentle waves. She was disappointed when they stepped into one of the inflatable dinghies and motored off in the direction of the yachts anchored a few hundred yards to the north up the beach. She'd been hoping that they were staying at the resort, but apparently, they were just visiting.

Now, though, they were here in the bar, obviously looking for what she was looking for. She glanced toward their table and caught the younger man staring at her. She smiled invitingly, and was pleased that he smiled in return. But then he looked away and resumed his conversation with the older man. She wondered for a moment about their relationship. They seemed to be an odd pair, unless they were related. When she had first spotted them on the beach earlier, she'd thought they might be a couple, but then she'd seen how they were both admiring the women in their vicinity.

～

"She looks like she's the pick of the litter," the older man said.

"Mm-hmm. Not bad at all," his younger companion agreed. "She was by herself on the beach earlier this afternoon."

"That's a good sign. Looks to me like she's on the prowl."

"I dunno," the younger one said. "I seen her give a couple guys their walkin' papers."

"Locals?" the older man asked.

"Yeah. Good-lookin' guys, though."

"Maybe she got a thing about blacks," the older one said.

"Possible, I guess, but it didn't look that way. She talked to them a few minutes, but it looked like there just wasn't any magic there."

"Think you might be the lucky one? You got the magic fairy dust."

"Yeah," the younger one said, "but that ain't the kind of magic I was talkin' about."

"Who gives a shit? She'll do. We got to keep movin', don't forget."

"Yeah, I know. She's runnin' a tab. Why don't you go see if you can slip the barkeep a bill and get her room number?"

"The hell I want to do that for?"

"Well, two reasons. One, it'll get your sorry ass out of my way. She doesn't look like the type would be interested in two guys at once."

"Yeah, okay. But why her room number?"

"You could go check it out and call me on my cell."

"Check it out for what?"

"Make sure she's traveling' alone. See if there's any sign of somebody might miss her right away. You know the drill."

"All right, lover boy, I'll check it out, but that means you get the check."

"Sure. No problem. If she checks out clean call me and then wait down by the dinghy dock."

~

MARY WAS DISAPPOINTED at first when she saw the older of the two men slide his chair back and get to his feet. The men exchanged a few words. The younger one laughed, and the older man walked over to the bar. He spoke to the bartender for a minute, and Mary saw him hand the man some money. She assumed he was settling their tab, but he walked out and left the younger man nursing his drink. Maybe she was about to get lucky after all. She sipped her rum punch and sat back, inhaling the clean, fresh scent of the sea that wafted through the bar on the light, onshore breeze that came every evening after sundown. Even if the hunting had been a bit disappointing so far, at least she couldn't complain about the venue. Grenada was a beautiful spot.

She heard the soft ringing of a telephone and looked up to see her quarry lifting a cellphone to his ear. He spoke in a quiet tone for a minute or two and disconnected, waving for the waiter. "Damn," she muttered under her breath, "he's leaving." She scanned the dimly lit room to see if there were other prospects, but she saw only couples. In a morose frame of mind, she picked up her drink and took a large swallow. "Can't get laid, might as well get drunk," she mumbled. She looked up, startled, as the waiter approached her table, a single rum punch on his tray.

He set the drink on a coaster in front of her and said, "Compliments of the gentleman across the way, ma'am. Enjoy."

"Thanks," she said, looking over at the man to see him giving her a big smile. She lifted the new drink without breaking eye contact, hoisting it toward him as she returned his smile. She took a small sip and returned the moisture-beaded glass to the coaster, never taking her eyes off him. He raised an eyebrow, and she nodded, watching as he rose to his feet with smooth grace and picked up his own drink. He glided across the room with a dancer's movements, keeping time to the calypso backbeat of the SOCA band that had just started playing. He stopped behind the empty chair across from her and leaned forward to speak so that he could be heard over the rising volume of the music.

"May I join you?" he asked.

"I was hoping that you would; thanks for the drink, by the way."

"My pleasure," he said, gazing into her eyes as he pulled out the chair and sat down.

She felt warmth spread through her as she held his look. "Your friend abandon you?"

"My uncle," he said. "Past his bedtime."

"I see. I'm Mary. Mary Nolan."

"Troy Stevens. I'm pleased to meet you, Mary. Where are you from?"

"Atlanta. You?"

"North Carolina, originally, but I'm kinda between jobs, and I'm spending some time down here with my uncle. He lives on his sailboat."

"Wow! Sounds like fun. What kind of work do you do?"

"Oh, I'm trying to make it as an actor, but it's tough. So I pick up whatever I can to pay the bills."

"I guess that leaves you as much time as you want to sail with your uncle. Where have you guys been lately?"

"Just kinda kickin' around the islands. You on vacation?"

"Yes. I'm celebrating."

"Celebrating? What're you celebrating?"

"Being single again," she said, batting her eyes.

"Divorced?" he asked in a sympathetic tone.

She nodded, grinning. "Right the first time."

"Sorry it didn't work out for you."

"Don't be. He was an asshole."

"Must have been a blind one to let you get away from him."

"Aw," she said. "Besides being the handsomest man I've ever seen, you're sweet."

She was tickled by his bashful smile as he looked away from her.

"Could you excuse me for a minute, Troy? I need to powder my nose."

"Sure," he said, rising to his feet and stepping around the table to help her up.

"Don't go 'way," she said, feeling the rum rush to her head. "I'll be right back."

"I'll be here, don't you worry," he said.

CHAPTER 3
SAILOR'S DELIGHT

Connie felt the boat shift slightly as Paul stepped off onto the finger pier on his way to the grocery store. She had been feigning sleep to avoid having to talk to him this morning; she knew it was cowardly of her, but she was playing for time. If she could avoid a confrontation with him until their guests arrived, she could use the time to collect her thoughts and let the wounds heal. She knew he'd be at the grocery store for a while; their stock of staples was running low, and shopping in Grenada was time-consuming. She rolled out of the berth and made it up neatly; she needed order in her world at the moment. Paying attention to the little things gave her the illusion of control, which was critical to her sense of well-being right now. The notion of Paul having some hidden relationship with that hussy rattled her more than she could have imagined.

She washed her face and brushed her teeth, studying her reflection in the bright sunlight that filtered through the head portlight. She thought about makeup, but rejected the idea; she normally didn't wear any, never having felt the need to improve on the looks with which she'd been blessed from birth. She gave the darkly beautiful woman in the mirror a wry grin and shook her head. She might be a few years older than Karen Gilbert, but it didn't show — not even in the harsh sunlight. Paul might have a different opinion, but she wasn't going to start painting her face. That would be admitting defeat, in a way.

She stepped out into the galley, taken aback when she saw the breakfast tray that Paul had left for her. "Guilt?" she wondered, and then gave herself a mental slap. It could be, except that the tray was typical of the thoughtfulness that had drawn her to him from the beginning. She had never known such an innately gentle, kind person as Paul. She brushed off the choking feeling as the image of the thong invaded her thoughts. She smiled at the small glass of freshly squeezed passion fruit juice nestled in a bowl of ice, reaching for it and raising it to her lips. He was a master of the little touches; the tray was artfully arranged, everything laid out just where she would expect it to be. She lifted the inverted saucer that covered the cereal bowl to find a carefully arranged array of sliced fruit resting atop the granola. She picked up the tiny pitcher of cream from another small bowl of crushed ice and poured it over the cereal.

She wondered how such a thoughtful man could be drawn to a tart like Karen Gilbert. She immediately quashed that thought; she had resolved not to get into that until after the charter. Nothing about Paul's relationship with Karen would change during the charter, except that time could work its magic. By the time their guests left, her shock would have worn off, and any feelings Paul had would likewise have moderated. At least, she hoped that would be the case.

Meanwhile, she wanted to go to the big, open-air market downtown and pick up some fresh flowers and a basket of fragrant, locally grown spices for each of the guests' cabins. She finished her breakfast and rinsed and dried the dishes, stowing everything as she worked. She got dressed and left the boat, intending to be gone before Paul returned. She didn't think she should be alone with him just yet; she might say something she'd regret.

～

PAUL WAS AMUSED by the chalkboard listing the day's specials outside the grocery store. He was self-aware enough to realize that he was seeking to take his mind off Connie's strange behavior, but he allowed himself a moment's indulgence anyway. "Fresh, wild, local iguana" was the special of the day, and he chuckled as he contemplated ways to cook it. If they didn't have guests coming aboard, he might be tempted to buy some, thinking that an exotic dish might distract Connie from whatever was bothering her.

This was the first time since they'd been together that he had seen her so upset. He was sad for her, as well as troubled that she didn't want to tell him what was bothering her. After 20 years as a detective, he read people well. He had seen the signs last night in the taxi; she wanted to be left alone. As he tried to imagine what could have happened in his absence to explain her withdrawal, he realized that he didn't know Connie all that well. They had been too preoccupied with falling in love and starting the charter business to spend time exploring each other's backgrounds.

Paul met Connie when she chartered *Vengeance*, the boat that belonged to Mario Espinosa's goddaughter. She had inadvertently stumbled into a money-laundering operation run by a crook named Sam Alfano, who was wanted for murder. Paul had gotten involved in the apprehension of Alfano partly through his final case for the Miami Police Department and partly through his connection to Mario and his goddaughter. He and Connie had become friends when he stayed in the islands for a few days of relaxation after wrapping up the arrest.

Before they met, he had investigated Connie at the request of Dani Berger, Mario's goddaughter. Dani's initial suspicion that

Connie was involved in money-laundering had proved unfounded, and the two young women had become close friends. Most of what Paul knew about Connie's background took the form of sterile, impersonal facts that had been provided by a fellow detective who had worked with Connie while shutting down a drug-smuggling operation that had included her former business partner. Beyond the fact that Joe Denardo, the detective, had given Connie a glowing recommendation for her help in putting away the smugglers and solving the murder of her partner, what Paul knew about Connie was that he wanted to spend the rest of his life with her.

"That'll be $523.12 E.C. Or you want to pay in U.S. dollars?"

"Sorry," Paul said to the cashier, surprised that he had finished the grocery shopping without being conscious of it. He looked down at the list in his hand, the items methodically checked off. "I'm a little distracted. I'll pay in E.C. dollars."

"I know you on a boat; you an' the pretty lady usually come in together. Can't remember the boat name."

"*Diamantista,*" Paul said. "You need the customs papers for the V.A.T. rebate?"

"No. Tha's okay. We got a copy on file from when the lady was in here the other day. Tell her Paula said hello. I know she glad you back. She been missin' you; I could tell."

∽

THE MAID RAPPED SHARPLY on the door, tapping with her passkey. It was midmorning; most guests would be out of their rooms by now, but after a few embarrassing episodes early in her tenure at the Grand Anse Beach Resort, she had learned to be cautious about opening room doors. After a second knock without a response, she inserted her key and opened the door just a crack.

"Good morning. Maid service," she called.

When there was no response, she opened the door fully and

stepped into the room, surprised to see that the bed had not been disturbed since the night maid had turned down the covers last night. That was a little out of the ordinary, but not unusual enough to alarm her. While she, like many of the islanders, was quite conservative, she knew that single guests often slept with people they met at the resort. She didn't approve, but she kept her judgments to herself. After all, they paid her salary, and she wanted to know as little as possible about the depravity that occupied them in the nighttime.

She checked the bathroom; the towels had been used since she had cleaned the room yesterday, and the terry cloth bathmat on the tiled floor was slightly damp. She looked around for a moment, thinking something was wrong, and then it struck her. There were no toiletries on the counter, and she remembered that this woman had left a substantial makeup kit out yesterday. She opened the cabinets, but there was no sign of the makeup kit. Stepping back into the room, she looked around, confirming that the woman's luggage was not in evidence. She checked the dresser drawers and the closet, but none of the woman's belongings were in the room. Now she was a bit alarmed; guests normally stayed from one weekend to the next. Midweek departures were unusual. She went to her cart outside the door and checked the schedule on her clipboard, verifying that Mary Nolan was expected to stay for three more days.

Frowning, she picked up the phone from the nightstand by the bed and dialed her supervisor. "Mary Nolan in room 132 has lef'," she said, when the supervisor answered.

"Hmm. She 's'posed to be here until Friday. Why you say she lef'?"

"She bed not slep' in las' night, an' —"

"Maybe she get lucky," the supervisor interrupted. "Tha's what the 'Mericans call it — gettin' lucky — when they meet up wit' somebody an' fool aroun'. None of our affair. Jus' you clean the room, an' — "

"No. Tha's what I t'ink at firs', but all her stuff gone."

"You sure?"

"Yes."

"Hol' on, then. I check wit' the office an' call you back there."

The maid sat on the edge of the bed, waiting. In a moment, the phone rang. "Yes, hello?" she answered.

"Room paid t'rough Friday; she don' check out. They say mebbe she go stay somewhere else fo' a day. Jus' clean it up an' leave it; mebbe she be back. If not, we make it up clean on Friday, okay?"

"Yes."

∼

As CONNIE STEPPED out of the taxi in the marina parking lot, she saw Paul walking up the dock from *Diamantista*. She paid the driver and reached into the back of the minivan to collect her purchases, stealing a glance at her watch. Their guests should be arriving from the airport momentarily. She walked past the guard's shack and entered the marina grounds, flowers in one hand and spice baskets in the other.

"Good afternoon, Connie," the guard said.

"Good afternoon, Louis."

"Your guests will be here in a minute; Felix called. He say 'bout five minutes. I called Paul on the boat; he comin' to greet them."

"Thanks, Louis," she said, marveling at how cell phones had replaced the coconut telegraph as a means of keeping everyone informed. A stranger had no hope of slipping around unnoticed in the islands, where everybody knew everybody else's business.

She started down the dock toward *Diamantista*, watching for Paul to come around the corner. When she saw him, she felt her face melt into a genuine smile. They stopped a pace apart on the dock.

"The Regans will be here any minute," he said, returning her smile.

"I heard. I ... "

"Want me to take that stuff to the boat?" he offered.

"No, that's okay, thanks. You greet them. I want to get these arranged in their cabins. I'll hurry; maybe I'll be back up here in time. Or I'll just meet you all when you bring them back."

Paul nodded and made his way to the gate, glancing back to admire her as she walked gracefully toward *Diamantista*. By the time he reached the parking lot, a dark green minivan with "Felix" emblazoned across the top of the windshield came to stop near the marina gate. He reached for the handle on the side door, sliding it open.

"Good afternoon, Mr. and Mrs. Regan. You too, Ms. Regan." Paul smiled as the pretty teenager blushed at being called Ms. Regan. She flipped her shoulder-length blond hair behind her ears and grinned.

"Welcome to Grenada. I'm Paul Russo; I'm the first mate on *Diamantista*."

"Hi, Paul. Luke Regan," the man said, crouching as he climbed out of the van and offered Paul his hand. "Call me Luke, please."

Luke was about Paul's height and looked lean and fit. His hair was black and curly, shot through with a few strands of gray. Paul guessed that he was in his mid-to-late thirties.

"Thanks, Luke," Paul said, shaking hands.

"Meet my wife, Monica, and my daughter, Julia."

"My pleasure," Paul said, beaming at the ladies. "How was the flight?"

"Not bad. We spent the night in Miami, so we just had a few hours flying today," Luke said.

Paul opened the back doors of the minivan as Luke was paying the driver. He loaded their three duffle bags into a dock cart, finishing as the Regans came around behind the van to join him.

"I'll take your things down to the boat; let's get you settled. If you're hungry, there's a good restaurant right here in the marina, or I can whip up something quick if you'd prefer."

"Thanks, Paul, but we bought sandwiches on the plane," Monica said. "I don't know about Luke and Julia, but I'd like to stretch my legs. Is there anywhere we could take a good walk?"

"Sure. Just follow the driveway back to the road and take a left. There's a nice sidewalk that will take you all the way around the Carenage and into St. Georges. That's the town over there," he said, gesturing across the harbor. "It's a pretty good hike, but if you get tired, just flag down a bus; they're minivans, just like the taxi, except they'll stop and pick up and drop off passengers anywhere along the route, and they're cheap. The driver or the conductor can tell you how to get wherever you want to go; just ask."

"Conductor?" Julia asked.

Paul smiled. "They have a person who opens and closes the door and stops traffic for you to cross the street, if he needs to. He'll also collect the fare."

"Cool," Julia said. "Can I change into some cooler clothes before we go?"

"Good idea," Monica said. "I'd like to do that, too."

"Let's go with Paul, then," Luke said. "We'll put our stuff away and then go see the town."

CHAPTER 4

SAILOR'S DELIGHT

"Nice touch, clearing out her stuff," Troy said. "What made you think of that? Old habits, you thievin' bastard?"

"Watch yourself, pretty boy. I figured if we left her stuff in the room, the people at the resort would get suspicious after a day or two."

They had delivered Mary Nolan early this morning and were sailing south along the west coast of St. Vincent. Troy had the helm, and his companion had spread her belongings out in the cockpit as he pawed through the medium-sized suitcase. "Nice camera and some high-end costume jewelry," the older man muttered.

"Might as well keep the camera. I can't think of anywhere to sell the rest of it. Can you?"

"Nah. Mostly just didn't think it was a good idea to leave it. Made it look too much like somebody coulda snatched her. This way, the hotel will just think she ran out on them, see?"

"Yeah. Five thousand bucks — not a bad score for our first time," Troy said.

"Not too bad," his companion agreed.

"So how much do you think we need to buy enough coke to make it worth the trip north?"

"Hundred grand or so. We get that much uncut shit into Miami an' we can retire an' live large," the older man said.

"That's a shitload of women," Troy mused. "Lots of exposure. Somebody's gonna notice, man."

"Nah. The man said spread it out; never twice in a row at the same island, remember? Stick to loners, like this broad. Nobody misses 'em for a while. Cops on one island don't talk to their neighbors on the next island unless somethin' tips 'em off."

"Still, that's a lot of time and trouble."

"Shit, Troy, it's easy work, man. Besides, there's always virgins."

"What? What're you talkin' about, virgins?"

"You don't fuckin' listen, do you?"

"I missed somethin', I guess. What about virgins? They want virgins?"

"Yeah. He's got a buyer — guy that specializes in Asia and the Middle East."

"How much?"

"Twenty-five grand for a white teenager. Five grand bonus if she's blond."

"Now that's more like it," Troy said. "We can snatch a few like last night for pocket money — keep us in dope while we look for virgins. Only gotta score a few of them, and we'll be set to make that Miami run."

"How we gonna score teenage girls without getting in trouble? Old farts like us?"

"Speak for yourself, man. I can pass for late teens, no trouble. Just need the right haircut and some moisturizer to cover the sun damage. Stick with me, old fart."

"We'll see," the older man said, putting Mary's things back into the suitcase with a few large rocks for ballast. He took out a knife and punctured the nylon in several places after he zipped it closed. "Heave to for a minute. Let's be sure it sinks."

Troy spun the helm, turning their bow to the port, through the wind. After the sails rattled for a few seconds, they filled on the opposite tack, the jib back-winded. The boat stopped, held steady by the pressure of the breeze in the sails, which were working against each other now. The older man dropped the suitcase over the side and they watched it sink from view beneath the clear, indigo-blue water, leaving a momentary trail of bubbles. He turned and grinned at Troy, nodding his head.

Troy cast off the sheet that held the jib back-winded and sheeted the sail in on the opposite tack. The boat began to pick up speed, and he returned to their original course, trimming the sails as his companion watched. After a moment, the older man went below and returned with two moisture-beaded bottles of Carib beer.

"To virgins," Troy said as they clicked the bottles together and drained them in one long draught.

∽

END of the excerpt from *Sailor's Delight – a Connie Barrera Thriller (Book 2)* ...

IF YOU'RE ENJOYING *Sailor's Delight* and would like to keep reading it, just visit www.clrdougherty.com

Other Books by C.L.R. Dougherty

Bluewater Thrillers

Bluewater Killer
Bluewater Vengeance
Bluewater Voodoo
Bluewater Ice
Bluewater Betrayal
Bluewater Stalker
Bluewater Bullion
Bluewater Rendezvous
Bluewater Ganja
Bluewater Jailbird
Bluewater Drone
Bluewater Revolution
Bluewater Enigma
Bluewater Thrillers Boxed Set: Books 1-3

Connie Barrera Thrillers

From Deception to Betrayal - An Introduction to Connie Barrera

Love for Sail - A Connie Barrera Thriller
Sailor's Delight - A Connie Barrera Thriller
A Blast to Sail - A Connie Barrera Thriller
Storm Sail - A Connie Barrera Thriller

Running Under Sail - A Connie Barrera Thriller

Sails Job - A Connie Barrera Thriller

Under Full Sail - A Connie Barrera Thriller

Other Fiction

Deception in Savannah

The Redemption of Becky Jones

The Lost Tourist Franchise

Books for Sailors and Dreamers

Life's a Ditch

Dungda de Islan'

For more information please visit www.clrdougherty.com

Or visit www.amazon.com/author/clrdougherty

Made in the USA
Lexington, KY
05 May 2018